Master Cornhill

Before the Great Plague swept London in 1665, eleven-year-
old foundling Michael Cornhill had led a sheltered, happy life
with his foster family and seldom wondered about the parents
he had never known. Sent hastily from the city when his foster
mother succumbed to the dread plague, Michael survived; but
eight months later when he returned, all his family and friends
had perished. Homeless and penniless, he brooded now about
his unknown origins and worried about his future. Two new
friends made life possible for him—Tom Godfrey, a carefree
young man who sang ballads on street corners for a living, and
Susanna, a sturdily independent girl who kept house for an old
Dutch map-maker. Though Michael liked helping Tom sell
ballads, he knew—and Susanna often reminded him—that this
was not really the way to spend the rest of his life.

Then another disaster struck the ancient city. A fierce
conflagration, known to history as the Great Fire of London,
swept everything before it in a gigantic holocaust. How
Michael and Tom struggled through it, attempting to reach
Susanna and the old map-maker, and how Michael found the
direction his life should eventually take make up the conclud-
ing section of this absorbing story, brimming with authentic
detail and swift in its dramatic conclusion.

MASTER
CORNHILL

LONDON
1666

■ SUNDAY
□ MONDAY
▨ TUESDAY

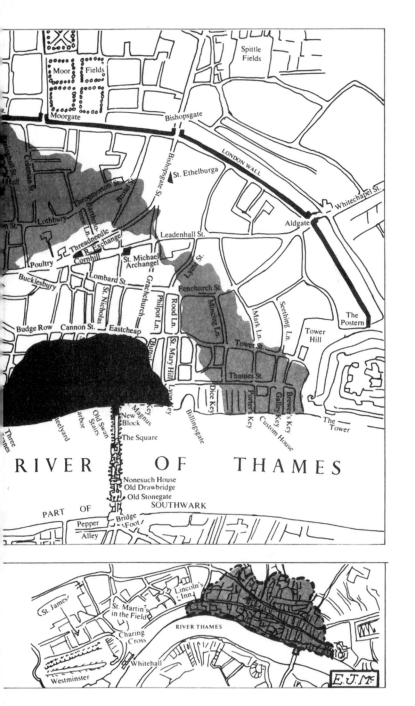

MASTER CORNHILL

Eloise Jarvis McGraw

ILLUSTRATED WITH A MAP AND REPRODUCTIONS OF OLD PRINTS

Sonlight Curriculum, Ltd.

We wish to acknowledge use of the following illustrations:

The Great Pit in Aldgate by G. Cruikshank, page xiii
Detail from *Panorama of the City* by Wenceslaus Hollar, page 57
The Great Fire of London, Courtesy of Bettmann Archive, page 127

Printed in the United States of America

Library of Congress Cataloging in Publication Data
McGraw, Eloise Jarvis. Master Cornhill.
Reprint. Originally published: New York: Atheneum, 1973.
Summary: Victim of both the Great Plague and the Great Fire of London,
a homeless, penniless eleven-year-old must decide what direction his
life should take.
[1. London (England)—Fiction] I. Title. PZ7.M1696Mas 1995 [Fic]
ISBN 13: 978-1-887840-00-2
ISBN 10: 1-887840-00-1

For a catalog of Sonlight Curriculum materials for the home school,
write:

Sonlight Curriculum, Ltd.
8042 South Grant Way
Littleton, CO 80122-2705
USA

Or e-mail: catalog@sonlight.com

For the middle ones,
Billy and Adam

Contents

PART I

The Turnip Cart

The spring frosts were over now, and from all directions, by water and along the jolting, boggy roads, Londoners who had fled their plague-ridden city the summer past were heading home, thanking God they'd finished with 1665 forever. Every highway crawled with them—rich and poor, in carts and coaches, on horseback, afoot—and a sober crowd they were, in spite of their ribbons and periwigs and an occasional brave plume. It was a lonesome thing to be creeping back in this muddy April, not knowing at all what you'd find or who was left, if anyone, after the worst plague in London's memory had run its course.

On the Oxford road, at half-past eight of a morning, one such band of travelers was nearing Uxbridge—a lurching stagecoach, a straggle of riders and pack animals, a tinker festooned with pots and pans, and a one-horse cart that wrenched, pitched, and creaked along the rutted way, its left wheel ever plunging into a mud-hole as its right one climbed a boulder. In the cart a boy of eleven, named Michael Cornhill, bounced perilously atop a dozen knobby sacks of turnips, clinging hard to the crate of squawking hens beside him. He was a trustful-looking boy, with a saddle of freckles over a fine straight nose, and shoulder-length hair the color of new thatch tucked impatiently behind his ears. His knee-breeches and jackanapes, good sturdy garments a year before, were outgrown and outworn now; the ribbon-loop trimming looked as if mice had been at it. Its ruin continued as Michael embraced the splintery hen-crate, his dark-blue eyes, wide and serious, straying once more to the road behind.

Not a sign of High Wycombe now, even the steeple was long gone—it must be two leagues back. Also two leagues back, Michael was telling himself with what bravado he could muster, was that gloomy little house with silly Mistress Schoonmaker and her pious, penny-pinching husband and her sniffling Alphy-boy, and prayer-saying all day and wearing Alphy's cast-off shirts and longing for London and the Truebloods. Eight months of it—all behind him. Very abruptly, behind him.

Behind him, too, the prospect of being handed over to the parish workhouse as an indigent waif, on Tuesday next—a plan Michael had heard nothing of until yesterday morning when Master Schoonmaker had informed him without preamble that the money sent by his foster-father for his support eight months before was nearly exhausted. The austere voice still echoed in Michael's ears, the sharp, pink nose still wavered before his eyes. "Only twelve shillings fourpence is left for you . . . I am not a rich man, Michael. The workhouse will teach you a useful trade, you will be better off there. Indeed, since God in his wisdom has now for the second time left you destitute, without kith or kin, it is plainly His will. . . . Yes, of course, you may return to London if you prefer—though in view of the sadly changed circumstances, and with only twelve shillings in the world—"

Sadly changed they were, with no Truebloods alive to welcome him home—no home, either. But Michael would have preferred leaping into a deep well to remaining in High Wycombe one more day. And one day later, here he was, irrevocably, in the turnip cart. . . . The sun was mellowing the air now; the scent of mud and horses and hens rose strongly; a blackbird whistled; the harness chimed through the squealing of the wheels. Ahead, the carter bellowed hopefully that it was getting fine and warm a-days now; the tinker bellowed back gloomily that it was still cold enough a-nights.

Michael drew a long breath, putting the Schoonmakers from his mind. As he faced front again, he glanced at the girl riding beside him, clinging to the other side of the hen-crate. Still asleep, she was. . . . For a moment his eyes lingered curiously on her bobbing head, her snub-nosed, cheerful profile. The Gold-and-Silver Maiden, he'd been calling her to himself; he didn't know her name. She had joined the company at the last crossroads inn, emerging amid a flurry of farewells in the wake of a tall, stern-faced old man dressed all in black. In the little inn-yard the two had conferred briefly, the old man handing her a coin, she dropping him a curtsey. Then he had mounted into the stagecoach, and she, picking up her bundle and making a rapid survey of the higgledy-piggledy cavalcade that milled about the muddy yard, had headed straight for the cart. A moment later she was handing the carter her coin and climbing up onto the turnip sacks beside Michael with a brisk, "Good-morrow," spoken in a quaint, husky voice. He had replied shyly, almost inaudibly. Whereupon she had wedged herself firmly against the hen-crate and gone to sleep. They had not exchanged another word.

Sighing, Michael looked away. Once back in London everything would surely seem better; he wouldn't feel so all alone. The Bottses were bound to take him in, at least until Uncle Penwood came. They were longtime neighbors, after all. And Uncle Penwood was bound to turn up in London *this* summer. . . . Michael's hand crept into his left breeches pocket to touch his money-purse with its meager hoard—reduced by the carter to ten shillings and ninepence—and the sharp little lump that was The Shell. He wished he knew Mistress Trueblood's uncle better, was surer how he felt about— well, boys and things. But never mind that. He had his own, true family to search for. Michael wasn't a destitute orphan without kith or kin, not really. Somewhere in London there were other Cornhills, and he meant to find them.

Meanwhile, he *wished* the girl would wake up, though she'd disdain his company when she did, as like as not. She was sixteen at least, and when girls got sixteen—pretty ones—they grew mightily scornful of boys of eleven. And she was remarkably pretty. Or rather, not pretty, like Mary Botts, but—well—*remarkable*. Gold and silver. It was her hair that was silver, and her skin that was gold. He had never seen hair as pale as hers; the wisps and tendrils all around her hood's edge were shades lighter than her rosy, freckled face, and looked flax-white against the rough dark cloth of the hood.

She suddenly opened her eyes and encountered his intent and frowning gaze. At once her whole face went pink with merriment, making the tendrils look lighter than ever, and her eyes narrowed to sky-blue slits between their thick, fair lashes. "Lawks, are you putting a spell on me?" she demanded.

Flushing, Michael stammered that it was nothing of the sort, that he craved pardon for his rudeness, that he was only—only looking at her hair.

"My hair? Good faith, I suppose it's falling down, is it?"

"Oh, no—well, I can't tell if 'tis or not. I was only—only thinking it's pretty. I mean the bits that show."

She seemed to think that the funniest of speeches or else Michael the most absurd of boys—and who could blame her, he thought furiously, scowling away northward at the far horizon and feeling very overheated about the ears. He wished one of his friends from school were in this cart instead of this stupid girl—preferably Edmund Botts, or even Mary, for all she was sixteen and scornful of him now. At least he was used to her, she was part of the old, familiar life in Bartholomew Lane. Oh, he would be glad to see the Bottses. Except for them, there wasn't any old life left him, everything was changed. . . .

"Lud, you're vexed now, aren't you?" said the girl beside him ruefully. "Pays me out for my rattle-brain ways. I vow I never meant to mock you."

"Oh—I took no heed of it." Michael felt his ears heating up again in spite of his urgent wish to appear indifferent. But her grin was so impenitent that he couldn't help grinning sheepishly back. "I suppose I did sound like a silly bobchin," he admitted.

"And I like a lack-wit! Come, that's better," she added with satisfaction. "A long face never shortened a long journey."

"Had I a long face?"

"Long and lonesome, that you did. Like a Puritan at King Charles' court."

"Like Master Schoonmaker." Michael's giggle spilled out of him at the thought of Master Schoonmaker's pale, pink-nosed face and pious black hat among a courtful of periwigged Westminster dandies, with Charles II in crimson satin, standing elegantly by.

"Master who?"

"Oh—just a Puritan I know."

"Ah, so do I know a few of them still!" she exclaimed. "Whether they'll own to it now or not. You can't mistake that look they have, as if they smelled something nasty and it was all your fault."

"That's Master Schoonmaker to the nail!"

"And my landlord back in Noble Street, too."

They exchanged a companionable glance, and Michael's opinion settled for good and all. She was not stupid, but as jolly and easy as he had thought from his first glimpse of her. "That tall old man," he said. "The one in black, that you came from the inn with—is he a Puritan?"

"No, no, not him! He's Dutch, is Master Haas. I grant you he does look stern, and there's that voice of his—sounds like the Lord Almighty's! Lawks, but I was scared of him, at first! But he's ever so good, when you know him. He's been six months with his daughter at Piebald Farm—she's the squire's widow—and he used to walk to the inn every morning to drink his burnt-wine. That's how I got to know him. A sad old man—lost his son and son's wife to the plague. Now there's only one grandson left, for his daughter's childless. I'm to be servant at his house in the city— cook and look after the grandson and him at the Golden Buckle."

"Then you're bound for London too."

"If I had to walk all the way!"

It was just how Michael felt, himself. "Still, it'd be a fearful long walk in this mud, it would."

"No matter! I've been ten months back there at that crossroads inn, sweeping the floor and carrying the country folk their ale. You'd not find me balking at a little mud—or even a mountain of it!"

Perhaps, thought Michael, they could share another cart on to London from Uxbridge, where this one stopped. "What's your name?" he asked her.

"Susanna. And what's yours?"

Michael told her, adding proudly, as he had been taught, "Foster son to Master William Trueblood, the draper, at the White Hind, top of Bart'lomew Lane, near Throgmorton Street." Then with the still-sore drag at his heart, he added, "Master Trueblood's dead now, though, and Mistress Trueblood and both maidservants and John the 'prentice too."

Susanna nodded sympathetically. "So is my Old Joan and half of London, I guess. How did they get you out, then?"

Out of the house, she meant, before the examiners nailed it tight shut, with everyone in it, and painted the dread red-ochre cross on the door beside the despairing words, *God Have Mercy on Us.* Once a plague-stricken house was shut up and a watcher with his white staff posted by the door, it was a rare thing that anyone got out of it except in the dead-cart.

"It was my father's quickness—the day he found the plague-tokens on my mother's shoulder." Michael's memories of that hot August day were broken but terrible: Master Trueblood, white-faced, emerging from the bedchamber and quickly closing the door; the sound of Mistress Trueblood's bitter weeping within; the shocking, unnatural, silent speed with which his always-deliberate, always-talkative father moved—first downstairs to the shop and his strongbox to get a paper with a big seal, then hustling Michael through the streets to the stable behind an inn, to hold hurried, low-voiced talk with a man there and give him the paper and five gold pieces—an amount that made Michael's eyes bulge. "There was a man in Milk Street—I think he used to be our coachman— and he had a coach and horses. And my father had already got a Lord Mayor's health-pass somehow." Michael knew only that before he could sort out anything that was happening he was inside the coach and off for High Wycombe, without so much as a spare shirt, without even a loving touch in farewell, so fearful was Master Trueblood that the plague might have clung somehow to his hand. The last Michael saw of him was his stooped back, as he hurried, head down and grieving, back to Bartholomew Lane and his sick wife. And there he had died with her four days later. Master Botts had sent a letter to tell Michael so and to warn him to stay on with the Schoonmakers until London was clean again.

Susanna heard all this and nodded again. "God's mercy you had some place to go," she remarked.

"Hadn't you, then?"

"Not I. But then, I found one soon enough," she said briskly. "By chance they lacked a servant maid at that Green Man Inn and by chance there was I. It was early then, folk weren't so frighted of the plague that they'd bolt and bar the doors the minute they clapped eyes on a Londoner, the way they did all summer."

"You left London *before* the summer?"

"First week of May. We lived near Cripplegate, Old Joan and I —the sickness came earliest round about there. And one evening along toward the end of April I came back to our lodgings, and there was Nancy, a girl who lived just above us, crying from the window not to go in, Old Joan was dead—of spotted fever, she said, of course. Everybody said that then. But we both knew it was plague. I slipped in anyhow and got my petticoats and cloak, and five shillings I had hidden in the chimney, and Old Joan's paper with her will. She had some gold, Old Joan had, and she wanted her church to have it when she died. I saw to it, before I came away."

"Who was Old Joan, your granny?" put in Michael.

"All the granny I had," Susanna said with her husky laugh. "And all the mother or aunt or sister. Old Joan Peddler, everybody called her. Her name was Peach. She peddled combs and gloves and pins and suchlike trifles around the edges of London for near thirty years—and for ten of 'em, I helped her. So I'm Peach too, now."

"Mistress Susanna Peach," Michael said, liking the sound of it as well as he liked this cheerful, gold-and-silver girl.

"Better than Mistress Susanna Nobody," she said, and with twinkling eyes, bowed as well as she could in the lurching cart. "Well met, Master Michael Trueblood."

Michael laughed. That did sound so funny, Michael *Trueblood.* "Cornhill," he corrected her.

"What?"

"Cornhill. That's *my* name. I kept it when the Truebloods took me. Though I don't know who my kin are," he assured her, wanting them to go on companionably being orphans together, two of a kind. "So far, I don't. Master Trueblood always used to say they must have been grand, fine folk. Because of—well, you know— Cornhill Street. But—" He became aware that she was staring at him very oddly. *"You* know. Cornhill Street, in London."

"Yes, well I know it! But what—?"

"Oh, well . . ." Michael laughed uncomfortably, beginning to wish he hadn't brought it up. "Father—that is, Master Trueblood— he used to say the street must have been named for my family. Of course, I think he was only gulling me," he added hastily.

To his dismay, she gave a whoop of laughter, throwing her head back so that the hood fell away from her great knot of silvery hair.

"Oh, my faith, so that's the way of it! 'Master Cornhill!' Lawks, I always wondered how that street was named!" She went off into another irrepressible gale.

Michael, bewildered in his turn and desperately embarrassed, could only mutter, "I said he was only gulling me." And how ridiculous the story sounded, now he thought of it. Of course, he had never quite believed it, not really, not since he was much younger anyhow. It had just been a sort of loving joke of his father's, to make him secretly feel proud because his family *might* be a grand one. He frowned hard at the hen-crate, his ears turning to fire, wishing with all his heart he had never brought it up.

Susanna's hand closed warm on his. "Ah, Master Cornhill, I'm not mocking you. But that's my name too, you know—or was, once."

"Your name is Cornhill?"

"It used to be, till I was five years old or so—a gutter-brat sleeping in doorways and getting my bread anyhow. Then Old Joan caught me one day, nipping a tortoise-shell comb from her stall, and scolded me hard and took me home to live with her, the good old soul. . . . So, we must be sister and brother, hey? Master and Mistress Cornhill—and only just finding each other after all these years!" She watched his astonished face, her own alive with mirth, then softening as she shook her head over him. "What a coney you are! Don't you know every babe abandoned on the porch of St. Michael Archangel Church in Cornhill Street—and there's a-many of 'em—is christened 'Cornhill'? They must call us something."

"Oh," Michael breathed, after quite a long pause during which his brain stumbled about in unfamiliar territory.

"Didn't your Truebloods ever tell you where they got you?" Susanna asked him gently.

"Yes." Michael swallowed. "From a widow-woman in Mark Lane, who fell ill and couldn't keep me."

"And before the widow-woman?"

Michael's brows knotted with trying to remember. But finally he had to shrug. He knew nothing of where the widow-woman had got him. Nor had he known that all St. Michael Archangel foundlings were christened "Cornhill." The Truebloods had never mentioned it, nor had anyone else. Maybe nobody had wanted him to know that his own, real mother had simply abandoned him on a church porch like a discarded shoe.

He wished he *didn't* know it. Oh, how he wished he had never told Susanna what his name was, that he had his Cornhill family back—fine folk or paupers, it wouldn't matter. But the Cornhills were deader than the Truebloods now. There'd never even *been* any Cornhills.

"What about me, then?" Michael burst out. "I'm not Cornhill, either. I haven't got a name at all, I'm not anybody."

"Don't be a goose, you're the same nice lad you were five minutes ago. That's enough, isn't it?" asked Susanna.

"No!" Michael told her passionately. "It's *not* enough. I must have been somebody once—*had* somebody once—" His panic subsided. Of course, he'd had somebody in the beginning. He'd had the person who left him on that church porch. His mother probably. It was just that her name wasn't Cornhill. He didn't know what her name was—or anything else about her, except that she hadn't wanted her baby. It wasn't much of a recommendation for a mother. Or for the baby either. Maybe she hadn't even liked him.

On the *other* hand, Michael told himself rebelliously, maybe she'd liked him ever so much but had to give him up because she was sick or dying or too poor to feed him or afraid to admit he was hers. Why, maybe she'd been a grand, fine lady, a lord's daughter—an *earl's* daughter, even, and had run away and married a poor—well, a poor . . . Oh, well, that was silly, he supposed. But she *could* have been just a nice, loving woman with too many children to provide for, so she had to give one away—or several. Why, in *that* case . . . Michael's mind explored this surprising vista. He turned to Susanna, wide-eyed. "D'you think we *might* be brother and sister? Why, suppose we are! Wouldn't that be a—"

"Miracle? Yes, it would be, Master Cornhill! Do you know how many Master Cornhills are left on that church porch every year of the world? It must be hundreds. And more hundreds of Mistress Cornhills like me."

"What happens to them, then?" Michael demanded. "There's not one other boy named Cornhill in the whole Merchant-Taylor's school."

"I suppose most of us change it to something else—like Peach."

"Oh," said Michael sadly.

"Or else they die. Ever so many babies die, even rich, fine babies with mamas and nursemaids, let alone parish foundlings. Old Joan, when she was young and had her husband still, she had eight babes, one after t'other—seven boys, one girl. And not one of them lived to a year."

"Well, you and I lived. And we're *still* alive," Michael retorted. He didn't want to talk or hear any more about death, whether from plague or anything else.

"We are! And healthy!" Susanna agreed heartily. "We come of sturdy stock, the both of us. Don't you say so?"

"Yes. We both have fair hair, too," Michael pointed out. "And we both have blue eyes, and we both have—"

"Freckles. And holes in our stockings. And mud on our shoes."

"Yes. And do you know what else?" Michael had been studying her closely. "We both have little brown moles on the left side of our necks!" Michael raised eager eyes and stared intently into hers. "We *might* be brother and sister, you know. It's not *impossible.*"

She was already shaking with laughter at him again, her face flushed pink in its frame of pale tendrils. "You are the absurdest young one! An hour, at most, since you first clapped eyes on me—and straight off you must have us kin!"

"But we might truly be. I'd like you for my sister, you're ever so jolly," Michael told her earnestly. "Anyway," he went on after a moment, "I'd like *someone* to be kin to. Whatever their name is. Maybe just a cousin or an uncle or . . . I do have a sort of uncle, but he's not my own . . . I haven't anybody all my own, now. And nor do you."

"It doesn't fret me," Susanna said, but gently.

"It does me," Michael confessed. He peered coaxingly into her face. "We could adopt each other, couldn't we?"

"Ah, Master Cornhill, a fat lot of good I'd be to you! Not a sixpence to my name, no home—except old Master Haas's, and I'll likely have to sleep on the kitchen table there. But never you mind, there'll be someone in London to look after you, won't there?"

"Oh—yes, some neighbors. . . . Friends. Master Botts is a draper, same as my foster father was."

"Ah, then, you won't need *me*."

"I suppose not," Michael mumbled. It was just that he wished somebody or other needed *him*. He fell silent, thinking ahead to London and the Bottses and Mary, who was scornful of him now, and Elizabeth—married and gone—and Mistress Botts who was a sharp-tongued scold. Well, there was Edmund. Edmund would be glad to see him, Michael was sure of it. But neither Edmund nor the other Bottses *needed* him; they had one another.

Jangling and creaking, the cavalcade topped a little hill, and Uxbridge Tower, rising over a huddle of roofs, came into view. Susanna sat up, pointing. "There, Master Cornhill! We'll break our fast in a tick now, and thank God for that!"

Parting In Uxbridge

Michael was as glad as she to straighten his cramped legs when they slid off the turnip sacks in Uxbridge a few minutes later. It was near ten o'clock, and he had been traveling since dawn. As the cart rattled away toward the marketplace, he and Susanna followed the rest of the company into the cobbled yard of the King's Head Inn. It was an old, old building that rose about them in galleried tiers, all mellow brick and diamond-paned windows and black, carved oak. Swinging from the lowest gallery was a weathered sign showing King Henry VIII in a funny flat hat. Michael squinted up at it, half-smiling. On inn signs, at least, the eighth Henry always looked jolly. Perhaps he really had been—think of the jolly songs he wrote that Master Trueblood used to play on his flageolet or on the new virginals.

And what, Michael wondered, had happened to the new virginals now? And the beds and their bolsters and the chairs and stools and tables and candlesticks and the settees that used to stand either side of the hearth and all the spoons and kettles and . . .

"D'you mean to stand and dream all day, Master Cornhill, or will you come in and drink your ale with me?"

Waking abruptly, Michael hurried after Susanna, narrowly avoiding a horse that suddenly sidestepped almost on top of him. The courtyard rang with voices and the sound of hoofs on cobblestones, as the riders dismounted, the coach-passengers crept stiffly from their vehicle, and the inn's ostlers and servants scurried about trying to answer everybody's summons at once.

Inside the ale-room it was cool and dim. Michael stopped to let his eyes adjust, smelling the good, sourish malt smell and feeling his stomach contract with hunger. Susanna was already settling herself on a bench near the front window, throwing off her cloak and reaching up to secure one of the pins that held her heavy knot of hair. The light filtering crookedly through the circular leaded panes made a halo of the crisp, individual hairs that would not lie smooth against her head. Michael joined her, announcing that he meant to have toast as well as ale today, his stomach was that empty.

"Is your purse also full?" she inquired.

"Well—I can spare an extra groat for toast. There'll be enough for you, too," Michael added, feeling that somehow that made it all right. "Anyhow, I've nearly eleven shillings left, and only my dinner and fare from here to London yet to pay. *Maybe* a night's lodging too, if I can't find a carter going on soon." Uneasily he pulled out his purse and emptied it on the table, catching the shell as it rolled. There would be only ten shillings sixpence left after he paid for his ale and toast, he saw. Still, that was enough.

"What's that speckled thing?" Susanna asked, as he began to scoop coins back into his purse.

"This? Ah, that's my shell." Michael gave it a loving polish on his sleeve and held it out for her to see—a small, ivory-colored, brown-speckled cone with a throat of glowing peach. "Uncle Penwood brought me that from Virginny—found it himself on the shore there after a storm. He's captain of the merchant ship *Medusa,* is Uncle Penwood. He's not *my* uncle, a-course, but Mistress Trueblood's."

"Fancy!" murmured Susanna. She made no comment as he returned the shell to his purse and the purse to his pocket, but when the innkeeper's wife had set their ale and toast before them and hurried away, she added, "I'd think he'd be looking after you, not just neighbors."

"Oh, he will," Michael said quickly. "That is—he's in Virginny now or someplace betwixt there and here. But he will, when he comes back to London." He's bound to, Michael assured himself, stuffing his mouth with toast. He raised confident eyes to Susanna's and suddenly *felt* confident, enough to smile through his chewing. "Likely he'll 'prentice me, too, when I'm old enough. I might have a ship of my own someday! Here, have some toast."

Susanna laughed and helped herself. "Seems we've landed on

our feet again. That's twice in our lives for the both of us." Teasingly, she added, "It's the luck that runs in our family, hey?"

Michael returned her grin, but privately he saw no reason at all why the two of them might *not* be kin, close kin—and more and more reasons why they might be. He even *felt* kin to her, as if they belonged together. He was trying to phrase this in terms she would not laugh at when he realized she was on her feet, bobbing a curtsey to the old man, her new master, who had suddenly loomed up beside their table. How tall he is, thought Michael, peering up at him—and he looked taller in those black clothes. He was big-boned, too, with an impressive, craggy face, and a voice so deep that Michael was reminded of summer thunder and was too entranced at first by the sound of his talking to listen to what he said.

But then the dark, frowning gaze was bent on him, and Susanna said, "Oh, no, Master Haas, he's none of mine, we only rode in the cart together. Am I to come straight-away, then?"

"Nay, finish your ale, *meidje,*" rumbled the summer thunder. "The coach I bespoke is not come, and Philip must see to his horse yet. It will be a quarter-hour." He gave a brusque nod and turned away to join a handsome, ruddy young man who was waiting nearby. The two disappeared into the innyard, and Michael tugged at Susanna's sleeve, feeling suddenly uneasy.

"A quarter-hour—what does he mean? Who is that Philip?"

"His grandson, come from London just to meet him! So all the plan's changed, and they've hired a coach."

"A *private* coach? You'll not be going by cart, then?"

"No, didn't you hear him?" Susanna slid onto the bench again, her eyes bright. "We go south a few miles, to stay with their kinsman. And tomorrow or so, when our highnesses are rested, we board a riverboat and sail straight home. That's traveling in style, that is! And we'll be set down at Old Swan Stairs, y'see, right at their doorstep as you might say."

"Master Haas's doorstep?" Michael repeated. He felt alarmed and confused, as if he were being rushed along, dragged away from something he must cling to at all costs.

"It's Philip's home too—and Philip's shop since the plague took his parents. He's a haberdasher and toyman, same as Old Joan was —and his shop's the Golden Buckle."

"Is that where you'll live?" Michael asked anxiously.

"For a twelvemonth, for I've promised Master—and I keep my pledge, I do! After that—well, who knows! I might have other plans!" Susanna finished her ale and threw him a sparkling glance. "I've a mind to be an actress!"

Wide-eyed, Michael looked to see if she were serious. He knew there *were* actresses nowadays—real women, playing the women's roles always before played by boys or men—Master Trueblood had told him so. But . . . he studied her tip-nosed profile as she wiped her mouth on the back of her hand and reached for her cloak. "Ah—you're gulling me," he said with a grin.

"I'm not. I've thought and thought of it. That Nancy I spoke of —the girl upstairs—her sister Moll acts with the King's Company and lives in Westminster Town. But she came home once to see Nancy, and oh! the gown she had on—laced all over! And a little black velvet coat edged with white fur—and a muff! All because she's learned to sing and dance a bit! Well, why can't I?"

Why not, indeed? Michael was mightily impressed. He had never before met anyone who even knew an actress, much less had resolved to be one.

"Only trouble is," Susanna added, "I don't care over-much for Moll. It may be that what suits her wouldn't do for me at all. I'll wait and see!" She was up and flinging the cloak about her. "I'd best go out now, Master Cornhill—"

"Wait—I'll come along—" Michael scrambled up too, his food forgotten.

"No need," she was beginning, when a light coach rattled into the cobbled yard so smartly that it all but took off the open ale-room door. "That's ours, I'll be bound," Susanna exclaimed. She shot an amused glance at Michael as they hurried out into the sunshine. "A sixpence says I'll have to ride in the basket."

Before Michael could take the wager or refuse it, Master Haas was beckoning imperatively. Philip was already climbing into the coach, and the stable boys were hoisting luggage onto the narrow rack perched above the rear wheels.

"Good-by to you, Master Cornhill," Susanna cried. "Good luck, and I hope we meet again someday." The next thing Michael knew, he was enfolded in a quick embrace that smelled of ale and beeswax, and for an instant the silvery hair tickled his cheek. Then she was running across the innyard, her cloak flying back from her sky-blue skirts.

Oh, wait—oh wait—oh wait! cried something inside Michael. But he stood tongue-tied and helpless as the last strap was fastened about Master Haas's boxes and—sure enough—Susanna was boosted up to settle herself as best she could on top of them. The stable boys fell back, the coachman flicked his whip, Susanna clung tight to the buckled straps, and the carriage was moving—out of the innyard and, no doubt, straight out of Michael's life.

"Good-by!" he yelled, finding his tongue at last and flinging up a hand to wave.

Susanna waved back—perilously, letting go the straps with one hand to do so. Then the coach turned with a lurch into the street, and she grabbed again for dear life. Her laughter floated back to Michael as the coach disappeared.

For some moments he stood listening to the scrape of its wheels receding down the cobbled street. Then he started desolately back into the inn to finish his ale and toast. Never mind, he told himself crossly. The world's not ending; you can search her out next week.

It was then he realized he had not asked her where the Golden Buckle was, and she had not thought to tell him. *We'll be set down at Old Swan Stairs . . .* and then what? There were a thousand streets and alleys and lanes and . . .

Never mind. He could look in every single alley. Plenty of time —a whole year before she left to be an actress. An actress, just think of that. Resolutely, Michael thought of it, to keep from thinking of anything else. He himself had never been in a theatre, but Master Trueblood had seen real actresses in a play. "And shocking it did seem, at first," he had confided to Michael and Mistress Trueblood. "But bless His Majesty, he's opened the theatres again, and after twelve years of Master Cromwell, *that's* such a delight that he might have monkeys acting in them, for all of me—eh, Michael? Ah, it's good to have a proper king again, and colored cloth on my shelves, and be done with Puritans and all that purse-mouthed piety. . . ."

That was the way Master Trueblood's talk used to be—rich and various, with one thing leading jovially to many others, while Mistress Trueblood sat smiling agreement to everything, with her chair drawn close to the hearth and her fingers flying over some broidery work, or a neck-band she was hemming. How cozy, how safe and certain it had been in Bartholomew Lane. Michael wished, oh, how he wished, that the plague had not come. Or that there really had been a Cornhill family once, with maybe a great-aunt or third cousin still left around. Or that it were really true that Susanna was his sister—and most of all he wished he had asked where the Golden Buckle was.

His unfinished ale and toast were no longer on the table. The table was now occupied by somebody else—a large man, a large woman, and a whining small boy.

Dismally, his stomach growling as if to reproach him for not filling it when he had the chance, Michael went back outside, across the innyard and out to the street, his hand stealing into his pocket to touch his purse and the shell.

I have the Bottses, he told himself. And Uncle Penwood, someday or other. And I'll find Susanna again, I will.

Walking rapidly he set off to locate the marketplace and, with luck, a carrier's cart starting soon for London.

Welcome Home

Michael had poor luck with carts and carters. It was mid-morning of the next day before he achieved a seat with a goods-carrier, and nearly six o'clock when at last the square towers and vast hulk of St. Paul's Cathedral loomed up ahead amid the hundred spires and massed red roofs and chimneypots of London. When the goods-carrier's cart finally rattled over Holborn Bridge and into the yard of the George Inn, Michael jumped down, stiff and sore from jolting, and gladly set off on his own two feet toward Holborn Conduit at the crossroads.

Though he and his carter had dined at noon on bowls of peas-porridge, Michael could have eaten again this minute. But his ten shillings had shrunk to less than eight; besides, it was hours before anybody's normal supper time. The Bottsses would give him a fine supper at nine or ten this evening, he was sure of that; there might even be eel-pie if Mary was still fond of it.

At the Conduit he turned down Snow Hill, passed through London Wall at Newgate, and headed toward Cheapside, walking briskly because he had most of the width of the city to cross—a mile at least—and he was eager to arrive. As the familiar stench of Fleet Ditch faded behind him, that of the Shambles in Newgate Market assaulted his nostrils, and both traffic and noise increased. Dodging carts and chairmen, water carriers and shoppers, he pressed on into the meat market proper—a once broad street made almost impassable by a line of butchers' shops called the Middle Row running straight down the center of the way. Each shop was hung all around with joints of beef and legs of mutton, which in turn were hung with flies. The two narrow lanes remaining on each side of the Middle Row would scarcely accommodate a smallish coach—and a largish one was squeezing through the back-side just as Michael, hugging the wall of housefronts and using his elbows freely, arrived at the entrance to Stinking Lane. He ducked nimbly into the little passage, in company with an equally nimble housewife and an old-shoes-for-brooms man. They stood huddled together while the coach scraped by, then went their ways.

Michael scampered through the rest of the Shambles and edged past the equally crowded stretch of Blowbladder Street, emerging triumphant into Westcheap with a feeling of exhilaration. It was his first use in nearly a year of the Londoner's skill in walking unscathed through the city's streets, and it gave him a sense of homecoming as warming as it was unexpected.

Whatever the sad changes in Bartholomew Lane, London was the same as ever. It smelled right; it felt right as it jostled and shoved against him; it sounded right, from the clatter of wheels and the eight-toned wail of the oyster-sellers to the peal of the six o'clock Angelus that suddenly rang out all around him—rang from St. Peter-the-Poor at his left hand, from St. Matthew's Friday Street to his right, from every quarter of London in a wonderful clangor. The bells of St. Swithin's, St. Sepulchre, St. Agnes, St. Faith, St. Paul's, and scores of others whose voices he knew, chimed out against each other from near and far—loudest was St. Antholin's, most beautiful the six perfect bells of St. Michael Arch-angel, Cornhill.

And at first he thought London looked right, too. Cheapside was broad and fine as ever, with its tall, top-heavy white houses criss-crossed with age-dark timbering, their overhung gables peering down onto the street over their own bow windows, like stout old gentlemen craning to see past their waistcoat buttons. The signs were the same, too—the Mitres and Chained Swans and Mermaids thrusting out from shop and tavern to creak and sway over his head. The people who passed him seemed the same, so did the hackneys rattling by; even that chambermaid emptying slops out of an upstairs window might be last year's chambermaid; and the garbage clogging the street kennels might be last year's garbage, still waiting for a rain to move it along to somewhere else.

Nothing has changed, Michael told himself firmly.

But he could not help noticing some things, and the more he

noticed, the more there seemed to be. The gilt was peeling from many of the signs; shuttered windows and boarded-up doors stared like blind eyes here and there all along the street. In Goldsmith's Row, six out of the fifteen shops were closed. Perhaps their owners had not yet returned from wherever they had fled last summer—or perhaps they would never return at all. And now that he was noticing, he thought the hurrying Londoners seemed fewer and their faces sadder than he remembered. His own uneasiness—a vague dread he did not explore—dragged at his footsteps as Cheapside merged into Poultry to bring him ever closer to his old home. Then, crossing the end of Conyhope Lane, he suddenly stopped in his tracks, as a gust of the fitful northeast breeze that had been playing with the signs brought a new and dreadful stench. It could only have come from the churchyard of St. Mildred Poultry just ahead.

Michael knew about the churchyards, knew more than he cared to, from all the plague stories he had unwillingly listened to on the road. There were a hundred and nine churches in London, each with its burying-ground; and every burying-ground was choked and heaped with plague-dead. In many, the level of the soil was now raised two or three feet above normal by the pitiful carpet of dead beneath, covered by such a scanty layer of earth and winter's sodden leaves that they stank of death yet. Even so, there had been far more dead parishioners than churchyard earth to bury them in. During the nightmare of last September, there had been five or six thousand deaths each week, and finally the dead-carts had trundled day and night out of the city, forced to dump their loads in open pits in the fields.

Michael had heard all this. But hearing a dreadful tale is different from being confronted by evidence of it that you can smell with your own nose. Now every tale came back sharply and so did his own too-vivid memories, which he had been trying to forget for months. Suddenly he felt he could not bear—not yet—to walk through Bartholomew Lane, past the house where he had lived so long. There were other routes to Throgmorton Street and the Botts's.

Wheeling so abruptly that he nearly knocked down a periwigged gentleman walking along with his nose in a book, he returned to Old Jewry Lane and hurried up it, past St. Mary Colechurch perching queerly on its high foundations, and past St. Olave's and its churchyard beyond, trying neither to smell nor think, then around the corner into Lothbury and the din of the metal foundries. There was still St. Margaret's Church to pass, then he was in Throgmorton Street, anxiously peering ahead to find the familiar Sceptre sign that hung above Master Botts's door.

It was there, swaying in the little breeze. Slowly Michael walked toward it, noticing with pounding heart the boarded-up windows above it, the blind, shuttered shop below. Then, with a surge of relief, he saw that the door stood agape. They were there—maybe only just returning from the country, like himself. Eagerly he ran forward and burst through the open door into the musty-smelling dimness of the shop, calling, "Edmund! Mistress Botts!" Some unseen obstacle tripped him up at once; he went sprawling, with a flash of pain in his shin.

In the silence while he was recovering his breath, he heard a voice from above stairs, almost a whisper: "God's mercy on us—who is that?"

"It's me—Michael Cornhill," Michael panted. He staggered to his feet again, rubbing his shin. "Is that you, Mary?"

A sharp intake of breath from above but no response.

With a sinking dread, Michael repeated, "Mary? Please come down."

"God's mercy on us," the voice whispered again, but then footsteps sounded quickly on the stair, and a young woman came into view. It was Mary's older sister, Elizabeth—Mistress Osborne she was now, since marrying a young mercer a year ago. She paused on the landing, staring at Michael with a very strange expression.

Michael stared back at her, trying to smile. "I've come back. From High Wycombe. Is—is Edmund here?"

Slowly, she shook her head.

"Or Mary?" Michael persisted. "Or—Master Botts?"

"Dead," she said gently. "Mary, Edmund, my father, my mother, little Sarah, the servant girls, two of the apprentices—all dead. All in a fortnight's time, all in this house together. There's nobody left but me."

Michael was silent, as confidence, expectation, hope blinked out like candles in a vast, unknown night.

Elizabeth faltered, "I—I don't live here now, y'know. I only

came from Deptford to see what was left, if any thieves had been—
and to fetch the silver candlesticks and—whatever's left to fetch.
I—we've only a small house, Michael, Joseph and me—" Her voice
rose a little, sharpened. "And we've only a small shop, and there's
the baby to think of—*I* can't look after you, we've barely enough
for ourselves—"

"Yes, a-course. Yes, I know," Michael was mumbling, conscious
only of an urgent desire to remove himself at once and forever from
Throgmorton Street. "I know, I know. . . ."

Somehow he was out of the shop and stumbling back across the
street. Edmund, *dead.* How could that be, how could it? And Mary,
who was so pretty—and *all* of them. Everything had changed now,
all his plans were blown away like straws.

He walked without purpose or direction, struggling with his
disbelief, with a frightening numbness that gripped his mind and
refused to let him think. He did not know that his feet had turned
of themselves into Bartholomew Lane until he found himself looking straight at the house he had lived in for seven years.

It, too, had changed. There it was with its familiar top-heavy
attic thrusting out over the lane, but the garret window that had
been his own was tight-shuttered now, like a blinded eye. So was
the row of casements just below in the main chamber, where they
had dined and sat of an evening before the fire, and where his
foster mother and father had slept in their high rose-curtained bed.
And there was the shop on the ground floor—stark empty—he could
see the shelves through the window—and so must the house be,
too. The White Hind sign was rain-streaked and shabby, two of
the panes were broken, and a shutter hung from one hinge. There
was the intimately-known stone doorstep with its chipped corner,
the latch Michael had lifted innumerable times—and on the door,
traces still of the red-ochre plague cross, along with a fluttering
scrap of the quarantine notice bearing the faded words, *God Have
Mercy*—

Houses died too. A whole part of his life was closed like that
door. Michael turned and, without glancing back, walked on toward Threadneedle Street. As he walked, he began to turn over
in his mind the new and painfully unfamiliar questions of what
to do now, where to sleep during the night that was fast coming on,

and how to eat tomorrow and all the other tomorrows. Few answers occurred to him, and he liked none of them.

Directly ahead of him lay the Royal Exchange, wedged between Threadneedle Street and Cornhill to the south, with its graceful, slim tower rising high into the air. From long habit, Michael's eyes lifted to the big grasshopper crouching at the very tip-top of the spire. It was merely the family emblem of Sir Thomas Gresham, who had built the Exchange, but Michael had always taken a private, personal pleasure in it. It looked so brave there, shining with gilt, a homely, commonplace insect perched so merrily high above its betters—even now Michael's heavy spirits lifted slightly at sight of it. And as his glance returned to the building below, a face sprang into his mind.

Master Westercott, the mercer—longtime friend of the True-bloods—how could he have forgotten Master Westercott?

He was already darting across Threadneedle Street and through the arched entrance. The Exchange was four stories high, built around a vast arcaded courtyard that swarmed with people and glittered with fine shops. Michael sped for the left-hand stairway, dodged his way up it through the crowd, and found the mercer's shop where he remembered it.

He did not find the familiar rotund figure with the kindly face. There was an assistant, a lady customer, an apprentice rolling green silk onto a bolt. Uneasily, Michael approached the apprentice and asked for Master Westercott.

"Not here, my bully. He's not come back from Nottingham since the plague."

The boy thrust the green bolt onto a shelf, smoothed out a heap of topaz satin, and began rolling it, thumping the bolt over and over, while Michael stared at him in dismay.

"He's in Nottingham?" It might as well have been China.

"Might be home around Midsummer's. I couldn't say."

The topaz bolt landed on the shelf. Michael turned away.

On the street again, he braced his mind against hope and panic alike and tried to think of someone else to turn to. Master Simmons was dead last summer; Doctor Burnet too; and that pinch-mouthed Mistress Short across the lane, *she'd* hand him to the parish, sure. And the parish meant the workhouse and ending up a parish apprentice, bound to some drunken, ill-natured master, perhaps for life. Michael's skin crawled. He must, at all costs, avoid becoming a charge on the parish.

He must take charge of himself. Beginning now. There was nobody else to do it.

The sun had set, and the air was growing chilly. The great hive of the Royal Exchange still buzzed with shoppers and dickering merchant-bankers, but the country folk had sold their produce and were heading out of the city, their carts thriftily reloaded with the rich compost available in any gutter. Threadneedle Street was crowded with hoofs and wheels and voices and smells, all making for Bishopsgate. Above, in the clear lavender sky, a star hung silver and trembling; here and there in the dusky lanes a linkboy's torch bloomed golden. Michael's eyes followed one such golden blob dancing away down the narrow tunnel of Bearbinder Lane, where it was night already under the overhanging gables.

I could be a linkboy, he thought doubtfully.

A heaviness sank through him as he considered it. Never, especially in chilly weather, had the shivering linkboys with their pallid faces, their wind-chapped hands, and their piping cry, "D'ye want light?" aroused in him the slightest twinge of envy, not even at times when he had felt school a prison and his bedtime unreasonable tyranny. If you were a linkboy, you lived in dusk and dark alleys, forever exposed to the dangers your light was supposed to protect others from. Suppose a cutthroat *did* leap out at your gentleman as you were lighting him to his tavern or to the river stairs? What could you do except watch murder done—or be murdered yourself? And where did you sleep if you were a linkboy? Indeed, where did you get your link?

Never mind, Michael told himself, plodding on down Poultry. There are lots of linkboys, they live somehow, they sleep somewhere; I could be one too. Better that than the workhouse.

You got links down near the river, of course. They were made of tow and tallow, weren't they? A chandler's shop was what you wanted. In one of those narrow alleys near Old Swan Stairs. Old Swan Stairs! It was there Susanna and her new master would step off their riverboat; she had said so. She might be in London already. But where in London? *Never mind.* He could not go to see her now, anyway; she might think he wanted pity—or even alms!—and a servant's wages were small enough without . . .

Michael halted so suddenly that the porter just behind bumped into him, and a water-carrier bumped the porter, liberally splashing all three. "Look watcher about, young 'un!" exclaimed one or the other in exasperation as Michael hastily got out of the way, muttering apologies. He jumped over the chain looped between posts, which set off the footway from the coachway, crossed Cheap by the great hulk of Mary-le-Bow Church, and headed for St. Paul's, almost giddy with relief. He had suddenly realized what he must do—he must hire out for a servant. And he knew just how to set about doing it. Someone was bound to need a boots-boy or stable-boy or scullery lad; that someone was bound to come to Paul's Walk to pick one out; therefore, Michael Cornhill would station himself in Paul's Walk for the someone to find. It was all going to be simple, after all, or anyhow simpler than he had thought. He might even be busy at his new work by this time tomorrow.

Therefore, he could afford at least a *small* bit of supper tonight. Promising himself that he would wait till real suppertime to eat it—say, when Bow bells had rung at nine—Michael turned down Friday Street, found a little cook-shop, made a cautious purchase of bread and green cheese, then walked on to Watling Street, and turned west again toward the vast, dilapidated pile of St. Paul's Cathedral. He now had only six shillings ninepence between him and the void.

But since the void was so soon to become gainful employment, he was tempted to part with another penny a few moments later when he reached Paul's Churchyard and found a ballad-seller offering his wares with the usual knot of listeners around him. Michael paused too, because it was the jolliest sort of ballad, new verses set to the tune of an old catch Mistress Trueblood used to hum as she sewed. The ballad-seller's tale was about a highwayman's servant, who asked so many admiring questions of his conceited, thieving master that he learned all the tricks of the trade, whereupon he neatly robbed the highwayman and made off. The rhymes were wonderfully witty, and the old tune as merry as ever. The singer took Michael's fancy, too—a tall man, slow and elegant of movement like some large member of the cat family, with a droll expression and a careless, good baritone, which he used with humor as he played his lute.

His eye fell on Michael, who stood giggling away at the edge of the little crowd, and he smiled and aimed a specially funny bit right at him, raising his eyebrows so astonishingly high that Michael laughed aloud, starting a sympathetic ripple among the others. That ballad was surely worth a penny—even when one's purse was rather flat. Michael went so far as to take his purse out of his pocket and count its contents again; then he reluctantly put it back. He heard the song through to its end, too absorbed to resent the jostling as someone pushed rudely past him and out of the crowd. He turned away only when the singer bowed and began to sell his printed sheets.

The north side of the cathedral had been partially cleared of the dozens of small shops and sheds that over the years had filled the space between the giant buttresses as honey fills a comb. Michael vaguely remembered that the Bishop or King or somebody was trying to restore the old building's grandeur, though he had heard Master Trueblood say they'd do better to set a torch to it and start over. But the door leading into the north aisle, known as the Si Quis door, was as always covered with notices, offers to buy or sell, announcements. Somebody had lost a tortoise comb-case, somebody else a fat amber necklace; a third somebody had found one black leathern gauntlet, which he promised to return if given a ha'penny for his trouble. Nobody seemed in need of a boots-boy—at least, nobody who had posted a notice on the Si Quis door.

Never mind, Michael told himself. Tomorrow, in Paul's Walk, something would turn up. It had to. After considerable exploring and groping in the dark among the sheds he found a cranny, sheltered from the wind by an age-worn buttress and big enough to sleep in if he curled up rather tight. Since he was cold anyway, this suited him. He crept into his dirty bed just as Mary-le-Bow's bells rang out nine o'clock. Gratefully he dug into his pocket for his bread and cheese, then dug again wondering where his purse had got to—then with sudden panic felt in the other pocket, with fright and hurt and disbelief felt in all his pockets.

The purse was gone. His six shillings ninepence were gone. The shell was gone. The bread and cheese had generously been left him by the thief.

Michael's stomach contracted sickeningly as if he had plunged from a great height. His mind flashed back to the somebody who had jostled him as he stood engrossed by the ballad-singer, and he knew just when he had been robbed.

He was half out of his cranny, tears of outrage scalding his eyelids and anguish filling his heart, before he realized the futility of giving chase. He had not even glimpsed the jostler's size or shape. He sank back with a very strange feeling in his middle. The purse was gone, and that was that.

After a long time he ate his supper, trying not to think about it, trying hard not to think at all. Tomorrow—tomorrow everything would be all right.

The Serving-Man's Log

Michael awoke at six to the familiar clamor of the Angelus ringing out all over London—three groups of three beats sounding thunderously from Paul's bells directly above him, and in the pauses, weaving through the tangled skeins of overtones, the voices of other churches all over the city—and every voice he knew. It cheered him as he crept out of his cranny and stretched his stiff limbs. High Wycombe had churches too, and the churches had bells, but this was the authentic London uproar that he had waked to all his life, and he had not heard it in seven months.

As the last peals rolled away into throbbing silence, he remembered about his purse and the thief, and his shillings and the shell. *Never mind,* he thought instantly, before the panic could rise and overcome him. Never mind, never mind. All that was yesterday. Today he would be employed.

The day was already well begun in the huge open area of Paul's Churchyard, which differed from all other churchyards in that it was populated by the living instead of the dead. A few of the many little stationers' and booksellers' shops were open and doing business; the shutters were clattering up on others. Wives with their shopping baskets hurried past in a short cut to Cheapside; clerks and teachers were beginning to arrive at Paul's School near the east gate. An old man peered at the notices posted on the Si Quis door, then opened it, and went in. Michael adjusted his frayed jacket, tucked his hair behind his ears, and resolutely followed.

The vast gloom inside at first seemed total darkness. He paused; in a moment his eyes adjusted to the daybreak light creeping through the great rose window at the east end of the cathedral and the narrow ones along each side, and he could make out the massive pillars marching two by two into the dimness far down the nave, their heads lost in the murkier reaches high above. Like giants, Michael thought, as he started toward them—a column of soldier-giants turned to stone on their way to the war.

It did not occur to him, because things had always been so, that this huge, echoing, stone-chilled, dusk-filled nave was a curious place to be a hub of London life. To him, it seemed only natural that here, in Paul's, more business was transacted than in the Royal Exchange. In the North Alley, Londoners consulted their lawyers, in Paul's Walk between the columns they met their friends or struck their bargains or simply promenaded. Westminster fops eyed one another's coats or periwigs; ne'er-do-wells stalked "Duke Humphrey's Walk" in the South Alley hoping to cadge a meal; and men in a hurry led horses or mules clomping straight through the transept and out the other side, rather than go a quarter-mile around by streets.

And beside a certain pier, at the corner where the South Transept crossed Duke Humphrey's Walk, stood a bench called the serving-man's log. Here the old man whom Michael had followed through the Si Quis door had already stationed himself.

Michael sat down beside him rather diffidently. In a moment, after a sidelong scrutiny, he ventured, "God give you good morrow, sir."

The old man, who had been staring vacantly straight ahead, turned slowly, inspected Michael with rheumy, tired-looking eyes, began to nod delicately and rapidly—rather as though his head were trembling—and still nodding, slowly turned away. "God y'good morrow, boy," he said in a thin and mournful voice.

Wishing that he had got somebody more cheerful to sit beside, Michael turned away too, ready to let the conversation lapse for-ever. To his surprise, the old man spoke again immediately, though still mournfully enough. "Offering for a servant, are ye?"

"Yes, sir," Michael answered.

"Ye ben't old enough for a ostler, be ye? They allus want ostlers."

"Well—I'm eleven. I could be a stableboy, I think."

"They won't want stableboys, not they. They allus want ostlers."

The conversation languished. Michael asked presently, "What are you offering for, sir?"

"I be a footman, boy." The old man paused, started his head

nodding again, and when he had it quivering rapidly went on, "Allus have been, allus mean to be. Wait on table, open the door —yes, and ride up behind on the master's carriage, I'll do that, yes, I will, freely. But sleep in the stable I won't. Nay, I'm no ostler, boy, And I'll *be* no ostler, that I won't. Nay, not I."

"Yes, sir," Michael said drearily. The monotonous tone and rhythm of the old man's talk was almost putting him to sleep. He stopped listening and began to watch the people going and coming among the giant pillars, in and out of the shadows. Shafts of sunlight dancing with dust-motes slanted down now from the rose window, dramatically gilding at one moment a face that vanished into gloom the next. One of the faces he glimpsed was that of the ballad-singer he had listened to last night. An expensive few moments of pleasure *that* had been. I might as well have bought his whole stock and given him the purse too, Michael reflected. Better a nice and funny singer had his money, than a sneak thief. His eyes followed the tall, jaunty figure in its dashing, if somewhat fantastic, collection of clothing, no item of which seemed to match another in fabric or even age, though the total effect was wonderfully becoming. Then he lost sight of the ballad man behind the columns of Duke Humphrey's Walk and with a sigh turned again to watch for possible employers.

He found a burly, worried-looking man standing in front of him, inspecting him with fists on hips. With a leap of hope, Michael sprang to his feet.

"No, no, you're too young, lad," the man muttered, waving him back down. He transferred his stare to the old man, muttered, "And he's too old," and strode away down the nave. Deflated, Michael resumed his seat.

Gradually Paul's Walk filled with bustling life, the shafts of light slanted down more steeply, the whole cathedral buzzed with voices like a gigantic wasp's nest. The ballad-singer passed again, noticed Michael, and smiled at him, raising his eyebrows in that exaggerated, droll way. Two more prospective employers came and went. A down-at-heels ostler sauntered along and sat down beside the old man. He was hired within ten minutes. Michael glanced with reluctant respect at his aged companion, who set his head a-tremble and said, "I told ye. Ostlers, that's all they want."

By mid-morning Michael felt as if he had spent a long lifetime on that bench and was beginning to believe he could spend eternity there without coming any closer to employment. He was also beginning to wonder how hungry a boy could get before he actually fainted away or died or something and was making a rather panicky effort to imagine how he could acquire sixpence, without actually stealing it, when he again saw the ballad-seller striding across the nave. This time, he deliberately peered toward Michael, then with a slight frown changed course, and walked up to stand in front of him.

"*Still* no luck?" he asked, as Michael scrambled rather shyly to his feet.

"No, sir."

"You've been sitting in one spot a long time for a fellow your size and weight."

"Yes, sir!" Michael agreed with feeling.

The ballad-seller looked amused, but his gray, speckled eyes continued to run over Michael's person with puzzled interest. "What's the trouble, don't they like your looks? Or don't they bother to tell you?"

"They mostly say I'm too young. But they never say what *for*," Michael said bitterly.

"To the devil with all of 'em! May their souls roast like chestnuts in the seventh level of the Inferno! Like mutton chops! Like pigs on a spit!" said the ballad-man.

Michael lifted startled eyes to the other's calmly dispassionate face and felt a small warmth begin to ease the cold, pinched place in his middle.

"Ah, I thought that might help a bit," the singer remarked. "Quite a handicap, not to know a good full-throated curse when you need one—and you've not had time to pick up many at your age. I've others, if you want them. What is your age, if I may ask it?"

"Eleven, sir. Eleven and a *half*."

"Hmmm. And have persons of eleven and a half got clean out of the habit of having a draught or bite of something at mid-morning? I used to be eager enough, as I remember."

Michael swallowed a mouthful of saliva that presented itself at the very thought of a good, filling mug of ale. "No, sir, but *this* morning I thought I'd best stay here at the bench, in case—"

"Pockets to let, are they?"

"Oh, no, sir, I—"

"Come, don't try to bubble me. Let's see your purse."

Michael had been taught to hold his chin high, never to whine, and not to burden strangers with his troubles. But this stranger had him properly pinned down. After a brief internal struggle, he burst out, "Well, I can't let you see it, sir! Some sneak thief got it off me last evening—it was while I was listening to you sing." Seeing a very strange expression pass over the ballad-seller's face, he added quickly, "All my fault, sir, I wasn't paying heed."

The singer's odd but attractive speckled eyes regarded him fixedly for a moment. Then he said, "See here, Person of Eleven and a Half—what's your regular name, by the by?"

"Michael, sir."

"Well, see here, Michael. What sort of work are you wanting, exactly? What have you done before?"

"I haven't done anything before," Michael confessed. "But I'm sure I could learn to be a boots or a scullery boy or—"

"Would you consider at all becoming a ballad-seller's assistant—just temporarily until something better turns up?"

A wave of astonishment washed over Michael, warming every cranny of him, body and soul. "Oh, *yes,* sir!" he said earnestly. "But—do you need an assistant, sir?"

"I'm almost certain of it. I suggest we go in search of a very large glass of something while we discuss the matter."

Joyously, Michael agreed. With a solicitous farewell to the old man, for whom he now felt deep pity—but who was gazing vaguely elsewhere and did not notice—he followed his new friend through the crowd and out across the great churchyard. The singer headed up the nearest lane, his long, lazy-looking strides covering the distance so efficiently that Michael had to skip a bit to keep up. As they went, he studied his companion surreptitiously, admiring the short, swinging, claret-colored cloak, the shabby high boots with their frayed bunches of scarlet ribbon, the wide-brimmed hat with its broken bottle-green plume that was somehow indescribably jaunty. But there was something missing that he had been wondering about, and presently he ventured a question.

"Where is your lute, sir? The one you were playing last night?"

"At home in bed," said the other. Before Michael could do more than stare, he added, "Y'know, it's time you called me something besides 'sir.' My name is Godfrey, Thomas Godfrey. I suggest you try 'Tom.' "

"Yes, sir—yes, Tom."

"Much better." As he led the way into Paternoster Row, Tom added absently, "How much money was in that purse of yours?"

"Six shillings and ninepence—it was all I had. And . . . my shell was in it, too."

"Your shell?"

Michael nodded, tried to dismiss it with a shrug. "Just a—a shell I had. But it came clean from Virginny. I've had it ever so long . . . now I'll never see it again."

"Oh, you might, y'know," Tom said in a careless tone. As Michael looked up at him in surprise, he added, "People do, now and again. I know a fellow who's had great luck finding purses that were lost or stolen. We'll have to ask him. Was the purse itself of any value?"

"I don't know—but it was pretty," Michael told him. "Scarlet leather with a little gilt dragon on it and a *very* good clasp. My father gave it me when I began in school."

The ballad-man, turning in under a sign portraying a golden lion, paused with his hand on the door-latch. "School?"

"I go to the Merchant-Taylors' school. *Used* to go there, I mean. My father is—my *foster* father *was*—a draper in Bart'lomew Lane, his name was—"

"Wait—patience—I can see we have much to find out about each other. I suggest we break our fast first, then take lesser things one at a time."

Like all Tom's suggestions, this one met with Michael's complete approval.

They spent an hour at the Golden Lion, finding out all about each other. Or rather, Tom Godfrey found out all about Michael—and the Truebloods and the Bottses and the Schoonmakers, and the long and lonely months away from London, and the half-longed-for, half-dreaded journey back—and about his name, Corn-hill, and what Susanna had said, and then in glowing phrases a great deal about Susanna herself, how she looked and talked and turned pink when she laughed and meant to be an actress, and how extremely jolly it would have been if she'd really been Michael's sister. It was easy to talk to Tom.

It was less easy to make out what Tom thought of it all, though what he thought of Michael himself was reassuringly obvious from the warmth in his speckled gray eyes. He sat on the other side of the worn plank table, left shoulder against the sill of the grimy window, right foot propped up beside him on the bench, his hat with its broken-backed plume perched up on his knee. Occasionally he asked a question, but mainly he just drank his ale and listened, and little of what he was thinking showed in his face. It was an attractive face—framed in his own chestnut-brown hair, which he wore with the careless confidence of a man who has an eighty-shilling periwig at home—but its habitual expression was pleasantly noncommittal. The eyebrows he could lift so drolly high tilted upwards naturally above his nose, giving him a look of innocence and mild interrogation; the ironic curving of his mouth belied the eyebrows. But you could not wish a more attentive listener—at least, so Michael thought, as he finished his story and admired his new friend over the edge of his tankard.

"Yes," Tom sighed. "I rather thought you were not the usual London street-sparrow." He drew a deep breath, toyed a moment with the hat on his knee, put it on his head, tossed it back onto his knee. "And you have literally no one to go to? You've thought of all your father's friends, all his associates?"

"All the ones *I* knew. Except Master Fitzmary," Michael added reluctantly, remembering a fat, pompous face, a chilly smile. "He's beadle of the Drapers' Company. I met him once."

"And would prefer never to meet him again," Tom said in an accurate reading of his expression. "And this uncle you mentioned —will he come soon?"

"I don't know," Michael confessed. He hesitated, then blurted out what he'd been afraid to say even to himself. "I don't even know—not for certain-sure—if he'll 'prentice me when he does come." Swallowing, he went on. "He's never in London long. Not often, either. I—I've scarcely seen him a dozen times."

"No family of his own?"

"Oh, no. He's wed to his ship, he always says."

"But he's fond of you?"

Fond? Uncle Penwood's face floated up in Michael's mind—leathery-brown with iron-gray tufts of eyebrows, strong teeth showing as he laughed down at Michael. "I—I guess he likes me well enough. He always calls me 'bully' and asks if I mean to be a sailing-man when I grow up. And he gave me the shell."

"That shell. A sort of lucky-piece, is it?"

"Oh—no—just a shell," Michael mumbled awkwardly. Impossible to explain how he felt about the shell—how many times he had studied it, turned it in his hands, how intimately he knew its shape and color, how merely to touch it conjured up that distant shore where it was found, and all the other faraway, entrancing shores a sailing-man might walk along. . . . "He found it himself, one morning in Virginny. That's where he's gone now, to Virginny, to take woolen cloth and bring tobacco back."

"And he'll bring it straight to London?"

But for that Michael had no answer. The *Medusa* sometimes called at several ports before turning homeward—Bermuda, Barbados. . . . "He never put in to London at all last summer, because of—how things were here."

"Very wise," Tom said. "Well-a-day, we'll inquire at the Custom House when we're next in the neighborhood. They'll have some knowledge of the ship I daresay—despite how things were last summer."

They were silent a moment. In a rather subdued tone, Michael asked, "Did you stay in London, all through the plague?"

"I did—though I slept on a wherry in mid-river, not in my lodgings." Tom finished his ale, set the tankard down with a thump, and went on briskly, "And that brings to mind another matter—where are *your* lodgings at the moment? Ah, yes. Under a loose board somewhere in Paul's Churchyard or in an old bird's nest—I thought so. You had best come home with me when our day's work's done."

Michael, suddenly choking on his ale with amusement at the

idea of the old bird's nest, managed to sputter, "Yes, sir—Tom."

"You do have a mightily contagious giggle, d'ye know that?" Tom remarked thoughtfully. "It's what caused me to mark you last evening, there in the crowd . . . you liked my ballad, didn't you?"

"Oh, yes!" said Michael. He liked all ballads; they were bound up with his earliest memories of Bartholomew Lane. Mistress Trueblood had liked to sing them; his garret room, like many another, had been papered with them. Their woodcuts were crude but interesting, and the verses as good as a hornbook when one was learning to read.

Putting a few diffident questions of his own, he learned that Tom himself wrote a fair number of the ballads he sold and got others from Master Bennet, the stationer at the Lamb and Inkbottle in Paul's Churchyard, who printed the work of a dozen different versifiers on his long, flimsy sheets. "Low doggerel, in the main," Tom said, with a disdainful gesture that invested the ragged flounces on his wrist with the elegance of lace. "I prefer to peddle my own rhymes." As an afterthought, he added that his commission on his own rhymes was somewhat more generous as well—though only somewhat.

"My earnings are not princely, Michael. Nor will yours be, if you accept my offer of temporary employment. You will receive"—Tom paused to frown—"let us say, thruppence a day and your keep—which, I may as well warn you, *may* not include supper *every* day. In a word, my financial affairs sometimes become financial embarrassments. However, I do contract to buy you a new jackanapes. This afternoon, before the seams of that one actually burst. There. Those are my terms. They may seem harsh, but you may accept or reject 'em, no offense either way."

Michael, to whom they did not seem at all harsh, accepted with enthusiasm, and asked about his new duties. He was told that he would learn them when Tom decided what they were. "They will include giggling," Tom added. "Now, if you've finished your glass, I suggest—" He broke off as his glance halted on something beyond Michael's left shoulder, and a curious gleam came into his eyes. Michael turned to find out what he was looking at and after a puzzled search through the dim and crowded interior of the tavern finally noticed a nondescript little man peering toward them around a taller man's coatsleeve.

"He does look surprised, now doesn't he?" Tom murmured with evident amusement. "I think we'll give him a real turn, what d'you say?" Without waiting for an answer, he gave a beckoning jerk of his head that made the little man stare in consternation, glance quickly around, then start toward them with a bewildered expression.

"But who is it?" whispered Michael, who was bewildered himself. This scruffy and weasel-faced nobody sidling through the crowd looked as though he could not possibly have anything to do with Tom.

"It is my friend who is so lucky at finding lost articles," Tom answered cheerfully. "His name's Jack Stubbs, and he's wondering where in the world o'marvels I got me a Person of eleven and a half since yesterday supper-time. Aren't you, i'gad, Jack Horner?"

"Now, hush, now, Tom, lad!" exclaimed the little man under his breath, sliding an agitated glance to either side of him and attempting to smile reproachfully at the same time. "Please, now, none of your odd humors, lad."

"Hates that nickname, Jack does," Tom remarked pleasantly to Michael. "Well, I must have my jest now and again, Jack. I'll tell you a better joke, though. Somewhere in London this morning there's a foist biting his thumb at himself for a Tony—he drew this boy's flat purse last evening instead of some rich coney's fat one. Six shillings ninepence—and a shell—is all he got for risking a trip up Heavy Hill."

"A Tony he was, sure!" Jack Stubbs mumbled. "Likely some nip, though, lad, not a foist. You meant a nip."

"I mean a foist. And 'twas all Michael had, those shillings. He liked the purse, too—scarlet leather with a little gilt dragon. *And* the shell, most particularly. Think you could find it for him, if you were to look about, Jack? He's my new assistant, Michael is. I do hold a poor opinion of a man who robs children! I say 'man,' but 'clapperdudgeon's' a better word, now don't you agree?"

"Oh, I do. I do agree," Jack said hastily. "Assistant, did y'say, lad?"

"Temporary assistant. Until he can make shift to repair his

fortunes—or find a position more in keeping with his rearing. He wasn't born in the gutter like you, Jack, and didn't choose it like me. So we'll just boost him out of it, d'ye see? I know I can count on you."

"Oh, y'can, y'can, lad!" Master Stubbs turned to Michael rather as if he had a stiff neck and made a try at a winning smile. "I'll just have a look 'round for your purse, young sir. I might be lucky, I might. You just rest easy."

"We'll both rest easy," Tom assured him. "Rub off, now, Jack," he added with a brisk display of cuff-flounces in a gesture as of shooing away flies. "There, we're rid of *him,*" he said to Michael without so much as a pause. "And as I was about to suggest some moments ago, let us rub off, ourselves, and begin the day's business."

As he spoke he plucked his hat from his knee and clapped it carelessly on his head, where it assumed, apparently of its own accord, the dashing attractiveness of all his clothes. Michael, whose brain was exceedingly busy with the events of the last few minutes, glanced around as they were leaving the tavern to have another private look at Master Stubbs, but the little man had vanished as if through a hole in the floor.

Tom

"Can he really find my purse, d'you think?" Michael asked Tom doubtfully, as they started along Paternoster Row. He felt very doubtful about Master Stubbs, in a great variety of ways, most of which he did not clearly understand himself.

But Tom said, "Jack? Oh, I'd not be the least surprised, y'know. He's got the devil's own luck. Now—what color would you fancy for your new jackanapes?"

But Michael was not to be diverted just yet. "How did you get to know—that man?" he asked uncomfortably.

Tom glanced down at him, half-smiling, met his troubled gaze with a thoughtful one, and looked away again. "If one sleeps in the dog's bed, one gets fleas," he answered.

Michael considered this odd response a moment—and the odd, contemptuous tone in which it was uttered—then said in relief, "He's not *really* your friend then."

"No more than the flea is the dog's. But by the same token, we know each other very well, Jack Horner and I." They walked in silence a moment, Tom keeping an eye on Michael's profile, and saying presently, "Come—let's have it."

"Oh—I was only wondering . . . you said you *chose* the—the dog's bed."

"I said gutter. Never evade words, Michael. Yes, I chose it. And you're asking yourself why any bobchin fool would do a thing like that."

But suddenly, in a burst of comprehension, Michael thought he knew why even a person of Tom's obvious breeding, intelligence, and education might do such a thing. "Was it a duel?" he exclaimed in hushed tones. "You killed your man and had to flee or hide?"

Tom laughed aloud. "I'm not really a fool, boy. *Or* a hot-head."

"You fled your debts, then? Or your kinsmen?"

"That's closer," Tom admitted. "Though I'd have borne with them if I'd been my father's eldest son. Unfortunately, I'm his youngest."

"Oh," Michael said—and this time he really was enlightened. This explained everything—from Tom's educated accent to the way he wore his clothes. Visions of spreading estates, liveried servants, a stately country house, flashed through Michael's mind as he raised wide, respectful eyes.

"You've heard of entail, I see," Tom remarked. "My eldest brother inherits all. My second went into the church. My third was bought a sinecure on the Navy Board. I was given a year at Cambridge and told to fend for myself thereafter. Fend how? It was ship out for Virginia and live with the savages—which I think my father rather hoped for—or settle for London and the fleas. As you see . . . I settled." He smiled down at Michael, suddenly hoisting his eyebrows up as high as they would go, then looking pleased when Michael giggled. "I've never once regretted the savages, y'know," he added. "Nor my dear pompous parent, either, I'm bound to say."

"Who is your father?" asked Michael, who was burning with curiosity to know if he would turn out to be "Lord" Somebody, or merely "Sir."

But Tom said, "No, that I won't do—drag his name down with me. Here we are," he added briskly. "Now. I insist that you concern yourself with your new jacket. Cut? Fabric? Color? I say 'new.' I mean new to *you,* as I'm sure you understand."

Michael, who had not understood, looked around him in astonishment. His whole previous experience with clothes had consisted in being told that some bolt-end of cloth in his father's shop would make him a nice suit, then standing still while the tailor measured him, then later wearing the suit. Without giving it a conscious thought, he had assumed that he and Tom were on their way to a tailor's shop. Instead, they were standing before one of the old-clothes stalls that half-blocked Kerry Lane, and Tom was fingering, holding out, frowning at, scornfully flipping aside, a variety of jackets hanging there fluttering in the April breeze—any one of which, Michael grasped at last, might belong to him within a very few minutes.

His first impulse was to cling to his own familiar one, outgrown and outworn though it might be. But his second was to dart a rather keener glance at Tom's own imaginative and admirable costume, to decide it had undoubtedly been assembled by this very method, perhaps from these very stalls, and to look back at the lines of gaily dancing garments with a new exhilaration growing in his heart. He might choose for *himself?* Choose any color or style of jacket that caught his fancy, without reference to such hampering considerations as suitability or durability? He could perhaps even have a red one? A red *silk* one?

But the new freedom was not to be quite so free as that. Tom's guiding principle, as he sorted through the wares on display, was quality. Whatever a garment's age and condition now, it must have once been excellent to attract his connoisseur's eye, then it must satisfy that eye's stringent demands in regard to cut and style. *Then* it must fit and be becoming, and Michael must like it. With practiced dispatch, Tom set aside three jackets that met his first requirements and called Michael into consultation about the last few. The delightful result was that the outgrown jackanapes, plus two shillings sixpence, ended up in the clothes-merchant's hands, and a new one—new to Michael—of a stylish cut that showed a great deal of white shirt about the waist and forearms ended up on Michael's back. It was cloth, not silk, but it was poppy-red, with only two of its gilt buttons missing, and the gayest possible fringe of multi-colored ribbon loops around each elbow where the new sleeves ended. Best of all, a broad, once richly embroidered velvet sword-belt that had riveted Michael's gaze—though he had said not a word about it—now slanted grandly across his chest, needing only the addition of a short sword at the left hip, in case he ever chanced to acquire one.

"Hoyday! Now, that's something like, that is!" Tom said, with a clap of his hands as he stood back to admire Michael. "Very good indeed. And now we must work like little spinners to make up the price."

So Michael, much entertained by the vision of himself as a little spider in a scarlet coat, strode proudly beside Tom back to Cheap and down Old 'Change—but not into Paul's Churchyard as he expected. "Are we not to sell ballads today, then?" he asked in disappointment.

"We are. Master Bennet is doubtless asking himself the same question. But I go to work when it suits me. Just now it suits me to fetch my lute—and arrange for your accommodations."

This meant, Michael found, to have a short, private conversation with Mistress Floss—or Mother Floss as she seemed to be called —the very blond and very fat alewife of the Boar's Head tavern, while Michael waited rather uneasily outside in Knightrider Street, dodging both foot and wheeled traffic, trying to ignore the smell of nightmare hanging over nearby St. Mary Magdalen churchyard and wondering what he would do if Mother Floss refused to let him share Tom's lodgings. But it was all right. Tom emerged promptly, led him around the corner into tiny Dolittle Lane, and up the rickety back stairs of the Boar's Head. Adjoining the tavern at the rear was a stable where a hackney-man kept his horses and Mother Floss her cow, and above the stable was a garret of two rooms. One was the hay-loft, no more than a rough-floored shelf over the stable below; the other, imperfectly partitioned off from it by a sagging curtain, was Tom's home.

A home less like the house on Bartholomew Lane would have been hard to find. Hesitantly, Michael followed Tom through the curtain and stopped, feeling very much a stranger. The room was barely middle-sized, but gained a certain airiness from the steep pitch of its ceiling, which slanted down from a central beam above the makeshift partition and was in fact merely the underside of the stable roof. You could see the rafters and the sooty hollows of the tiles, festooned with ancient cobwebs. Ranged beneath were one bed with faded green hangings, one sagging chair, one stool, one washstand, and one battered table on which a stub of tallow candle was stuck into a pool of its own drippings. On one of two nails in the age-darkened wall hung Tom's other shirt. Beside it, on a crude shelf, stood half a dozen books. The whole place smelled oddly countrified from the hay stored beyond the curtain and the clean straw strewn over the floor—nice, though not a proper "home" smell, Michael thought, only half-certain what he meant. (Wax tapers, cloves, and roasting meat at the Truebloods', rushlights and cabbage at the Schoonmakers'.)

The one window, a dormer thrusting out over Dolittle Lane, peered straight into the garret window of the house across the way, to whose occupant you could have handed a bowl of soup without the slightest difficulty—or, if you had especially long arms, reached in and salted it for him. In that garret, Tom remarked, lived a puppeteer—a "motion-man" named Harry Hobson—with his wife and children. Michael, peering into their window with interest at this news, saw two small wooden-headed puppets lying abandoned on the sill.

The lute really was "at home in bed," tucked neatly between the blanket and the ragged coverlet, which Tom said was the best place for it when it was not in use. "But never put a lute between *sheets,* Michael. Sheets can be sweat-damp, and damp is the worst of all weathers for a lute." As he spoke, Tom drew the instrument out of its nest and ran his fingers over the strings, tuning a bit and tightening the pegs, then laid it aside, and from under the bed dragged a light wooden frame stretched with thickly braided straw.

"Oh! A truckle bed!" Michael said in tones of such relief that Tom laughed.

"Were you thinking you'd sleep on the floor? I've Mother Floss's promise of a mattress for it by tonight. Not a grand one—I daresay you're used to feathers. But you won't mind straw. Now. Let's have that bundle."

Michael relinquished it, self-consciously. Tom untied the knots and with some ceremony shook out Michael's spare shirt and underclothes, and his one tucker—all hand-downs from Alphy Schoonmaker and soft with wear, but sound linen nonetheless—and hung them on the second of the two nails, remarking that Michael was now officially at home. Then he slipped the lute-strap over his shoulder and led the way down the decrepit stairs to the lane.

Michael, feeling strongly that all this must surely be happening to somebody else, glanced once more around his strange new home and followed.

They walked directly to Paul's Churchyard where Tom disappeared into Master Bennet's shop to get his ballad-sheets. Outside, the stationer's apprentice, a hulking boy wearing a drab, durable jacket on which Michael gazed with scorn, was pacing about under the Lamb and Inkbottle sign, shouting, "What d'ye lack?" at every passerby, gabbling a long list of items his master sold, even catching a sleeve now and then to urge someone inside—in short, diligently performing his duties. Michael, who wished to be diligent in performing his, whatever they turned out to be, paced about too at a little distance and watched the boy covertly, meanwhile displaying his new sword-belt. Odd though his new work might be, it was as close to real apprenticeship as he was likely to come for a time, and he was resolved to give his best to it.

But business was again postponed. As Tom reappeared, carrying a sheaf of ballads, the first peal of the midday Angelus from Paul's rang out across the clear air, and seconds later the London-wide uproar was well launched. When each of the hundred and nine churches had completed its own nine beats, and the overtones were slipping away in a jangle of fading colors, Tom, who had merely smiled and directed Michael in dumb show toward Watling Street, said, "First we dine—because everybody else will before they have time or patience to listen to a song. Then we find a likely corner near some tavern favored by people with fat purses. As they stroll forth after dinner, full of swan-pie and human kindness, they may consent to fatten *our* purse a trifle."

They themselves filled up on brawn and cabbage at a cookshop, then walked up Bow Lane to Cheapside, where within a few paces of Mary-le-Bow Church they had a choice of good inns and taverns; indeed, every second sign seemed to be the long iron rod of an ale-house, thrusting out over the street to dangle a bush or bough in front of thirsty folks' noses. Tom chose a place at the Bread Street corner near the water-standard in the middle of the street, which was itself always busy with wives and watercarriers coming and going with their wooden pails. Handing Michael half the ballad sheets, he dropped the rest to the cobbles and put his foot on them. Then he unslung his lute.

"But what do I do?" Michael asked nervously, seized with sudden stage-fright as he glanced at the indifferent faces passing by.

"Just give me your ears and attention while I sing you a song," Tom told him with a smile. "If you can contrive to look like the beginning of a crowd, so much the better. By all means, giggle at the funny bits. But chiefly, enjoy yourself and let it show. When I've done singing, you can hawk our wares."

"Like an apprentice," Michael said eagerly.

Tom stayed his hand upon the lute-strings. "Not quite like an apprentice, Michael. You are *not* settled for seven years—or even seven months. You must remember, our arrangement is *temporary.*"

Michael, feeling a bit quenched, murmured, "Yes, sir."

But then Tom smiled again, hoisted his eyebrows, swept a bold chord from the strings, and you could no more resist than you could jump over Paul's—not if you were Michael, from whose head everything else promptly fled. The ballad was a witty one, the tune was fine and sprightly, and there were plenty of occasions for Michael to giggle at the funny bits. As for contriving to look like a crowd, he forgot to. But since he was standing transfixed with enjoyment, totally absorbed in the musical tale, and reflecting in his upturned face every slightest shift of emotion from sympathy to sudden mirth that the verses and Tom intended, people began to gather anyhow—pausing first, with amused faces, to watch Michael, then staying to share his laughter and Tom's spell.

As the final chords were sounding, Michael remembered his duties. He swung about with his face still merry from the finale and thrust his ballad-sheets aloft with a shrill, "Who'll buy for a penny?" Another laugh went up, and a good-natured gentleman bought two before Tom had straightened from his bow. A young girl bought another, a countryman three, and from a window above, the wife tossed down a penny to have a sheet left downstairs in her husband's shop for her. Pennies seemed to rain upon Michael; he was kept busy grabbing them and thrusting a ballad-sheet into outstretched hands and bobbing his thanks. When their little crowd had all filtered away into the larger crowd, he was left with only two or three ballads, and Tom's expression was almost stunned.

"Do we find a new corner now?" Michael asked him briskly. "There's that whole stack under your foot still."

"Yes. Yes, a new corner. You're a magician, Michael. Let's try Bucklersbury—right at the end by St. Mary Woolchurch."

Michael agreed with pleasure; Bucklersbury always smelled intriguingly of the apothecary shops and herb-sellers' stalls that lined the street. Tom sang a different ballad there, a dark, dramatic, gory account of a murder—a true account of a real murder; a woman had been stabbed to death in the alleys of Whitefriars only the night before. Some versifier had been scribbling before the blood was dry, though not Tom, who told Michael regretfully that he had not heard of the affair in time. It drew a larger crowd than the gay ballad because of the song's chilly horrors and its pious adjurations at the end, which as everyone knew were very improving to the character. Also because of Tom's spell-binding powers, for he was something of a magician himself in holding his listeners. It was when he stopped singing and began selling that he lost them, he told Michael. Here Michael shone. He was at once quicker, shriller, more persistent, and harder to say no to than Tom, and having had no previous experience, he had no doubts of his success. Together, Tom and his new assistant sold nearly all the murder-ballad sheets beside St. Mary Woolchurch.

It was as they were stationing themselves in Cannon Street a few minutes later that Michael spotted Jack Stubbs among the peddlers, housewives, rich merchants, poor watercarriers, maid-servants, clerks, thieves and a hundred other varieties of Londoners pushing past, many of them already slowing expectantly at sight of Tom's lute and ballad-sheets.

"Look, there's your friend—the one you called 'Jack Horner,' " Michael said rather loudly, to be heard over the clatter of a passing cart. He pointed at Jack, then, because he felt a bit guilty about disliking the little man so, turned the gesture into a friendly wave.

To his surprise, Tom spun him around and thrust a stack of ballads into his arms, muttering, "Sh-sh-sh—we don't recognize him unless I say so."

Before Michael could do more than gape, Tom swept his fingers down over the lute strings in one of the strong exhilarating chords that could stop passersby in their tracks and turn persons of eleven and a half into stone images depicting Anticipation. Michael did not think of Master Stubbs again.

"I'll tell you what it is, it's your new red jackanapes," Tom said half an hour later, as the last three or four listeners straggled off in various directions, reading their ballad-sheets and still chuckling. A bare half-dozen sheets remained in Michael's hand, and Tom's purse was fat with pennies, which he rapidly began to count.

Michael watched with satisfaction and a proprietary eye, remarking that they should have no trouble at all selling the next batch before the evening Angelus.

"What next batch?" Tom asked absently.

"Won't we fetch more now?" asked Michael, whose idea had been to hurry back to the stationer's for more ballads, then hurry out to sell those, and to repeat all this many times every day, thus getting rich as fast as possible.

He learned at once that such ideas were his alone. Tom said, "My faith, no!" and stared at him, astonished. "There's nine shillings here—nearly an angel. Why, that'll keep us handsomely— supper for both and a glass of canary for me and enough over for the printing tomorrow of whatever I might scribble tonight. Why work longer? Here's your thruppence, Michael—well earned, too. Go spend a bit of it, and we'll meet later."

"But—" Michael began in consternation.

"I've a bit of business that needs seeing to," Tom said hastily. "Personal matter. And you'll be glad enough to be free of my company for a while, I daresay. Just wander home to the Boar's Head whenever it suits you. The rest of the day is yours."

Michael, who did not want the rest of his day, stood holding his thruppence and watching Tom's tall, jaunty figure move with a cat's ease through the crowded street, until even the broken tip of the bottle-green plume had vanished. Then he started slowly in the other direction, wondering what to do with himself now, and trying very hard not to feel wounded and thrust aside. He had no right to feel so, he knew. Obviously, his new life was going to provide him with periods of freedom from Tom's company, whether he wanted them or not—because Tom would want some periods free of his. Fair enough.

For just a moment, though, he was filled with such a rush of longing for Master and Mistress Trueblood whose ways he had understood and to whom he had really belonged—*not* temporarily —that he could scarcely see through the tears that blurred the sunny afternoon. When he had blinked them away, angrily wiped his nose on the sleeve of his red jacket, and looked about him again, he found that his feet had carried him from long habit into Suffolk Lane. He stood almost at the doorstep of the great house—

once, long ago, the Duke of Buckingham's—called the Manor of the Rose, where the Merchant Taylors had their school and where he had construed his Latin and learned his Greek daily for five long years. The plague had changed all that, killed schoolmates and masters impartially and finally closed the school. He knew nobody there now. He gave the familiar doorway and the sculptured rose above it one long and homesick glance, then hurried on down the lane lest someone recognize him and turn him over to the parish.

If I had just one person truly blood-kin to me, he thought as he emerged into Thames Street. Just one grandmother, or fourth cousin, or sister—

A sister. It would be nice, ever so nice and jolly, to talk to Susanna right now, wouldn't it? If he could only find that shop. And if she hadn't forgotten him. No, she couldn't have forgotten him, it was only day before yesterday they had parted in the court-yard of the King's Head Inn.

Day before yesterday? It seemed year before last, so much had changed in his world since then.

He started eastward along the street, looking uncertainly about him. She had mentioned Old Swan Stairs, which was just yonder, down one of those riverside alleys. But a haberdasher's shop would scarcely be here in Thames Street, among the chandlers and fish-mongers and sailmakers. More likely in Lombard or Cornhill. Or it could be tucked away in any of the lanes between here and there. Michael turned into St. Martin's Lane and wandered northward, exploring as he went, looking everywhere for a Golden Buckle sign.

An hour later he emerged from Pope's Head Alley onto Corn-hill and stood wondering wearily which way to go—west toward Poultry, straight across the street into the Royal Exchange (but there was no Golden Buckle there, he knew), or east toward St. Michael Archangel.

His gaze lingered thoughtfully on the looming gray tower of the church whose name he bore, the church where someone, eleven and a half years ago, had laid him in a corner of the porch one foggy dawning, then hurried away. And suddenly he knew where to start looking for a trace of his own blood kin. He started toward St. Michael Archangel as fast as he could go.

The Fishmonger's Apprentice

"No, I know nothing about it, nothing, and so I've told you already," the verger said impatiently. "Nor would the beadle know, nor the curate, nor anybody else. As for bothering the vicar with such questions, the notion's a simpleton's! Now begone, child, begone—sss—sss—sss!"

Flapping both hands as if he were ridding the place of cats, he had Michael outside the church's side door, and the door closed in his face, before one could sneeze.

Michael stood a moment, scowling at the door. He had explained his request as civilly as he knew how, had taken up a mere moment of this supercilious verger's time; he had asked only to see the register or somebody who might remember eleven and a half years back—he did not know how to be less troublesome. Resolving to come back another day, he turned reluctantly away, cutting through the cloister and the churchyard just south of the great building. It was an extra large churchyard, so not quite as overcrowded and ill-covered as some others, but the smell of death hung over it all the same, and Michael's whole intent was to hurry through as fast as he could. But as he skirted the great pulpit-cross built by some medieval parishioner, he saw an old woman in front of one of the nearby almshouses, hobbling aimlessly up and down in the last of the sunshine. She looked very old, very much a part of her surroundings—as if she might have lived long in that almshouse, perhaps as long as eleven years. Almost without thinking, Michael started toward her.

She noticed him at once, halted to peer at him, and began to grin toothlessly when he came closer, nodding her head and clasping her hands with apparent delight. Diffidently Michael said, "Good morrow," and explained what he wanted, and something of why he wanted it—feeling more awkward all the time because she listened without a word, without the slightest change of expression, staring at his face as intently as if he had hypnotised her. "But—I suppose you might not remember—or even know anything about me anyway," he finished lamely.

"But I do, though," she said at once, in a voice as intent as her eyes.

"You *do?*"

"I do. Oh, I do. I remember your mother—a poor widder woman like me, she were, and with all them little children—and her name was Blake, and she was hanged."

"Hanged . . ." Michael repeated, or tried to, but his breath left him in the middle of the word, and he could only shudder and stare at the old woman as she had stared at him.

"Hanged, she was. Yes. Oh, yes. And for naught, neither, only that her husband was no Puritan, but a loyal King's man, and in Master Cromwell's day that was mightily out of fashion, that was. . . ." She talked on steadily, rambling a bit but never too much for Michael to follow her story—a story not unlike others of the Civil War years that he had heard when Master or Mistress Trueblood reminisced with friends. Ten children, Mistress Blake had been left to care for, when her Royalist husband had been driven out of London. "And most of 'em little children, y'mind— one was a wee babby only a month or two old . . . and then her little shop was broke into by them Roundhead villyans, yes, just ruint it was, and fourteen pound stolen, and her house plundered— and horses and men billeted on her when she could scarce find bread for them little ones without she begged for it. . . ." But at last, Michael gathered, the persecuted woman was hauled into the courts, tried and condemned as a Royalist, led to the gallows with other victims—"and Mistress Blake not knowing but her turn was next, standing all the while with a halter about her neck over against the gallows—and a soldier would have put the rope under her kerchief, to hide it, like, but she'd have none of it, she wouldn't. 'I am not ashamed to suffer in this cause,' she says to him, and in a voice all could hear—oh, a brave woman, she were, a brave widder-woman, fit for the Book of Martyrs, that she were!"

Shaken and half in tears at this sudden intelligence of the mother he could not even remember, Michael at last managed to break into the old woman's monologue to ask about the orphaned children.

"All gone, scattered—whether the poor cossets is alive or dead nobody knows, it's all in the Lord's hands—only three of them was brought here, I know naught of the girl, she ran away soon, but the big boy, Alan, he was raised in the parish workhouse, then put out 'prentice to a fishmonger. A good lad, they do say, and he looks the world and all like you! And the babby—that was you, little Master—why, you was put to a wet-nurse right here in this churchyard in that almshouse end of the row and raised up here till you was took away somewheres . . . used to be choirman's houses, these did, but almshouses now, God's mercy, for poor widders in the parish like me, I thank the Lord . . ."

"Mistress—please, mistress—this Alan, my b-brother—" Michael stumbled over the word, it felt so strange and wonderful on his lips. "Where can I find him? Who is the fishmonger he's apprenticed to? I—"

"Hawkins, that's the man. Paul Hawkins, down near Cock Key or it may be Buttolph's Lane. I know naught of what happened to the girl, though, she ran away. . . . Little Master, I'll take you up in the bell tower, I will, and glad to! Come along—I'll show you a wonder, where the Devil himself sprang through the window one night and knocked the bell-ringers on their faces and out o' their heads and left his claw marks plain on the windowsill. Yes, when the ringers come to their wits again, they saw the scratches there, right in the stone, deep enough to set a feather into. Come along, I'll show you—"

But Michael had already been shown this wonder by Mistress Trueblood several years ago. He managed to escape the old woman—Mistress Beasley, she said her name was—with difficulty but without rudeness, for he was overwhelmingly grateful to her, though he was very anxious *not* to stay and listen to her any longer.

The moment he was free he hurled himself down Birchin Lane as if the bell-ringers' Devil were after him, heading for Cock Key. *The girl,* she had said—the girl had run away, and she knew nothing of her, but it was plain there had once been a girl—a sister. What, oh, what if he should find this Alan, this brother, and they did really look alike, light hair and freckles and blue eyes, and even a little mole on the side of the neck . . . and what if Alan would be as overjoyed to find him as he would be to find Alan, and then what if they both went searching together this very evening and found the Golden Buckle and Susanna, and she would be overjoyed too, and it would *all come true!* . . . Michael, running headlong on his zigzag course toward the river—Lombard to Gracechurch, then Eastcheap to Buttolph's Lane—was scarcely aware of the coaches he dodged, the obstacles he avoided or leaped over, the people he brushed past, or even that his feet ever touched the cobbles.

Ten minutes after he had left the churchyard he was standing in a fish-reeking alley behind the mean little house and shop of Paul Hawkins, staring unhappily at the gangling, underfed, bitter-eyed, black-haired eighteen-year-old whose name was Alan Blake. The "brother" was gutting plaice, rapidly and expertly, with bloody, scarred hands, throwing the offal on the ground and the fish into a shallow basket, where they glittered like raw gold in the sunset light. And he was shaking his head, his dark eyes running over Michael with faint amusement but not much interest.

"Y'must be a bobchin, to believe all that," he said.

"But—d'you mean it isn't so? None of it?"

"Oh, yes, it's so. All of it. But it's nothing to do with *you*. How old are you?"

"Eleven. And a half."

"Well, can't you count? The Rebellion was over in '52. My mother—not yours—was hanged in '49. Five years before you were born."

Michael was silent, slowly and painfully trying to take this in. Sixteen-forty-nine was, certainly, five years before he was born. Yet old Mistress Beasley had been so *sure*—her details so convincing. "But—what of the girl? She said there was a girl—? And a baby. And that was *me*."

"There was a girl," Alan Blake said patiently. "My sister Fan, a year older than me. She ran away from the workhouse, and I've never seen her since. And there was a baby. I forget its name, but it wasn't you, because it died. You're somebody else." His bitter dark eyes flicked sardonically to Michael's face. "You'd best thank

God for it, and don't let the parish find you on its hands, or you'll
end up like me—apprenticed for the rest of your nat'ral days.
Or so *he* thinks, that sousing, lying, clabber-headed . . ." The
rest dwindled to a string of muttered curses as the boy darted a
glance of hatred toward the windows above him.

"You—don't like your master?" Michael said lamely.

"Oh, I love 'im, I do." A fish sailed, glittering, into the basket,
and the gutting knife plunged ferociously into another. "But the
next time the navy's press gangs are in the streets, I'm going to let
them take me. I don't mind fighting their Dutchmen for 'em. Not
if it gets me away from *him*."

A moment later Alan Blake picked up the basket and stalked
into a shed attached to the back of the house. And that was the
end of that.

Slowly, Michael walked on through the alley and out into Pudding Lane. It was hours yet till suppertime; the six o'clock bells were
just now ringing. But he was suddenly ravenous with such a hunger
as he had seldom known. From a baker's shop he was passing came
a fragrance that pulled him through the door, willy-nilly; he spent
a ha'penny on two fresh-baked "wiggs" and walked on again, de-
vouring them as if he had never eaten raisin-buns in his life. But
they were gone too soon, and somehow the hunger was still there.
Hands thrust deep into his breeches pockets—one tightly clutching
his remaining coins—he plodded along Eastcheap, crossing the top
of Poultney Lane without so much as a glance down toward the
river and Old Swan Stairs. He would not, after all, be going joyfully in search of Susanna with their "brother," this evening or
any evening. He was not sure he would search for her any more
at all.

Indeed, he was not sure where he was going now. To the stable
behind the Boar's Head, he supposed, and Tom's room. *My room,*
he thought experimentally. But it was not really his room, for all
that his nightshirt was hanging on that nail. He was a stranger
there—and for all Tom's kindness, a stranger to Tom, too.

Never mind! It was all only temporary—as Tom kept saying.
Only until the *Medusa* sailed home.

Meanwhile, he had no place else to go, so he wandered toward
Dolittle Lane. He encountered a funeral procession in Budge Row

and followed it up to Cheapside. He saw a thief being dragged toward Newgate prison—and a very old duchess, wrapped in innumerable shawls despite the heat, being borne in her crested sedan chair along Goldsmith's Row. He watched two hackney coaches jam royally in Blowbladder Street and listened to the ensuing loud and spirited quarrel and heard the cry of "Fire!" from somewhere up Foster Lane, where he ran with everybody else to gape at the smoke pouring out from a narrow house, and presently from its right-hand neighbor too, and then from the one built back-to-back with it in Gutter Lane, while the families ran out weeping and terrified, carrying pots and pans and bedclothes or something queer like a hearth broom or a feathered hat, which they'd snatched up only because it came to hand first. But after a while the parish constable struggled through the crowd with his assistants, who hitched up their hand-squirts to the conduit around behind Wood Street, and began to spray the houses and pull down the flaming timbers with their long-handled hooks, so Michael left, feeling certain they'd get the blaze out all right sooner or later—they always did. Besides, it was sweating hot there, like standing too close to a mammoth bonfire. He wandered back down Gutter Lane to Cheap again, and slowly, under a dimming sky, back to Blowbladder Street. He walked through Paul's Churchyard in the red of sunset-end, eyeing the cubbyhole where he had slept last night and feeling strongly that he would rather not sleep there again. And so at last, when it was nearly dark, he climbed the rickety stairs to the room above the stable, only half-believing that Tom would really be there, that this queerest of all days was more than some uneasy, lonesome dream.

Tom was there, lounging on his bed with one knee cocked up and his back against the bedpost, plucking at his lute. As Michael stepped uncertainly into the room, he turned quickly, and a strange look washed over his face—a look very much like relief. He stood up instantly, flung the lute onto the bed, and exclaimed, "Well-a-day! I thought you'd never get here! Indeed, I wondered if you were coming. Bad as I need you, too! You're just the one can tell me a rhyme for 'Herman'."

Surprised into a giggle, Michael stood considering this, feeling the heavy cold thing inside him warm and lighten, and his doubts begin to evaporate like dew in the sun. "Vermin?" he suggested.

"No, no, it can't be a funny one, this is a funeral-dirge. Sir Richard Herman was buried this evening—the judge, y'know."

"Oh! I saw the procession! It must have been his!"

"Did you, now! Why, you're invaluable. How many attendants were there? How many banners?"

So Michael described it all as accurately as he could, and in the midst of it, Tom suddenly shouted "Ermine!" and dropped into the chair by the table to scribble furiously on one of the sheets of foolscap scattered there, then stopped, gave Michael a quick, bland look, and said, "I'gad, I nearly forgot to give you this." As he spoke, he reached into his shirt, drew something out, and put it into Michael's hand.

And there lay the scarlet leather purse with the little gilt dragon. It was still warm from Tom's body—and of a familiar weight. Without even looking inside, Michael was sure it contained exactly six shillings ninepence, and the shell.

He stared at it, a dozen questions buzzing like bees around his mind, then with lips already parted to ask the first one, he raised his eyes. Tom had gone back to his scribbling. His quill scrabbled like a live thing across the foolscap, scratching and squeaking; he dipped it swiftly with a flourish of ragged cuff-flounces, made a blot and muttered at it, paused for a word, pounced on one, and scribbled again with a "ha!" of satisfaction. His hat, with its dashing sweep of brim and its broken-backed plume, flew like an ensign from the bedpost beyond him.

And Michael closed his mouth again. *Never mind.* Firmly he turned away, opened his scarlet purse to put today's coins in it, and slipped the purse into his pocket, where it felt reassuringly familiar. Then he took off his new red jackanapes and swordbelt and hung them on his nail. Some other time he'd ask Tom questions about his lucky friend and how he found the purse.

Or maybe never.

PART II

The Streets

Meanwhile there was a new life to get used to—and a very odd one it seemed to Michael, just at first. But soon it began to feel quite natural and ordinary to wake each morning to the thump of hoofs belowstairs, punctuated by the hack-driver's "Whoa, Laddie!" and the mournful bawling of Mother Floss's cow, and to go to sleep each night in the rustly snugness of the truckle bed after a day spent wandering the streets of London. Even the occasional afternoons of freedom from Tom ceased to burden him; it was sometimes good, he decided, to stroll away down a street, in-dependent as a man grown, and simply gaze about and think one's own thoughts. Nor did he worry for long about the extra ballads they could have fetched and sold but didn't. To think beyond the present was not Tom's way, and an easy, pleasant way Michael began to find it.

Of course, for him it was all only temporary, as Tom frequently reminded him. "Just until your uncle comes home," he said at first, until an inquiry at the Custom House informed them that there was no word at all of when the *Medusa* might be expected. Then it became, "Just until we find you something more suitable. You'd not want to accept just *any* situation. It's your future we must keep an eye on." However, Tom's notions of how to do this seemed as vague as Michael's, so the actual taking of any action in the matter remained comfortably in the future too.

For Michael, the present soon became absorbing. He had never known more variegated days or ones that flew so fast in spite of being almost idled away, with no school, few prayers, no errands or duties, and not overmuch ballad-selling either—just plenty of ballad-making and lute-playing and singing and amusement. It was as good as the life led by the grasshopper in the fable about the grasshopper and the ant printed in Michael's old hornbook that he had learned to read by. Indeed, every time he saw the grasshopper atop the Royal Exchange now, he thought of Tom. They sold just enough ballads to pay their keep, with a bit over for a treat or an occasional new shirt or tucker (new to *them*) and once gave the dinner-money for a nearly undamaged volume of Montaigne's *Essays* for Tom's tattered library—a cheap enough price, he told Michael, for the most civilized companionship in the world. Sometimes they peddled their ballads early, sometimes at midday, and occasionally after sundown when the pale evening light still lingered in the streets, for Tom hated doing anything in the same way twice. Most nights—though not all—he scribbled a new set of verses, trying them out on Michael to see if he giggled and demanding his help with rhymes. Michael was a dud at first, but he caught the hang of it, and before long his brain was swarming with lists of sounds and syllables—prayeth, payeth, slayeth, drummer, summer, mummer. Any unusual sight or event set him muttering rhymes for it under his breath.

London was a limitless source of such happenings, which Tom always got wind of if Michael didn't. After a free afternoon, Michael would come home in the gathering dusk to climb the stairs beside the stable, welcoming the honest smell of hay and animals as the street's stench faded behind him, and from the room above would hear the lute, sounding as if it were talking to itself. An instant later the curtain would be flung aside and Tom would peer down, saying, "Is that my Person of eleven and a half? Well, God-a-mercy, boy, guess what's happened—a calf with two heads was born today out near Spittal Fields. Still alive."

"Really? Two *whole* heads?"

"Two perfect little heads. Brown eyes in one, blue in the other— or so I heard. I haven't seen the wonder. But I'm making a song about it, and you must help me. Just now I'm wanting a rhyme for 'marveling,' and nothing comes to mind but 'starveling,' which won't do at all."

Some such excitement was forever turning up. Not a day passed but somebody would be murdered or somebody hanged or a great man buried or his daughter wed or his heir born. Or some Quaker would gloomily foretell that wicked London would perish in flames before the year was out, and folk would be talking of nothing else —just as if they'd never heard it before, though seers and prophets had been gloomily foretelling the same thing, time out of mind. Or, if all else failed, Tom like any other balladeer worth his salt could set into verse a tale from Ovid or Aesop or Robin Hood or an escapade of that liveliest of highwaymen, Gamaliel Ratsey.

"But a good fresh murder or hanging sells better," Tom admitted. "Something closer to home, d'ye see."

"Like the Rathbone Plot," Michael agreed.

That had been real news, a sensation during Michael's first days with Tom—the discovery of a full-blown plot to murder the King and restore the Commonwealth. Seven veterans of Cromwell's old army, led by one John Rathbone, had schemed to overwhelm the Horse Guards, seize the Tower, then close all the City gates, and set London afire. Michael, appalled, found it hard to conceive of such wickedness, but even harder to imagine waiting all summer to begin on it—for with the most cold-blood calm, the plotters had scheduled their *coup* for September 3rd.

"Why *September* 3rd?" he demanded, nearly incredulous. "That's four months off!"

"But the magic hour, nonetheless," Tom assured him, adding that Rathbone and company had prudently consulted Lilly's Almanac, even constructed a horoscope, before selecting their day. "If you're going to start a holocaust, you must do it properly, y'know. Can't go burning a hundred thousand of us in our beds on just any old inauspicious date." Tom smiled and hoisted his eyebrows and went on scribbling, as every ballad-man in town was doing at that moment. But Michael shivered, reflecting that all the Quaker fiery-doom prophets had come uncomfortably close to being right for once. Of course the conspirators were immediately convicted of high treason, and all London, including Tom and Michael, flocked to see them hanged. Then that seven-day wonder was over—to Tom's relief, for as he remarked to Michael, "Rathbone" was the devil's own word to find a rhyme for.

None of this silenced the seers and prophets, who continued to thunder that this was the year of destruction. In Michael's opinion, if last summer hadn't done for London, nothing could, but he found it easy to understand the mood of expectancy. Something was bound to happen in a year numbered 1666.

"Not destruction, though, or burning in our beds or anything. Not another comet, either," Michael added with a shudder. Last year's comet, eeriest of oracles, had ushered in the plague. "But it *could* be something nice for a change—like winning the war."

Tom agreed that a rousing naval victory over the Dutch, come summer, would serve very nicely. "Lacking that, we might stroll out to Smithfield this afternoon. I've heard the Red Bull Tavern has a monkey who can turn a full somersault while carrying a basket of eggs on his head."

It was this sort of suggestion that made the days fly. Tom's company was never boring, and his notions of a good way to spend an afternoon coincided marvelously with Michael's. If they were not strolling out to Smithfield or up and down the shady avenues of trees at Moorfields just to breathe the sweet-smelling country air, they might head down Lambert Hill to Trig Stairs, where a ferocious-looking, one-eyed waterman named Sam'l could usually be found, shouting for fares. Sam'l was one of Tom's strange "friends," of whom he had quite a collection—among them the lanky cunning-man Niggles, who was forever around the Boar's Head telling fortunes, and Sharp the mountebank, whose smile Michael distrusted from the bottom of his heart, but whose scruffy little monkey he loved and pitied. And there was a gypsy parson. . . . But Sam'l was Michael's favorite. Cutthroat though he looked, he would take them wherever Tom wanted to go, regardless of whether he got his sixpence that day or next week. When Michael marveled at this, Tom merely shrugged and said, "I did Sam'l a good turn once," but never explained any further. So they could take boat at will to go across to Bankside for a greyhound race or upriver to Westminster Stairs. From there one could go walking in St. James Park and maybe see the King (and once they did—strolling with a lady on each arm and three spaniels rollicking ahead and wearing a rich velvet coat and lace like cobwebs) or stroll along the Strand, where they went on May Day to watch the morris dancing. And once they went to Charing Cross to see the Italian puppet-show called Punchinello, which was ever so much funnier, Michael had to admit, than the simple playlets enacted

by the tiny creatures of Harry Hobson the "motion-man," their
neighbor across Dolittle Lane—though he never tired of watching
Harry's Poll and Paul and Baby.

Harry was another of Tom's odd "friends," a giant of a man,
with a vast, billowing, dirty shirt-front, a lot of tangled red hair,
and a strange hoarse voice that always made Michael want to clear
his throat. He was the cheeriest of neighbors, much given to calling
out greetings across the narrow space between his window and
Tom's, as he sat with tankard in hand and huge forearms propped
on the gritty sill. He could perform on any street-corner. His
theatre was only a ragged sheet that dropped from a hoop sus-
pended on a rickety standard; once inside his tubular "tent," Harry
vanished except for his battered boots, while above, the tiny
leathern figures of Paul and Poll capered at the sheet's top. When
the playlet ended, Paul and Poll subsided limply on their hooks,
and out ducked Harry to sell his penny whistles (which seldom
whistled an hour later, Michael discovered) or his Herbal Oint-
ment or his Elixir of Pure Gold, while the children, with whom
he was very popular, crowded around him in delight.

The odd thing was that his own five children were pale, thin
creatures, none of whom ever seemed to take delight in anything,
and all of whom avoided Harry as much as possible and stuck
close to their silent, faded mother. Michael found this puzzling
until the morning Harry came home, after a three-day absence, in
the condition Tom referred to as "spizzled." Then Michael, even
in his own room across the lane, found himself cowering away
from the window and behind the bed-curtains, enduring the sounds
he could not shut out—drunken roarings that made the air quiver,
blows and wild shrieks and cries for help, with an occasional crash
of furniture or tinkle of breaking glass to vary the liveliness. Tom
at length flung down his pen, stalked out to the stair-landing and
returned with an ancient shepherd's crook that always leaned
against the wall there, which he thrust out his window and, after
a moment's patient waiting, into Harry's window and around
Harry's neck. Ignoring the fresh roars this produced, he secured
the crook's other end on his own side and went back to his verses.
The noises from over the way then ceased; Michael, peering out
the open casement in astonishment, saw Harry snoring peacefully

on the windowseat with his neck still imprisoned, and his thin wife philosophically spreading an old quilt over his spraddled legs. Next day all was as before, and Harry jolly as ever.

It was a couple of mornings after this that Michael, walking with Tom down Milk Street, saw a familiar figure in Cheapside, just ahead—or thought he did. He caught his breath, then darted forward.

"What is it?" Tom demanded, striding after him.

"My uncle! I saw my uncle! Just yonder, in Cheap—in a blue coat . . ." Arriving in Cheapside himself, Michael halted to peer eagerly at the faces swarming past the tall water-standard in the middle of the street—water-carriers, housewives, sober-clad London businessmen on their endless errands up and down the City. "There! I think—" Michael was off again, dodging and shoving toward a blue coat now moving eastward past the stone hulk of Mary-le-Bow. Surely that was Uncle Penwood's straight back and high shoulders to the life.

But it was not Uncle Penwood's leathery face with its tufted eyebrows that looked down at him as he came panting alongside a moment later. It was only some stranger's. Falling back in bitter disappointment, Michael watched the blue coat lose itself in the crowd.

Tom's voice came gently from behind him. " 'Twasn't likely, you know. It's less than a se'enight since we checked on the ships' postings."

"I know. I just thought—" Michael turned away disconsolately, and they started back toward Paul's.

For a while they walked in silence. Then Tom said, "Might he have put the *Medusa* in to Dover?"

"He never used to. He always put in here. Always stayed at the same inn—Swan and Bridge on Fish Street Hill . . . the innkeeper was an old friend." Another thought struck Michael. "I don't suppose *he'd* have heard anything—?"

Tom shrugged ruefully; that wasn't likely, either. Still, I could ask, Michael reflected. After a brief inward debate, and a bit of vain rummaging among cobwebbed memories for the innkeeper's name, he parted from Tom in Watling Street, trudged back past London Stone to Eastcheap, and in a few more minutes was walking down the steep slope of Fish Street Hill, squinting at the array of signs swaying overhead. The street seemed full of inns; there was the Harrow, the Mitre, the Sun Taverne. . . . There! An archway flanked by windowpanes, under a sign depicting a white swan walking across a bridge lined with houses like London Bridge. Below was the name, G. Brandon.

Michael walked through the arch and into a courtyard full of sun and pigeons. In an open doorway stood a large, aproned man with brindled hair. Scattering pigeons in a cloud, Michael crossed the cobbles toward him, and two minutes afterwards was being overwhelmed with welcome.

"Cap'n *Penwood's* nevvy? Why, come along in this house, matey. My Bess'll want a sight of you, or I'm a Spaniard! Bess! E-liza-bess!" the innkeeper roared, sweeping Michael through a dark interior that smelled of ale and herrings. "Here, you, Tad! Fetch us a bite up topside—something a boy likes. Oh, Bess, m'love!"

In no time, Michael was nibbling "wiggs" and sausage in an upstairs chamber, wedged fast betwixt stout Master Brandon and his far stouter wife, and wishing he'd never come. Mistress Brandon had three rolling chins, earnest bulging eyes, and an alarming tendency to squeeze Michael ever tighter as she leaned toward him, overflowing the bench, spreading and settling like a sack of grain into her straining purple dress. What with chewing and swallowing, fending off her insistent offers of more food, and trying to break through her husband's steady flow of talk, Michael had difficulty even explaining why he had come. Finally he managed it.

"Fretting about the Cap'n, are ye?" Master Brandon said thoughtfully. "Well, I grant you, he's usually here by now. But it might be the fleet's delayed him, down along of Woolwich or Chatham. Why, the hull lower Thames's been that full o' navy you could near step from deck to deck! First-raters and sixty-gunners and fire ships, with ketches and wherries a-scooting around amongst 'em like water-bugs. Our son Jem, he signed on the *Essex* this year. Cap'n's cox's'n, same as I was once."

"But—I thought the fleet was gone by now."

"Aye, they've sailed, they finally sailed—about a fortnight back—"

"April twenty-third," put in Mistress Brandon precisely.

"—and they'll spend the hull month o' May a-tacking up and down, and seasoning the raw 'uns, and spying out the Dutch." The innkeeper sighed nostalgically. "May's the month for shaking down into a fighting crew, and June's the month for battle. Aye, we'll hear news a'plenty in June, I warrant you!"

"Just try a bite more cheese, ducky . . . No? The child eats like a sparrow!" Mistress Brandon leaned over Michael tenderly. "And how is it you chanced to think of asking us, ducky? Was't your father sent you?"

"No," Michael told her, edging away. "You see my—my foster parents died of plague last summer, and—"

"Saints bless us! La, the saints bless us all! Oh, poor ducky! What a pity—"

"Why, a shame that was, matey," exclaimed Master Brandon through the falling cadenza of his wife's commiseration. "But how was't *you* escaped?"

Michael told the tale of his long year's exile and his dismal homecoming, breaking off short as he suddenly realized his present circumstances might best be glossed over. But Mistress Brandon's eye had already sharpened, and her questions came like darts. Where was he living, then, if not with the Bottses? *How* was he living? Godfrey—would that be Master Stephen Godfrey at the . . . Oh, *Thomas* Godfrey. And who might . . . ? Oh, a musician, fancy! Exactly what sort of . . . ?

"Now, Bess, just haul in your tongue for a bit, eh? It's news of the *Medusa* the lad's come for, not t'Inquisition! I'm mortal sorry I can't tell you more'n what I have, matey. But my guess is, the Cap'n's just late. Don't give up hope."

Michael thanked him earnestly and managed to take his leave, saying Master Godfrey would worry if he weren't home for dinner. At that, he might not have escaped from Mistress Brandon but for the clock on St. Leonard Milkchurch obligingly singing out twelve o'clock, joined a few seconds later by St. Margaret's in a ragged duet. As their last notes faded, Michael was scattering the pigeons again, and back on the street.

"They sound like honest folk," Tom commented when he heard about it. After a moment, he added, "They might've offered you a home and work—if you'd asked politely."

"Yes," Michael said. He glanced away uncomfortably, hoping Tom weren't wishing he *had* asked. "Yes, but—"

"But Mistress Brandon gave you the vapors," Tom guessed with his usual accuracy.

"*Yes.* 'Twould've been like growing up inside a bolster!" said Michael feelingly.

Tom laughed and said his advice was to forget all about the *Medusa* for a while and simply take each day as it came. It was relaxing advice and, like most of Tom's, pleasantly easy to follow. Until a certain afternoon.

It was an afternoon in mid-May, hot and fine, with a brisk breeze snapping the ballad-sheets and everybody's coat-tails. The day's peddling finished, Tom had taken one of his genial but abrupt departures into the crowd, and Michael was left to his own devices. His mood was sanguine; business had gone so well he could have sold ten more copies of "True-Love Requited" if he'd had them. As he strolled aimlessly toward the river, he was still humming it, slightly off-key: *"There was a youth, and a well-belov'd youth, and he was an ESquire's son . . . He loved the Baylif's daughter dear, that lived in ISLington . . ."* Today, he felt it in his bones, something lucky would happen to somebody—perhaps to himself. Changing his hum to a cheerful whistle, he let the wind blow him east along Thames Street toward the Tower, thinking of the bleak prospect he had faced only a few weeks back of becoming a linkboy. Here was where he would have got his links, no doubt about it. Chandler's shops jostled one another all along the way, and rope-makers crowded back-to-back in the alleys and footways running down to the tall warehouses along the wharfs. How much tallow and wick might there be, Michael wondered, from end to end of Thames Street? Enough to make candles for all England—for all the world—for a world of giants. In his stretching imagination there appeared a vision of a mile-long row of candles, forty ells high and fat as church towers, thrusting up all along the river's bank—and of God's hand, holding a God-sized link of tarred rope, reaching down to light them, one after another.

The vision burst like a bubble as Michael jumped for his life out of the way of an overwrought hackney horse and almost fell into a huge basket of fish.

"Ol roight, ol roight, mind wotches about," grumbled the fish-monger's boy on whose toes he had trampled in his wild leap to safety. He gave Michael a push and started his chant again. "What d'ye lack? Will y'buy, will y'buy, any new great plaice or eeeeeels? What d'ye lack. . . ."

All London was crowded, but this end of Thames Street was crammed—with horses, with houses, with rats, with children, with coaches and carts and rubbish—and most of all with Londoners, half of whom were strenuously exerting themselves to sell some-thing to the other half. The street rang with their voices as they cried their wares or services, each with a special cry. It always made Michael feel as if he had strayed into the midst of some huge choir, singing a hundred-part madrigal, though a queer madri-gal it was, dominated by the shrill, insistent voices of the fishwives.

"New haddocks, *new!*"

"Ha'ye any old bellows or trays t'mend?"

"Lily-white mussels, *new!*"

"I have frrr-r-resh cheese and cream, I have fr-r-resh . . ."

"Have y'any work for a *coo*-per?"

"Will y'buy a very fine brush?"

"New oyy-y-y-sters, new Wallfleet oy-y-y-sters!"

"Quick, periwinkles, quick, quick, quick!"

Then over again from the beginning, with new bits added, and weaving in and out among the other cries, like dark threads in a bright tapestry, sounded the dirge-like chants of the prison alms-collectors, enough to make one shiver: "Bread and meeeat—for the poor prisoners of the Mar-shalsea . . . some bro-ken bread and meat . . ."

Passing the top of the alley leading to Old Swan Stairs, Michael was reminded, as usual, of Susanna. He paused to stare down to-ward the landing, puzzling once more over the riddle of her where-abouts, to which he had only this one provoking clue. It was the more provoking because it might be no clue at all. To land at Old Swan Stairs didn't necessarily mean you lived nearby; you might be going up New Fish Street toward Bishopsgate or around the end of London Bridge toward the Tower. Or onto the Bridge itself—it was just downstream from the Stairs.

The Bridge! Now that was a place he had never thought to look for the Golden Buckle.

And no use, either, he told himself stolidly, tired of the rush from hope to thudding disappointment that he had endured too often. Still, it might be there, it *might*.

He stepped into the alley and in a moment stood at the top of the Stairs, with the watermen below crying their "Oars!" at him, and his ears filled with the noise of the two great wooden water-wheels screeching and thumping and clattering away a stone's throw to the left. Above the wheels reared London Bridge, pride of the City and marvel of foreigners, stepping high, on its nineteen ancient stone arches, across the Thames. Its piers were protected from the rushing water by boat-shaped clusters of pilings called "starlings," which always reminded Michael of huge flat feet. And on its back, this many-footed London dragon bore houses and shops and people and traffic, in a long street as fine as any in the city, with houses often four or five stories high. It was at these houses that Michael gazed—or rather at the row of widely varied backs they presented to his view. Might Susanna now live in one of them?

If so, which? Some were narrow and venerable, weathered until they glowed velvet-brown in the low afternoon sun. Some were larger, some newer, some intricately half-timbered, boldly black and white. A number of turrets rose imposingly above the jumble of gables and chimneypots; here was a curl of wrought-iron, there a glimpse of crenelated stone, everywhere the sparkle of many windows, and a score of gilded weathervanes traced their delicate semaphores against the sky. Far toward the Southwark end he could make out the grim sprouting of poles angling helter-skelter above the Great Stone Gate, each pole topped by the pale skull of a traitor. Near at hand, in a third story window, someone's bedding lay airing over the sill, like a rude white tongue thrust out of a mouth.

We'll be set down at Old Swan Stairs, right at their doorstep as you might say. . . . Those were her words. Michael remembered them perfectly. He remembered everything to do with Susanna perfectly—including her saying to Master Haas, "Oh, he's none of mine, we only rode in the cart together."

Never mind, Michael told himself.

Climbing back up the steep little alley, he launched himself again into breezy Thames Street like a floating chip into a flood. One of the shrieking choir of peddlers was a gingerbread-seller, and after some serious doubts about the wisdom of tempting Fate, Michael spent a penny of his day's wages on a nicely gilded chunk of the dark confection. Along with a left-over ballad he had in his pocket, it would make a nice present—if he found Susanna.

If he didn't—well, he liked gingerbread himself.

The Bridge

Michael followed a hayrick down the last cobbled slope of New Fish Street and past the church of St. Magnus the Martyr. Then he stood on London Bridge itself, amid the full-throated clamor of the watermen, the waterwheels, and the Thames. It was a fine but congested street, the Bridge, and he peered about admiringly as he walked, squeezing close to the shopfronts because the traffic was murderous. Eagerly he craned his neck at the signs hanging above him, then stood tiptoe and even jumped up and down to peer across the way over the crush of coaches and horsemen and handcarts thronging the narrow street. This was the "new block," as everybody called it, the only section of shops rebuilt after a fire had burned nearly half across the Bridge thirty years before. There were Bibles and Dolphins, a Red Cock and a Black Bull and Three Neats' Tongues—but no Golden Buckle, not here.

Ahead lay the long razed stretch, still unbuilt and only ill-protected from the sweep of the winds down the river by a high, gap-toothed fence of palings. The fence ended at the open Square, beyond which the older houses began again.

Mindful of wheels and hoofs, Michael left the shelter of the new block, was all but knocked off his feet by the wind on its boisterous way to Greenwich, and head down, burrowed his way against it alongside the fence. He stopped once to poke his head cautiously through one of the gaps where a paling had blown off. Yonder in the Pool a great, high-sterned East Indiaman was turning slowly, weighing anchor, breaking out sails that filled, one by one, with a sharp report, as the ship moved like royalty past the Tower and on toward Gravesend with the sun glinting on her gilded scrollwork. Michael gazed after her, wondering where she was bound, thinking of the maps in Master Trueblood's study, with their enticing, unknown shorelines, their sea-serpents and puffing winds—thinking of the *Medusa*. Then he tucked his hair behind his ears and hurried on. Once across the Square to the next buildings, he began squinting at signs again.

He saw it at once, thrusting out on a curlicued wrought-iron arm from a house directly across the way—a blue rectangle bisected by a scarlet belt with a big gilt buckle. Above, black letters elegantly spelled out: "P. Haas, Haberd'sh'r & Toyman," and below: "In Ye Golden Buckel."

He stared at it with his mouth gaping open. There it *was*. The *very house*.

A handsome house it was, too—the second south of the Square and the tallest in its row. It had a graceful bank of windows at street level, a bow-windowed second story; the third story spanned the street in an *hautpas* to join with the house on the opposite side. Moreover, there was a garret above that.

Michael looked down at the slightly squashed gingerbread in his hand, then, uneasily, back at the grand house, feeling his confidence waver. Could it have been only three weeks ago that he and Susanna had shared the jolting cart and the ale and toast? It suddenly seemed a year ago, a century. He wondered if she would even remember who he was—and whether she would want him to remind her.

He was gazing uncertainly at the blue-painted door when it opened, and two chattering women emerged, followed by a maid-servant carrying their parcels. After them, in the doorway, appeared old Master Haas's handsome grandson in an elaborately curled periwig, gracefully (though somewhat indifferently) bowing them out. Philip, that was his name. Michael remembered it as he thrust aside his doubts, dashed across the cobbles almost under the hoofs of a pair of dray horses, and gained the doorway too.

"Good morrow, Master Philip," he said breathlessly.

Philip, who had been peering in the other direction, glanced around at him without a sign of recognition. Suddenly sure he should never have come, Michael asked if he might speak to Mistress Susanna and was told in irritable tones that he might if he could find her. "Who might you be, youngling?" Philip added with a frown, which cleared half-way through Michael's stammered explanation. "Oh, yes. The boy at Uxbridge. But I thought she told my grandfather you were none of hers."

"Nor am I," Michael muttered. "I only came to—came to—" Why *had* he come? The very idea now seemed idiotic.

Philip wasn't listening anyway. "Well, I'll give you a farthing to hunt her out for me. She was sent to Master Danforth a quarter-hour ago with a parcel—lazy wench, she's dawdling! Go on—the bookseller at the sign of the Angel, near the Great Stone Gate. Fetch her straight back. Well, run along."

An impatient hand reached out; Michael found himself turned smartly about-face, and given a careless clap on the shoulder, which sent him stumbling on his way down the street. He looked back indignantly, but Philip had disappeared inside, leaving him nothing but the door to glower at. He went on, though it was a damping beginning, and only a sort of obstinacy about finishing the whole pesky affair now he'd started kept him from turning back then and there. But nobody's spirits could have stayed damped long on the Bridge. The gay, swinging signs hanging at all levels, peeking around each other like children all eager to see the show—and the show itself, passing endlessly beneath the succession of *hautpas* that turned the street into a sun-striped tunnel—it was enough to cheer up a dead man. By the time Michael emerged into the sunshine of the old disused drawbridge, his natural buoyancy had combined with anticipation, and he was all but running. He glanced toward the Pool and the ships moving there with the sun in their sails—the East Indiaman was far below the Tower now—then turned for a look upriver and saw Susanna.

She was leaning against the opposite balustrade, her silvery head propped on one golden-skinned arm, her sky-blue skirts whipping about her in the breeze, and her attention focused on something in the river below—it could only be a boat—upon which she was apparently . . . that is, it *looked* as if she . . . Michael shaded his eyes against the low sun. No doubt about it, she was *spitting*. As he stared, she again leaned carefully forward, took judicious aim, waited for the right split second, and spat. Faint cries of indignation rose thinly above the river's noise. She straightened with an air of satisfaction—and Michael, suddenly dissolving in giggles, dodged across the roadway to her side.

"Mistress Susanna! Good morrow, Mistress Susanna!" he shouted.

She turned, and for the briefest second looked blank, then recognition lighted her whole cheerful, snub-nosed face. "Why, it's Master Cornhill! My soul and body! I thought you'd forgot me."

"Oh, no! I've been looking for you everywhere! You never told me where the shop was."

"Lud, *didn't* I? Well, I've thought of you often, and wondered where you landed—and whether 'twas on your feet again."

"Oh, yes, it was! Temporarily, I mean."

"And what a fine new jacket!" said Susanna, turning him about. "Or, anyway, it's a different one. . . ."

"It's new to *me,*" Michael explained quickly. "Here—I've brought you some gingerbread," he added, transferring the sticky mass from his hand to hers with some difficulty. "And a ballad. It's about a sailor whose ship is sunk by the Dutch, and he has to swim back to England, but he makes a mistake and swims to Holland instead, and he's captured—but later he gets away—and oh, it's ever so funny!"

"It sounds that," Susanna assured him, eyes twinkling, face pink with mirth in its frame of pale tendrils. "What a good fellow you are to bring me presents. Here, you have some too." She divided the gingerbread, and as Michael studied her eagerly, still half-breathless with feeling shy, she pressed a chunk back into his hand. "There. Now, however have you been? And did you find your Master Potter?—or was it Potts? No, Botts, I remember . . ." She broke off, watching his face. "Master Cornhill, dear—they *didn't* turn you away?"

Briefly, Michael explained about the Bottses, careful to keep his manner offhand and even rather distant, for fear she might possibly imagine he wanted her to feel sorry for him—though it occurred to him, deep down in a very private corner of himself, that perhaps he *did* want that, just a little. In any case, the distress on her face so comforted him that he forgot to feel awkward any longer. He found himself talking to her as easily as he had at the King's Head Inn, confiding that he had first thought he would have to be a linkboy, until he thought of Paul's and the serving-man's log, and sat himself down there, and sure *enough*, Tom had come by. . . .

By this time she was chuckling at him again and dividing her attention between his tale and her gingerbread, which perhaps made her lose the thread, for she suddenly broke in, "And who is Tom?" When Michael told her, she frowned down at him in concern. "A ballad-man? Now, how did you get mixed up with such a rogue as that, Master Cornhill?"

"Rogue? Indeed, he's *not* a rogue!" Michael exclaimed, as shocked as if she had hit him.

Susanna looked at him a moment, then smiled uncertainly and shrugged. "Well, then, I'm glad to know it. If you say he's not, I beg pardon and take it back."

She licked her fingers, and unrolled the ballad-sheet to study it, while Michael studied her, half-hurt and half-perplexed. "But what made you think he would be?"

"Oh—I don't know—a-many of 'em are. . . . Hoy, this is a funny verse, this is! What's the tune, Michael?"

But Michael had lost interest in the ballad. "How do you know a-many of them are?" he burst out.

She lowered the ballad-sheet and faced him squarely. "Now, then, Master Cornhill, I'm no Tony—I've seen a ballad-man or two, out at Smithfield, when it's Bart'lomew's Fair—"

"Oh, at the *Fair*, but—"

"Yes, and in Paul's Churchyard, too, and at the markets—wherever they can draw a good crowd for the foists and horn-thumbs."

"The foists and . . ." Michael swallowed. Into his mind flashed the dusky tap-room at the Golden Lion Tavern, Tom with one knee cocked and his hat perched on it, the startled weasel-face of the man Tom called Jack Horner. "Foists? I don't even know what—"

"Pickpockets, that's what foists are," Susanna said bluntly. "And horn-thumbs are the nippers that can cut a poor coney's purse straight through his pocket while he's gawking and guffawing at the ballad-man. Mind you, they're all in it together; the balladeer shares the purse at the ale-house later—and so does the motion-man, maybe, or the mountebank, for your nipper's not particular who collects his sheep for the shearing. Oh, I've seen it—Old Joan made sure I did. She knew all their tricks, did Old Joan, they never gulled *her*. They're a bad lot, mostly."

Michael was silent, firmly barring his mind against bits of memory that wanted in, stifling the uneasy thoughts that nibbled to get out.

"Master Cornhill?" Susanna said gently. "I only meant to warn you."

"I know." In a stronger voice, Michael added, *"Tom's* not a bad lot. They can't *all* be."

"I suppose not all," Susanna admitted, though rather doubtfully. "But what's this ballad-man to do with you? He first marked you, did he, as you sat in Paul's Walk that morning—?"

Michael had not yet mentioned joining Tom's audience the night before—or discovering his purse was gone. Nor did he mention either matter now. "And he hired me—I'm his assistant. He gives me thruppence a day, and my keep—and he bought me this jacket —and my sword-belt!" Michael began to smile, as affection warmed him. He told her all about Tom and his eyebrows and his hat with the broken plume, and the lute that went to bed like a person, and the old-clothes stalls and how mightily well Tom sang and how many ballads they sold.

"And he gives you lodging, too?"

"Yes, I sleep in a truckle bed. Oh, he's ever so nice, Tom is! You'll find out once you meet him."

Susanna nodded, studying him with a curious expression of mingled amusement and dissatisfaction. "No doubt he is, then," she remarked. Absently she reached over and untucked Michael's hair from behind his ears, then turned back to the balustrade with an air of putting the whole matter from her mind. A moment later she gave a whoop of laughter. "Look there, Master Cornhill!—another wherry full of popinjays!"

Michael, peering over the railing, saw among the usual clutter of small-boat traffic one six-oared wherry that seemed laden solely with brilliantly colored ruffles and ribbons and satin flounces. But closer inspection revealed living beings encased in this finery— though to Michael they looked more like Maypoles than human males. Obviously they came from Westminster and the Court; one would never mistake them for sober Londoners. Equally obviously, they meant to "shoot the Bridge"—a dangerous sport Michael had always hankered to try. Master Trueblood's prudent habit had been to land at Old Swan Stairs, walk in safety around the Bridge, and take boat again on the other side, quoting meanwhile the old London saying that London Bridge was built for wise men to go over and fools to go under. Plainly, these young Maypole-men were fools—but with courage enough under their ruffles.

"Here they come!" Michael shouted, as the three oarsmen, having chosen their moment, braced themselves and aimed the wherry straight at the Bridge. The torrent caught it up like a chip, lifted it high, would have dashed it against a great splayed starling-foot but for the furious exertions of the watermen—then suddenly hurled it like a spear through the eye of the stone arch. Just as it passed beneath them, Susanna spat, casually but precisely. Michael doubled up with mirth as he heard again the faint, indignant chorus from below and pictured some outraged dandy brushing at his ribbons.

"Hoy, there, what are you about, wench? You'll disgrace us all," exclaimed a voice. It was Philip, his ruddy face framed by the huge black wig, advancing hastily on Susanna.

"Rubbish, it's only court sparks. Did you see them? Bunches of ribbon big as mop-heads and periwigs down to their knees!" Susanna darted a glance at Philip, adding, *"Your* periwig's a bit longer than need be, an't it? You'll dip the sides in your porridge-bowl some suppertime unless you watch close."

"I'll dip you, if you don't mind that tongue of yours," he retorted. "Get you back to your kitchen, you're not to dawdle about like this."

"Who says I'm not to?"

"I say it, Mistress!"

"Let Master Jan say it, and I'll obey. He bade me take my time if I chose. It's his servant I am, and only his, and what he tells me, that I'll do."

Michael, following this exchange in some anxiety, was relieved to see Philip's frown give way to a shrug as he eyed Susanna. "All right, Pepper-Pot. But he'd take a stick to you soon enough if he caught you spitting on folk, and so I warn you! When will you come, then?"

"When I'm ready," said Susanna, then added peaceably, "Soon enough, soon enough."

Philip nodded and strode away toward the shop—without a mention of Michael's farthing, or even a sign of being aware of his existence. Resentfully, Michael demanded, "Soon enough for what?"

"For him to slip off to his greyhound-race while Master's gone to Stationers' Hall. Rantum-scantum as any 'prentice, he is—but there, he's only quit being one. I mind the shop for him now and then, if I'm not too busy. . . . Well, come, I've dilly-dallied long enough, Master Cornhill. I'll walk to the London side with you, then I'd best get me back. I dassn't push Philip *too* far."

Reluctantly Michael straightened from the railing, and they threaded their way back toward the Golden Buckle, conversing as they could in snatches and shouts. Susanna had more than landed on her feet, it seemed; she had a garret all her own, and she loved both house and shop, idolized her employer, and liked the work.

"You like scrubbing and cooking and—all that?" Michael said lamely, trying to remember what Mistress Trueblood's ever-exhausted maids had been so busy at, day and night.

"Oh, there's only the Master and Philip to do for, and I can order the house to suit myself, for *they* don't care, as long as food's on the table when they want it." But to Michael's eager questions about her becoming an actress, she shrugged and said she might have to change her plans. Not one theatre had opened since the plague, nor would, if the sickness started up again this summer. "Which God forbid!" she added fervently. "Anyhow, I'm promised to Master for a year, and I keep my vows, I do. And I love the Bridge, Michael—though what a din it makes!"

By now they had reached the long burnt-out stretch, so Susanna had to shriek the last phrases over the wind's whistling and the river's rush and the waterwheels' screeching and groaning. She threw back her silvery head and shouted with laughter, her eyes narrowed to sky-blue slits between their fair lashes as they met Michael's.

It was a din all right, but he liked the Bridge too. It was busy and full of life and even free of stench, for only here, out of all London, was no garbage dumped out of the front windows into the street—since it was far handier to dump it out the rear windows into the Thames. There was the Thames itself to watch too, the great ships in the Pool and the wherries and double-bowed Peter-boats and tiny fishing coracles, and the watermen, and even just the water, rising and falling with the tides and frothing white and swift as it rushed through the arches, often with a Bridge-shooting boat-load of people on its back. Oh, it was a fine, interesting place, the Bridge, and Michael wished *he* lived here.

But of course he didn't. He lived in Dolittle Lane, with Tom. Temporarily.

"Are you deaf or day-dreaming, Master Cornhill? I said, there's a friend of mine."

Michael turned quickly and found that they had reached the posts that marked the Bridge end. On the stairs downstream, a young waterman was waving at Susanna and flashing a very white grin, as he waited for a passenger to climb ashore from his little "oars."

"His name's Will Butling," Susanna was saying as she waved back. "He's a bridge-shooter, he is. And an honest fellow. Master Haas always hires him. It's not a bad life, is a waterman's."

"No." Michael eyed Will's big frame and powerful shoulders with awe. He was taller than Tom even and seemed as wide as two men across the chest. "That'd make a boy strong, and all, that would!" he said earnestly. "Learning that trade."

"It's what I was thinking," Susanna admitted.

Michael looked at her, wondering why she had been thinking it, hoping it might be the start of a sort of sisterly interest in him, even almost fondness—a kind of family feeling. "I'm not old enough to be apprenticed," he reminded her. "And anyway, Uncle Penwood will apprentice me—I think. When he comes home."

She turned to him with a little frown between her silvery eye-brows. "And when will that be, Master Cornhill?"

"I—don't know. But Tom'll look after me till he comes. He's *not* a rogue," Michael added, answering her expression, not her words. "You'd know if you only talked to him a minute. He's well-spoken—well-born, too. Of a fine rich family!"

That widened her eyes, right enough, but not with conviction. "Oh, my faith!" she exclaimed. "Yes, the black sheep, likely!"

Then, as Michael flushed painfully, she laid a hand on his shoulder in quick apology. "There now, perhaps he is."

"He *is*. It's true he—doesn't exactly—look so, but he sounds so, and . . ." Michael broke off. It was too difficult to explain.

Susanna studied him a moment, still smiling, then she sighed and shrugged. "Well, I wish he had an honest trade. But then, it's none of my affair. Now, mind you come again to see me!" With a final wave, she turned in a little swirl of blue skirts and headed back across the Bridge.

Michael watched till the traffic hid her, then slowly turned away. He found himself wishing earnestly that it were her affair, or that at least she could feel it so. He wished his welfare and his future were *somebody's* affair besides his own. And not just temporarily, either.

He started for Dolittle Lane but found himself dawdling, lingering at a wharf to watch some fisherboats spilling their catch like molten silver on the splintery boards. Scowling, half-hypnotised by the flow of the Thames past the pier, he leaned against one of the tarred posts, and suddenly all his vague doubts and unasked questions of these last weeks began surfacing at once, like that catch of fish dragged up squirming and wriggling from the depths. The six o'clock Angelus had long gone, and the daylight was going before he trudged back along the mile of Thames Street under a murky red sky and climbed Peter's Hill at a snail's pace. A few minutes later he was home.

Heat-Lightning

The bell-man was passing along Knightrider Street calling eleven of the clock that night before Tom flung down his pen and rose. "Enough! That verse'll not be done for tomorrow's printing, and there's an end to it. Sometimes they just won't canter along properly at all. Why d'ye suppose that is? The heat?"

Murmuring some answer, Michael closed the book he had not been reading and went to the open window to fetch their half-loaf and bit of cheese from the larder box outside, while Tom went down for the supper ale. It was hot indeed by now, less like mid-May than mid-July, and breathless; the wind had dropped at sundown, leaving some sluggish clouds gathered like wads of dirty cotton, and lightning without thunder had been flickering restlessly around the sky ever since. On his slow walk home Michael had seen another burning house—a common enough sight in wooden London, but an oppressive one in such weather when even the cheese sweated.

He turned from the window to find Tom standing with the foaming mugs in his hands, observing him. "You're quiet tonight. Is something fretting you?"

"Me? Oh, no. I—"

"Come, let's have it, we'll gnaw it over with our supper."

Michael stood unhappily, avoiding Tom's eye. Finally he said, "How did—you know Master Stubbs could find my purse?"

There was a silence. Then Tom drew a deep breath and exhaled it in a philosophical sigh as he set the mugs on the table. "By the world! That's putting a question squarely, that is. Well, I'll answer it squarely. I knew he could find it because I knew he must have nabbed it. Master Stubbs is a pickpocket, I regret to say."

"Oh," Michael said in a small voice. It was not, he realized, a surprise.

Tom regarded him a moment, then said, "Sit down, Michael. Eat your cheese. Y'know, it's no use being feared of a fact."

"No." Unhappily, Michael sank onto his stool. "It's true, then. Everything she said."

"Everything who said?"

"Susanna. You remember—the gold-and-silver one, that I rode in the cart with."

"Ah, that one. How comes it *she* suddenly turns up again?"

" 'Twasn't sudden. I've been looking everywhere for her." His gaze on the cheese he was crumbling, Michael explained the idea that had finally led him to the Bridge. "And there was the shop, sure enough, and she remembered me, and—"

"Ahh. And you told her all about your new employment—and your new employer—"

"Yes, and took her that ballad about the captive, and she thought it ever so funny! But—" Michael lifted his eyes. "But she said—"

"I know what she said. She told you all ballad-men are deep-dyed rogues, in league with the foists and the nippers and every cheating bully-boy in Alsatia."

"She—she only said a-many of them are."

"And a-many of them are, too," Tom said judiciously. "And you said—?"

"I said *you* were different. But . . ."

"But later you got to thinking. As well you might." Tom picked up his mug and carried it to the window, where he stood sipping at it and gazing out into the flickering dark. "Well, and I am different—I've no compact with Jack Stubbs. Oh, I know he's likely to be there, in the crowd, but that's nothing to do with me, is it? I follow my trade, he follows his, and that's an end to it. Except— well, there's an emergency now and again." Tom waved that away, took a thoughtful swallow. "Here—I have it. Jack's like a small bag of shillings I've got hid in the cellar—one I seldom need to touch. Think of him that way, Michael."

Michael nodded doubtfully, trying to obey. Tom watched him a moment, then came back, and dropped into his chair. "See here. It all comes down to the matter of live and let live. Jack's a foist—

admitted. And a paltry, fribbling sort of creature he is, hardly worth turning up your nose at. But we can't all be magistrates and dukes and respectable maid-servants, now can we? Foists must eat too. Why should I trouble myself about what's doing at the fringes of my little crowds and whose hand's in some hoddy-doddy's pocket? Let the hoddy-doddy keep his own there! And let Jack earn his living as he can." Tom sat back and filled his mouth with bread and cheese.

"You made him bring back *my* purse," Michael reminded him.

"Ah, well, God-a-mercy—birding from children! That's coming it too strong, and well he knows it. One more of those and he'll have to find himself another ballad-man. But children aside, Michael—and maybe one or two other types—it's a dog-eat-dog world, and every jolthead for himself! That's how *I* see the matter."

Michael nodded earnestly, wondering how *he* saw it. Tom's logic was persuasive. Of course, he knew well enough what Susanna (and Old Joan) would say, and no doubt Master Trueblood too. But none of them knew Tom. Or should that make any difference? It was all unfamiliar ground to Michael, and the footing felt precarious. The vocabulary, however, was diverting. "A foist, Master Stubbs is? Not a—horn-thumb?" he asked.

"Oh, no, never a nipper, not Jack . . . Ah, you're wondering why I called him 'Jack Horner' that morning. 'Twas to insult him. I was out of temper and pleased for him to know it." Tom leaned forward, lifting his eyebrows and dropping his voice. "Now, if 'twas a nipper I wanted to bite my thumb at, I'd call *him* Ralph Foister-Doister, or some such jesting slur. These rats have their different breeds, y'see—and their different skills, too, can't deny that—and so, their pride. Same as a balladeer has his." He finished his ale, studied Michael with an expression half impatient and half rueful, then banged the mug on the table, saying, "Devil wi' the girl, anyhow."

"Girl?"

"Your Susanna. A pize on her! She meddles."

"Oh, no, she never meant to! She was only warning me—to 'ware of rogues."

"For a maid her age, she knows a deal about them. *I* never taught you what a horn-thumb is."

"No, she did. She's *seen* 'em cut right through a coney's purse while the ballad-man's singing. They never gull her, she's learned their tricks."

"And between her and me you're learning their cant," Tom commented. "I doubt your Master Trueblood would care much for either of us. Well, if you heed me, you'll stay well away from her. She'll try to run your life for you—all females do!" He reached for his empty mug, drained a last drop from it, and sent it spinning and rocking away across the table. "What else did she talk about? Or was she just preaching and scolding the whole live-long afternoon?"

"Oh, *no*. We talked about all sorts of things. Then Philip came, scolding *her,* because she was spitting on the court dandies—"

Tom turned a startled face. "Because she was what?"

Michael explained, somewhat sheepishly at first, then with relish as he saw Tom's eyes twinkle and the corners of his mouth turn up irrepressibly. But when he mentioned Susanna's notion that he might 'prentice to a waterman, the twinkle was gone in a flash, and Tom was sitting bolt upright, glaring at him. "A *waterman?*"

"Yes," Michael faltered. "Maybe even a bridge-shooter, like Will Butling. That'd be a fine life—wouldn't it?"

"It's a brute's life—and you're as suited for it as Queen Cath-arine is for mine! God-a-mercy! Why not a street porter or an ironmonger? Has she never looked at you? Yes, those are a smith's shoulders, i'gad they are!"

Stung by this sarcasm, Michael pointed out that it would be some years before his shoulders were anything but a boy's—though re-membering the breadth of Will Butling's, he did privately wonder if he could ever aspire to anything so spectacular. "But not all watermen are made like smiths," he argued. "Sam'l's scrawny enough—and only one eye, too!"

"If you were made like Hercules, you'd still be a league above such work—as anybody but a purblind female could plainly see!"

"Susanna's not purblind. She was only thinking of my future."

"Well, if that's a sample of her notions, I can't say much for 'em! It's schooling you need and ought to have—Greek, and La-tin, and that. But trust a maid to see no further than a man's muscles and his morals! What of his intellect, his heart?"

Michael found no ready answer and apparently none was expected, for Tom turned away, muttering, "A waterman!" and, propping his feet on the table, fell to frowning at them—whether because his boots were shabby or his thoughts displeasing, it was hard to tell. Michael, who still saw little wrong with Susanna's notion and nothing at all with her intelligence, finished his supper in stolid silence. But presently Tom sighed and glanced around at him. "Well? Will it make a difference 'twixt us, all this? I freely release you from our bargain. . . . You'd best have a night's sleep on it before you answer."

"I don't need a night's sleep," Michael mumbled. "It'll make no difference at all." And why should it, he reflected moodily. The bargain was only temporary anyhow—as Tom himself kept repeating. He got up, brushed the crumbs onto the straw-strewn floor, and took the end of the loaf back to the window-box, conscious of Tom's slightly sardonic gaze.

"Mind you," the latter said abruptly, "I'll not be changing my ways, so don't expect it. A cat will be a cat, however much you whistle at him. And I'll be bound if a fatherless Tom-cat like me, raised in the alleys, isn't under a cloud to begin with. You can tell your Mistress Susanna—Now what's the matter?"

"Alleys?" echoed Michael, who had turned to stare at him. "Fatherless? What about His Lordship?"

"What lordship, God-a-mercy?"

"Your father! That is, you never said he was a *lord,* I—I made that up, I guess, or anyway exaggerated. But you did say—"

"Aaah, so I did!" Tom exclaimed softly. He removed his feet from the table with care. "So I did. My illustrious father."

"And your brothers—"

"And my unjustly favored brothers." Tom stood up, moved over to the bed to get his lute, and stood absently plucking and tuning it with his back to Michael. "Well-a-day. D'ye know, Michael, I fear I exaggerated, too?"

"But you—d'you mean—"

"I mean I've nary a brother—that I know of. My mother was a groom's daughter—then a cook's wife, a cook's widow when I was ten, a drunken beggar, and a corpse soon after. It's true I *served* a lord's youngest son one year, as his lackey, before he shipped out to Virginia. Later I was a knight's valet."

Michael's head was spinning. "Then why did you say—"

"Oh, why I say things is a mystery I've never solved myself," Tom remarked. "Perhaps I wished you to think well of me. Or wished to think better of myself. A man's a curious creature. . . . Come, enough talk. It's time for sleep."

He peeled off his shirt and wrapped the lute in it with his usual care, then dragged the truckle-bed out from under his own as if it were any other night. After a stunned moment, Michael undressed too, mechanically hung his clothes on their nail, knelt beside Tom to mumble his prayers, and got into bed, all the time thinking so hard, and so indignantly that he barely knew what he was doing. Alley-brat? Child of a drunken beggar-wench? *Tom?* Then where had he got that gentleman's accent—purer than Master Trueblood's, it was, even when he was talking thieves' cant.

"Unlikeliest tale I ever heard!" Michael suddenly burst out. "Think I'm a Tony, that you can bubble me so? Well, I'm not, then!"

Tom, sitting on his bed just reaching for the candle to blow it out, instead held it over Michael in his truckle-bed, blinking down at him with eyebrows high and astonished. "You disbelieve me? Now why, in the world o' marvels, d'ye think I'd spin you such a dreary, drab tale if it weren't the dreary, drab truth?"

"I don't know why! Nor do you, most likely," Michael added.

Amusement lighted Tom's speckled eyes briefly; then he blew out the candle and lay back amid the rustling and crunching of his straw mattress. In a moment he said, "No, likely I don't." And something in his tone—though a mild enough tone it was—told Michael that the subject was now closed.

Perhaps this time he wished me to think ill of him, reflected the boy. Or wished to think even worse of himself.

For a long while he lay wakeful, sweltering in the airless night, watching the lightning, wondering why it didn't thunder, wishing it would rain—wondering, too, at how strange life got sometimes and how puzzling were human beings, including himself. For it was true, what he had told Tom, and it would be just as true after a night's sleep, temporary bargain or not. It wasn't going to make any difference, knowing about Jack Stubbs. Not the least bit of difference at all.

Nor was any advice of Tom's going to keep him away from Susanna. His private but firm intention was to see her as often as ever he could.

The Esmeralda

Private intentions were one thing; good politics another. Michael let a whole day go by before paying a second call upon Susanna, fearing she might think him a nuisance if he came back too soon —or called too often, he warned himself, or stayed too long when he called. Still, she had invited him, so Saturday found him threading the Bridge traffic again. He was rewarded by a warm welcome and a friendly gossip in Master Haas's cozy oak-beamed kitchen, plus a morsel of gooseberry-cream left over from the Master's dinner. After that, Susanna announced that he might accompany her across-Bridge to the grocer's in Southwark, and help fetch the shopping back. So he went, stepping out gladly beside her through the alternate glare and tunneled shade of the Bridge, still humming the morning's ballad—a new Scottish one—with spirit if not much tune: "In *Scarlet* Town, where *I* was bound, there *was* a fair Maid dwelling—whom *I* had chosen to *be* my own, and her name was Barbara Allen. . . ."

"Now that's a catchy one, you might have brought me a sheet, you might," Susanna remarked, as they crossed the sunny open space of the old drawbridge.

"We sold the lot of 'em," said Michael. "Went like pork pies." He turned to walk backwards, dragging his fingers along the iron spikes of the fence as he squinted up at the fairy-tale turrets of Nonesuch House, the biggest and grandest house in the world (in Michael's opinion). It rose on both sides of the street, straddling it with a fancy arch and soaring up in a glitter of windows to onion-shaped cupolas tipped with gilt weathervanes, and had been Master Trueblood's unfailing standard of comparison: "Fine as Nonesuch House!" he had used to declare, even if he were speaking of a bolt of velvet or a new baby. *"I'll* have a house like that someday," Michael boasted, chiefly to hear Susanna's shout of laughter, with which she obliged immediately.

"Lawks, will you hark to Captain Puff! And when will 'someday' be? When you're 'prenticed to that uncle, you'll go sailing away for months and months and never need a house at all."

"That's so," Michael said thoughtfully. It was an aspect of a sailing-man's life he had not considered. He wondered if he would like it, never ever having a house like the one in Bartholomew Lane, but only a ship's cabin or a room in some inn like the Swan and Bridge for the brief, infrequent periods in London. He would miss London, that he knew. "I daresay it'll feel grand and free, being footloose like that," he said heartily.

"No doubt it will. And if you shouldn't care for it," Susanna added, after a shrewd glance at him, "no doubt your uncle will find you a master in some other trade."

"Ye-es," Michael agreed uncertainly. They emerged into the dazzle of the open space facing the Great Stone Gate, and he paused, shading his eyes for his usual fascinated but shuddery stare upward at the bleached traitors' skulls canting high on their poles atop the massive stone archway. Then he ran to catch up with Susanna. "But what other trade d'you mean?" he asked her.

"Oh, I don't know. Something you're clever at. . . . Hark, what's that?"

They both glanced around as a shrill squeal and the sound of laughter rose above the river's noise. There by the opposite Gate tower, in the nook formed by the stocks and the scold's cage, a little crowd had gathered around a raree-show man and a bagpiper. In the stocks sat a half-drunken girl whose crime had obviously been the selling of overripe fish, for a stinking specimen was hung around her neck under her nose, fairly bubbling in the afternoon heat. She seemed merry enough in spite of it, screeching with tipsy laughter at the antics of the bagpiper's little dog, who wore a frilled nightcap and pirouetted on his hind feet, barking incessantly to the squealing accompaniment of the pipes. The raree-show man, having unstrapped his coffin-like peepshow from his back, was loudly hawking the marvels to be seen for a penny. Michael had no penny, but he was gaping, enchanted, at the little dog's clown-

ing when he felt Susanna's tug at his sleeve and remembered they
had business to accomplish.

"Oh, did you see him, dancing like a person?" he cried as he
hurried after her.

"To tell the truth, 'twas that slut in the stocks I was looking at.
No older than me, she was." Susanna paused, her snub-nosed face
bleaker than Michael had ever seen it. "Lud, I was lucky to have
Old Joan, that I was, Master Cornhill! I might've turned out so
myself, otherwise. Or likely worse. And *you're* lucky to have your
uncle coming."

"Yes," Michael agreed, considerably sobered.

"Have they any word yet at the Custom House?"

"I haven't asked lately," Michael confessed.

"Well, you'd best keep at it. Since the fleet left, the Pool's filling
up with merchantmen—and a-many of 'em'll unload soon and sail
right out again, to Dover or somewhere. They don't want to be in
the North Sea in June—afeard of getting caught in battles. So Will
Butling tells me."

"Ods bobs!" Michael said in alarm. Imagine if the *Medusa*
should sail in and out again without his knowing! "I'll ask today,"
he declared. "I'll walk down by the Custom House before ever I
start for home."

He followed Susanna along Bridge Foot and down Pepper Alley
to the grocer's, absorbed in thought. What if he *shouldn't* care for a
sailing-man's life? The moment of finding out, one way or the
other, loomed suddenly closer than he liked. While he held the
basket for Susanna's purchases, he eyed the grocer's young apprentice, envying his apron and his air of confidence—and his
settled future. But that trade would never do for himself; it needed
a head for figures, and he'd been anything but clever at reckoning
in school. What had he been clever at? Only Greek, really . . . and
drawing slanderous pictures of the schoolmaster on his slate and
getting caned for it. What a worthless nupson of a boy I am, he
thought in disgust, as he lugged the basket out of the shop. It'll
be a sailing-man's life or nothing—and lucky I am to have the
chance of it.

"That's a solemn face you're pulling, Master Cornhill," Susanna
commented. "What are you thinking of?"

"Oh—nothing . . . Susanna, is there anything special you feel you're truly clever at?"

"Making gooseberry cream," she answered promptly. "And wiggling my ears."

Michael burst into giggles. "No, *can* you wiggle them? Let me see!"

At once she halted, lifted the silvery wisps and curls that fringed her cheeks, and demonstrated. She could not only wiggle her ears, she could move her entire scalp with quite spectacular success, and the sight of her concentrated face in the midst of all that silvery agitation rendered Michael so helpless with laughter that he had to set the basket down, and went reeling about the alley, his solemnity forgotten.

"Take care, you're bumping into folk!" Rosy with mirth herself, Susanna pulled Michael out of the way of a chimney sweep passing by with his awkward bundle of brushes and his sooty-faced, big-eyed boy. "Pick up the basket and come, Philip'll be having the vapors. I said I'd mind the shop for an hour."

"Again?" Michael exclaimed as they hurried on.

"Again! If I don't watch what I'm about, I'll find myself doing it half the time. Not that I'd care—I love a chance to handle the pretty combs and buttons and such-like. Wish 'twere my shop, instead of his."

" 'Tisn't truly his, is it? It's the grandfather's."

"Oh, no. The house belongs to Old Master, but the trade—that was Philip's father's. Now it's Philip's. Master Haas is no haberdasher, not he!"

"What is Master Haas, then?"

"Why, he's a map-colorer. That parcel I carried to Master Danforth, the bookseller at the Angel—it was maps he'd just got finished."

"A map-colorer!" Visions of puffing winds and far blue coastlines again flashed through Michael's mind.

"The best in London, so Master Danforth told me," Susanna said proudly. "That means in all of England, too. He's a guildsman of St. Luke, in Antwerp, and trained at Blaeu's."

"What's Blaeu's?" Michael asked, impressed.

"Truth to tell you, I don't know," Susanna confessed with a spurt of laughter. "A map-printer's, I suppose."

"But how does he color them? Have you ever watched him do it?"

"I? My soul and body, d'you think he wants a chit of a servant-maid hanging over his shoulder as he works? I've seen the maps, though, when he's finished—and ah, they're fine! All lovely blue and saffron and green with golden letters and such-like . . . Hoy! Look there under your foot, Michael! A sixpence!"

Stopping so suddenly he created another hazard in the clotted Bridge traffic, Michael spied the little coin between the cobbles where his foot had kicked it, and snatched it up in triumph. But when he tried to give it to Susanna, saying she saw it first, she insisted he keep it.

" 'Twas you who stepped on it. Keep it for luck. Maybe this is your lucky day! Lawks, there's Philip, craning out the doorway watching for me. How much faster does he think I can fly? Hand me the basket, Master Cornhill—or will you come in again?"

Reluctantly, Michael refused, reminding himself he mustn't become a nuisance. He would willingly have heard more about map-coloring and Antwerp, but it seemed prudent to avoid Philip's irritable eye. Besides, he must call at the Custom House.

Never mind, he thought. I'll see her again soon. I must tell Tom she can wiggle her ears—that was rich, that was!

Smiling, he walked on across the Square and back toward Thames Street, fingering the sixpence in his pocket. Maybe it *was* his lucky day. There'd be news of the *Medusa*—he felt it in his bones.

There was more than news of the *Medusa*. Incredibly, there was the *Medusa* herself, moored at Galley Key between the Custom House and the Tower of London—high-pooped, weather-beaten, with a broken foremast and a lot less gilt than when she had sailed away two years ago, but with the same familiar snake-haired Gorgon figurehead that Michael would have known in China. He gave a cry, squirmed his way past laboring navvies and a group of quarreling seamen, and had reached the wharf before he saw the name in fading scarlet letters on the barque's prow—not *Medusa*, but *Esmeralda*.

He halted, staring from the peeling letters to the battered figurehead. *Esmeralda?* That was the *Medusa* all the same. Unless there were two ships having snake-haired figureheads with old, well-remembered chips off the ends of their noses—unless that man standing yonder watching the navvies unloading was not Uncle Penwood's first mate Simon Cotter but his twin brother.

Michael found himself beside the man, pulling at his sleeve. "Master Cotter! Master Cotter! Where is my uncle?"

The man looked down at him, puzzled and at first quite uncomprehending. He wore a tucker of fine lace, Michael now noticed, and his stockings were silk—but it was Simon Cotter all the same. "My Uncle Penwood!" Michael insisted. "What's happened to him? I'm the Truebloods' boy, don't you remember?"

Then recognition and a startled consternation broke over the broad face. "By my right hand! So I do, then! The captain's little nevvy, an't it? My oath! But you was killed off by the plague a twelvemonth past—now wasn't you? Captain, he never got answer to his letters—and then some neighbor wrote and said the hull fambly was wiped out."

"They were—except for me. Oh, please—where *is* he?"

Master Cotter squinted thoughtfully into space, and pursed his lips. "New Amsterdam, he'd be by now," he answered. "Or so I judge—less'n he figures to run clean to the Bay Colony this month, but I misdoubt that. Captain be'nt overfond of them dripnose Puritans at Boston. He—"

"New Amsterdam? You mean he—he isn't here in London? He didn't even come? But why did he send his ship if—"

"Ah, but she's not his ship now, laddy!" exclaimed Master Cotter, opening his black eyes wide and beaming down at Michael. "She's *my* ship, that she is! My *Esmeralda*—bless 'er for a fine lass, too!"

"She's the *Medusa*," Michael whispered, seeing his future fall to pieces.

"Used to be the *Medusa*, aye. But she's the *Esmeralda* now, and Simon Cotter's, hull, spar and bowsprit! Your Uncle Penwood's got him a new lass, and her name's 'Virginny.' " Master Cotter winked elaborately and roared with laughter. "Aye, Captain's settled down in the New World—got him a piece o' land and a piece o' beach and a schooner-rigged pinkie for carryin' goods up and down the coast, and he's a happy man! I doubt me he ever comes back to London. . . . Hoy, mind whatcher about there, you ninnyhead!" he roared, lunging past Michael to clout a navvy who had fumbled his heavy load and nearly dropped it into the river. He righted the man's load, scowled suspiciously at the next one coming down the boarding plank, shouted something to a seaman on deck, and presently hurried up the plank himself. Michael was forgotten.

With a last look at the snaky-haired figurehead who had now become a stranger, Michael turned away. He had no further business with Simon Cotter. Nor with the *Medusa*—nor with Uncle Penwood. All that was over—indeed, had never been. He wondered how he could have believed in it and decided he never really had. He found it suddenly hard even to picture Uncle Penwood's face.

He emerged from the tangle of wharfside alleys into Thames Street and slowly started the long walk home—that "temporary" home in Dolittle Lane, which had abruptly become his only one. What would Tom say when he found out that "temporary" might stretch on and on for years? Perhaps he'll turn me out, Michael thought. Or turn me over to the parish . . . But Tom would never do that. Would he?

Michael found himself painfully unable to answer with any certainty. He knew precious little about Tom, when you came down to it.

He was still musing upon this point as he emerged into Knightrider Street at the top of Peter's Hill and spied Tom himself, turning into Dolittle Lane just ahead. Nothing was more familiar than that tall, easy-moving figure, the tilt of the hat and the angle of the broken plume—and nothing more mysterious than the man inside. Everybody was a mystery inside, really, Michael was thinking. A mystery to everybody else.

It was a lonesome, wearisome sort of thought, and his feet were dragging as he climbed the stairs a few moments later to find Tom just striking a spark from his tinderbox to light their evening candle.

"Well-a-day, there you are then! Dogging my very footsteps, were you?" Tom fixed the candle in its pool of drippings and tossed his hat onto the bedpost. Then he turned to Michael, and his smile vanished. "What ails you? Something wrong?"

Michael could only nod and swallow.

"What is it? Hoy! You've not had news of the uncle?" At another nod, Tom let his breath out in a long, comprehending "Ahhh." After a moment he added, "Bad news. He's dead? What was it, shipwreck?"

"No—he's not dead. Though he thinks *I* am. But he's not coming back. Not ever. He's sold the *Medusa*," Michael said bitterly. "She's here, tied up at Galley Key, I saw her myself! But she's not the *Medusa* now, she's the *Esmeralda,* which is a stupid, jolthead sort of name, and Simon Cotter's her master—so he says—"

"Wait. Go back, Michael—tell me everything."

So Michael told all he knew of the matter, which was not much, but, as Tom said thoughtfully, quite enough. They were silent for a long, uncomfortable moment, while Tom digested the news and Michael watched him do it. Unwelcome news it was to him, there was no doubt of it.

Michael swallowed again, hard and painfully. "I could—go out to him, maybe," he faltered. "Out to Virginny. If I could find out just where he is—"

"And had the passage money," said Tom. "And any assurance he'd be in the same spot when you arrived . . . if you ever did arrive. No, Michael, it won't do. You'll stay right here with me, until we fix on something better." He glanced at Michael and added recklessly, "If necessary, until you're old enough to 'prentice. So don't be fearing I'll turn you over to the parish."

Michael, releasing his pent-up breath and feeling a flood of relief rush over him, ears to toes, could only stammer that he *had* been a little a-feared because of their arrangement being temporary.

"As I've kept saying." Tom's smile was rueful. "And I own it's what I'd planned. But events alter cases, don't they? Well-a-day, lay out our supper, Michael, I'm going below to fetch us some ale."

Abstractedly, Michael obeyed. So the arrangement was temporary no longer—unless the half-mythical "something better" actually did turn up—or unless events again altered cases. Hugging the loaf as he absently sawed off ragged chunks with Tom's very dull dagger, Michael found himself wondering what sudden blow would descend next time. Events were always altering cases and plans and people's lives out of all recognition and without the slightest warning. Look what the plague had done to his—and after that, the purse-snatcher. Now he and Uncle Penwood were altering Tom's. And Tom did not want his life altered. Who could blame him?

Michael was still standing by the table, frowning down as he rubbed at a stain on the dagger, when Tom came back carrying two foaming mugs of ale and wearing a resolute expression.

"What it means," Tom announced as though he had never left the room, "is that we must bestir ourselves about your future. I mean to do so, you may rely on it. Enough of this feckless drifting and postponing, pleasant as it has been. Tomorrow—no, i'gad, this very evening!—we shall bend our minds to it."

"But—what can we do?" Michael asked, as they sat down to their skimpy meal.

"We shall compile long lists of possibilities," Tom told him grandly. He took a deep draught of his ale and wiped the foam from his lips with a flick of his cuff-tatters. "Tot up in one column all your talents and abilities. In another, all the possible crafts, trades, professions, avocations, pastimes—"

"But I haven't any talents or abilities," Michael said rather desperately.

"Nonsense, of course you have. Both actual and potential. Consider your talent for giggling—it won you your present employment, now didn't it? What's more, you've no mean skill at finding rhymes. And," Tom added, examining a lopsided chunk of bread with critical approval. "We must not overlook your skill at slicing a loaf with my dagger. 'Tisn't everyone that could make it cut at all, y'know."

By then Michael was giggling a bit between bites and beginning to feel himself not quite such a burden—or at any rate, a burden he might soon relieve Tom of, somehow or other. Tom saw to it he continued to feel so, keeping up a flow of cheerful nonsense during supper, and afterwards actually beginning to compile the lists —an exercise that led into such an interesting discussion of the myriad occupations of Londoners, from pin-making to rat-catching, and such an absorbing one of Michael's personal qualifications for this trade or that, that it was bedtime before they knew it or had fairly got started. But as Tom said, there was no need in the world to settle the whole thing in one evening; it would do them good to sleep on it.

So Michael settled into his truckle bed with his head stuffed with possibilities instead of uncertainties, and it was only after Tom's straw mattress had ceased its rustling that he suddenly remembered he had never mentioned about Susanna wiggling her ears. He reared up on his elbow, lips already parted to do so—then thought better of it, and lay down again. Tomorrow would do as well. The only thing of real importance was that he was still here in Dolittle Lane, fed and housed and earning his thruppence and safe from the parish beadle—and still with Tom. That was best of all. There was *nobody* quite like Tom. Or ever would be. And someday Michael would pay him a hundred-fold for everything, make it all up to him, give him a hundred fine presents, or a new lute, or whatever in all the world he wanted most. Someday.

Trials and Errors

Naturally enough, Michael's first gropings for some trade or future unconnected with the *Medusa* began at the haberdasher's shop. He was in and out of it as frequently as he dared as May passed, in a succession of bright days one very like another—all unnaturally hot and dry. It was disquieting weather to anyone who remembered last summer's heat and the dreadful clanging of the plague-bell. One Thursday afternoon on his way to see Susanna, Michael stopped by the Parish Clerk's Hall, as most Londoners did regularly this summer, to pick up the weekly Bill of Mortality, and found fifty-three plague deaths listed for the previous seven days. While not abnormal for this time of year, that was an unsettling jump from the mere sixteen or so of a fortnight earlier. There had been reports, too, that the sickness was gaining in places outside the city.

"You'd best spend more time here on the Bridge with me," Susanna advised him as she frowned over the list. He had found her alone, again left in charge of the shop. "It's the healthiest place in London, the Bridge is."

"Philip's parents died of plague here," Michael reminded her.

"But they were the only two who did! There's scarce another street lost fewer than ten. Hand me that packet of shop-bills, Michael."

Michael ripped off the printer's paper band and set the stack of small cards before her on the counter, admiring their neat, copperplate engraving and the good paper they were printed on —so different from the flimsy ballad-broadsides with their smudged woodcuts. Each bill showed a picture of the "Golden Buckel" sign; below was a close-written list of all that crowded the shelves behind Susanna and the drawers in front of her:

"Ye best Taylors and Glovers Needles, Needle Boxes, Taylors Shears, bodkins, Brass Thimbles & all sorts of Buttons for Liveries, Awl Blades & all sorts of Shoemakers Tackle, Inkpots, Inkhorns, drinking Horns, Sand Boxes, Snuff Boxes, Shoe Buckles, Cork Screws, Jews Harps, Shirt Buckles, Comb Cases, Nutmeg Graters, Hunting Horns, Dog Collars, Hawk Bells, marbles, trumpets, balls . . ."

". . . It's the water being so plentiful, all that dabbling in cold water—that's what makes the Bridge healthy," Susanna was saying as she placed a stack of the shopbills at the end of the counter so Michael could give one to each departing customer. "Master Thomas Soaper—he's the apothecary across the way—he told me fishmongers and watermen and such folk never catch any contagion at all. And it's from all that using of cold water and washing themselves."

"Well, maybe," Michael said, but he felt dubious. Mistress Trueblood had taken frightful cold one springtime, all from too much washing of her feet, because it was a fad just then, and Master Trueblood had warned Michael sternly against such follies.

"It's so!" Susanna insisted, adding, to Michael's dismay, that she meant to see to it *he* had a good wash before he left that evening, since she was sure that ballad-man would never think of it. "That— Ralph, or John, or whatever his name is."

"His name is Tom," Michael told her firmly. "And I don't want a good wash, I might take cold of it."

"Oh, lawks! That's a good one—when we're like to melt into our boots from this hot weather . . . Hoy! Look sharp now, here's a fine lady coming."

The matter of the good wash was shelved, to Michael's relief, and both of them concentrated on the customer, who bought six ha'penny buttons and an expensive comb-case before departing with one of the shop-bills to remind her to come back soon.

"A silver comb-case, it was," Michael told Tom that evening. "The best in the shop! Philip was pleased about that, I can tell you!"

"No doubt," Tom remarked. "Is Master Haas also pleased at

having you there, handing out bills and behaving as if you owned the place?"

"I don't behave so! Anyway," Michael confessed, "Master Haas doesn't know I'm there—not in the shop. Or that Susanna is, either. He doesn't know Philip's away to his silly friends the minute he's gone off-Bridge for an hour."

"And when he finds out?"

"Oh, he won't blame *us!* Master's ever so fair, Susanna says so . . . He's a map-colorer, Master Haas is, did I tell you? The best in England!"

"Susanna says so," murmured Tom.

"But he is! Ods bobs, you should see what he can do with just a little wee brush and some scarlet and a bit of gold leaf."

"D'ye mean to say he shows you his work?"

"Well—I . . . not exactly," Michael admitted. "I stole just a peek one day. Susanna sent me up to his chamber with his fresh-ironed tuckers, and there was his big table in the bow-window, with maps and color-pots all spread over it. . . . Oh, they were beautiful, and d'you know, something smells of garlic in that chamber, though I couldn't find what. . . . It was one day when he was gone."

"Hmmmm. The prickling of my thumbs says you'd best stay right away from the Bridge and out of trouble. But then, I don't suppose you'll heed me."

He supposed correctly. The more Michael saw of Susanna the better they got on. Peppery she might be, but she was always ready to laugh and tease and could not only wiggle her scalp but throw both thumbs out of joint, and was showing him how to do it. And she could whistle—sweeter than a thrush or shrill enough to pierce the din on the Bridge. Oh, Michael liked her fine.

He loved the old house, too, what he'd seen of it, which was: the stairway hall behind the shop; the warm, black-timbered kitchen overlooking the river at the rear, where he pared turnips and scoured pots for Susanna; and glimpses of bedchambers he caught whenever he followed her up the three flights of polished, tilting stairs to her tiny slope-ceilinged attic at the top. And of course, that one stolen, memorable look into the Master's bow-windowed chamber with its work table. As for the shop, with its bewildering array of wares, he liked it well enough too. When Philip wasn't in it.

It wasn't that Philip treated him rudely—rather that he took no notice of him at all. His careless black eyes would sweep across Michael to Susanna without pausing, leaving Michael smarting under the sensation of being invisible, a creature too insignificant to count. But short of hurling the bowl of turnip-parings at Philip's head, or thrusting out a foot to bring him crashing down—both sore temptations—Michael found nothing to do but smoulder. And to hope, privately, that Master Haas would someday catch Philip heading for Southwark and his friends of the bear-garden and race tracks. They were an expensive, hard-drinking set, too swift by far for Philip, according to Susanna, who drew her own conclusions from his boasting to her. Once or twice, she told Michael, she had heard him and his grandfather quarreling after Philip had stumbled home drunk late at night.

"And what Master would say to him jauntering off half the afternoons too, I don't know!" she added one day as she slid behind the counter, smoothing her hair. "Wagering for stakes 'way above his purse . . ."

"You don't—think you should tell Master Haas?"

Susanna hesitated; obviously she had considered it. "If I did, Philip'd turn me out of here afore morning. Oh, he'll settle down. He's just craving excitement—same as I did in that country tavern, that Green Man or whatever 'twas. Lud, how I missed London— and the bells!" she added, as the six o'clock clamor started up from Paul's and spread to both sides of the river in a rich-colored fog of sound.

Michael could understand that well enough—and even, he had to admit it, Philip's tedium. He was discovering that he did not quite share Susanna's love for shopkeeping. Ballad-selling was twice as lively, and more to his own taste. Aloud, he remarked only that shopkeeping was nothing like as jolly as being an actress would be.

"Nothing like as chancy, either," Susanna retorted. "But then, I might find a husband to look after me. It's you has the chancy future, now your uncle's sailed clean off the map—if you mean to stick with that Stephen or John or—"

"Tom," Michael said, but he smiled a little to himself as Susanna tossed her head and changed the subject as though she cared nothing about it. He had begun to think she did care—a little—about what happened to him, no matter if they were kin or not. Only a day or two before, she had boxed his ears for saying "damme," in a way that had reminded him powerfully of Mistress Trueblood, and she was always untucking his hair and pulling his collar straight as old Susan the cook used to do. The more a female pestered you, the fonder she was of you, so Michael's experience had told him. "Don't vex yourself," he said, "I'll not end up a ballad-man, for I can't carry a tune. Tom says he'd sooner trust a crow to carry a bowl of porridge." I'll not end up a shopkeeper either, he added to himself. But the question remained: what in the wide world could he be?

A day or so later, hanging about the kitchen at the Golden Buckle, he cautiously asked Susanna how one went about learning to be an actor. "Would they just, well, take on a likely boy, or—"

"Now whatever flea have you got in your nightcap this time, Master Cornhill?" she exclaimed, turning with the spitted joint in her hands to stare at him. "A proper-reared lad like you in such company? Why, what would your Master Trueblood say to such a notion? Here, down with you on the hearth and be turnspit for me, and no more vapors!"

"A turnspit is what I'll likely end up," Michael grumbled, settling himself reluctantly in the room's hottest spot. "Turnspit in a cookshop—and my Master Trueblood's not here to say *anything* to it! But it's likely all I'm good for."

"Oh, go on with you!" scoffed Susanna, as she reached down to untuck his side-locks. "Play-acting's not what you're wanting anyhow. You're needing some decent, hard-working trade."

"So you keep saying!" Michael retorted. "And Tom keeps saying I need Latin and Greek!"

"Latin and Greek!" Susanna's silvery eyebrows arched high. "Well, I'm sure I've nothing against that. And when does His Loftiness mean to send you to school?"

"Ah, give over, won't you?" Michael begged. "How can he, except through the parish? 'Twixt the two of you, you'll have me in the workhouse yet!" There was no answer. After a moment he raised alarmed eyes to Susanna's rosy, snub-nosed profile. "You *wouldn't* have the parish get me—would you, Susanna?"

She tossed her head impatiently. "Lawks, Master Cornhill, the way you talk, a body'd think the workhouse was the gates of hell and the parish beadle the devil! . . . Now, then, don't go having a fit o' the mother! I'd never turn you over to them, and so you know! But they'd teach you what a day's work is—and that's more than your precious Tom's doing!"

Michael left the Bridge that afternoon feeling restless and troubled. The day itself was oppressive, airless, and so hot even now at nearly sundown that his shirt stuck to his shoulder blades. The wharfs reeked of pitch and tar in the sun's low rays, and the old houses smelled like tinder, so dry was London in this strange un-London-like weather. If only it would rain, Michael felt, everything might seem more natural, and Susanna might not be cross. He knew she was not really cross at him, only at Tom for not being more like Old Joan—and perhaps at herself, Michael thought, for caring one way or the other. He wished he could persuade her to meet Tom face to face and see for herself that he was not the 'scape-gallows she thought him, but she became haughty whenever it was mentioned. And Tom, amused but faintly mocking, refused to embarrass her by turning up unasked.

"Well-a-day, I thought you'd decided to change your lodgings," he remarked when Michael wandered in at last. "You've been to see that girl again, I can tell by your face. *Now* what has she been saying about me?"

No use trying to parry that question, Michael had learned by experience. With a sigh, he sat down and repeated Susanna's latest criticisms. "Now don't *you* start talking about the parish and my own good!" he implored Tom.

"Parish be hanged—if she thinks they'd send you to school, she's badly mistaken."

"And nor do I want to go!"

"Well, there *you're* mistaken. All persons of eleven and a half with a head on their shoulders should be wanting to put something in it—and you do have a head on your shoulders, Michael." After a thoughtful moment, Tom added, "And she's right, you know. If I preach Latin and Greek, I should do something about it. So suppose I solve that little equation right now. Then what would she scold about, hey?"

Michael stared at him uneasily. "Solve it how?"

"I'll show you." Tom arose, plucked his hat from the bedpost, and clapped it on his head with a flourish of cuff-tatters. "Come along up to Paul's Churchyard before Master Bennet puts up his shutters. He'll likely have a Lily's **Latin Grammar** for a groat or two. Greek I can teach out of my head."

"*You* mean to teach me?" Michael said in astonishment, stumbling after him down the shaky stairs.

"Why not? I tutored a baronet's sprig once, later a rich pepper-merchant's young ones . . . in truth, at one time I was quite in demand among the quality—being especially esteemed," Tom added grandly, "for my accent in the French tongue."

"But—when was this?" demanded Michael, who was struggling to fit yet one more variant into the contradictory saga of Tom's life. "Before you were the lord's son's lackey, was it?"

"Oh, no, 'twas after. I'd come up in the world a bit. My father gave me a leg up, as you might say—"

"Your father? The cook?" Michael shot a skeptical glance at Tom's profile, blithesome under the sweeping brim of his hat.

"Oh, God-a-mercy, that cook was never my father—merely my mother's husband. My father was a French artist—a portrait painter. He enjoyed quite a vogue, here, I believe, before he returned to Paris . . . leaving me with a sound French accent but nothing else. The man was a spendthrift. Died without a *sou*—all his possessions gone for debt—imploring the bailiff's men to leave him his bed to die in."

Michael did not ask how this affecting information had reached Tom—all the way from Paris. He did not question the story at all. Bits of it had an odd ring of truth; it was easy to picture an improvident French portrait-painter as Tom's father. But he strongly doubted if any of Tom's stories was wholly true. He wondered why Tom told them. Perhaps his real past was so shameful, or so painful, that he could not bear to face it? Or perhaps merely dull—Tom could never face that.

"Can you speak French, truly?" Michael asked as they turned off Carter Lane toward Paul's.

"Mais, oui, certainement!" Tom exclaimed, adding a fluent rush of other remarks that quite dazzled Michael. They certainly *sounded* like French.

" 'S faith, that's ever so fine! Could you teach me French too, d'you think?"

"Why not?" said Tom.

"French? That ballad-man?" cried Susanna a few days later. "Lawks, that's stolen the wind from my sails, that has!" She giggled suddenly, her face going pink and her eyes vanishing in a thicket of silvery lashes. She took up a corner of her apron to wipe them, adding, "Not but what a French-jabbering rogue is still a rogue! . . . Well, Master Cornhill, I'll educate you too! You come to the Bridge here regular, instead of only hab-nab, and I'll train you proper around this house and shop."

"You mean let me dust the Master's table?"

"Well, anyway, his chamber."

"Agreed!" Michael said, before she could change her mind.

So the easy tempo of Michael's life became a bit more brisk. Each day, over the breakfast ale or while walking down Cheap or taking boat up-river, he learned his Latin and Greek and French from Tom, whose methods were as unorthodox as his schoolrooms but surprisingly effective. And every second afternoon, he went to the Bridge for an hour or two and learned shopkeeping and housekeeping and a great many of Old Joan's strait-laced precepts from Susanna—besides how to wiggle his whole scalp. In between, the ballad-selling and varied amusements went on as before. But Michael began to learn a lot—among other things, that he would rather watch old Master Haas brush delicate indigo over a map's lakes, or draw the four winds' puff-cheeked faces in the corners, than eat gooseberry cream or even listen to Tom sing, even when he had to do his watching from across the room while industriously flicking a feather-duster over the bed-curtains. One day when Susanna caught him hanging over the table in the Master's absence, touching the fine brushes with one finger and sniffing at the paint-pots in search of the mysterious garlic smell, she declared he must be going simple over that one lone subject. Michael agreed—and was at once struck forcibly by a desire to make the craft his own.

"Why not? I'd never like anything else so well! I could learn to paint, I *know* I could. Master Haas might even take me as apprentice, mightn't he?" he asked Susanna, greatly excited. "I mean, when I'm old enough—only one more year and a sixmonth, then I'll be thirteen. Susanna—ask him! Just say somebody you know has a boy—a *likely* boy, of eleven and a half—and does he think he might be wanting a 'prentice year after next. Please, will you?"

Dubious, but willing, Susanna put her question to the old man, who saw through the transparent little ruse at once and reacted with amusement, though not unkindly. "So 'somebody' has a boy, eh? But of course, it is not that small brother of Susanna! Oh, I have spied him there in the kitchen, that flax-hair *jongen* who is 'none of yours,' scrubbing the pots for you or creeping behind you up the stairs like a mouse. *Ja*—and sometimes finishing my eel pie, eh? Now, no need to blush the cheek so, *meidje!* Of food there is plenty, I begrudge not. But your question of the apprenticeship—that is another matter. I am an old man, I take no apprentices. But Philip is master haberdasher now, he is the shopman here. The *jongen* should ask Philip, not old *grootvader!* Eh? *Ja, ja, jawel . . .*"

". . . And then he went away," said Susanna, reporting all this to Michael later. "Laughing, only gently, y'know, but—well, I think he didn't take it serious."

"No," said Michael sadly. He could almost hear the old man's summer-thunder voice, the rumbling of kindly laughter, which had yet slammed a door in his face. For he felt he would sooner die a pauper than to ask Philip for anything, even supposing Philip wanted an apprentice, or he himself wanted to be a haberdasher, neither of which was so. With a sigh he put the whole matter from his mind, only adding slyly to Susanna, "You let him think I was your brother?"

"Oh, 'twas easier than explaining. I'll set him right one day."

Michael smiled and let it go—it didn't matter anyhow. But that evening, wandering along Cheap on his meandering way home, he heard the bells of St. Michael Archangel and stopped to look back toward Cornhill and the square stone tower and listen to the sweetest peal in England. He had never gone back there to press his questions on the vicar; he told himself it was useless. But at moments like this, with the evening pale about him and the clear, pure notes silvering the air, his heart swelled with shapeless longings until it seemed too large to hold in his chest. He thought back, half wistfully and half in derision, to the time when he had been Tony enough to believe Susanna might be his sister. Then he walked on, wondering who he really was—and if he'd ever find out.

Battles Far and Near

"Hsst! What's that? D'ye hear anything, Michael?"

Michael flung down his Latin book and ran to join Tom at the window. "Is it the guns again?"

"I'm not certain. Hark a minute." Tom pushed the casement open a little wider, and they both listened intently.

"All I can hear is those horses and all, in Knightrider's Street," Michael said in disgust. "But it couldn't have been thunder," he added, leaning out to squint up into a perfectly cloudless sky.

"No. Though it could well have been my fancy," Tom remarked. "I'm full of vapors these past few days, I own it frankly. . . . Good morrow, Harry!" he added as the motion-man's flushed round face and untidy mop of red hair appeared in the window opposite. "Did you hear guns?"

"Ehhh—not guns, but I did hear a bit o' news, when I was down to t'Three Sails for m'draught," Harry confided, thrusting his head and shoulders so far out the window that Michael held his breath in alarm. "The fight's on—and it's a-going famous!" he whispered hoarsely. "Famous! 'At's what they're saying."

"Another rumor," Tom said. But he reached for his hat and lute, adding, "We'll go investigate it all the same. Bring the rest of those ballads, Michael. Sure to be a crowd in the Park again . . ."

It was June—the month for battles—and they'd had a week of flying rumors, jumpy nerves, and sudden excursions to St. James's Park to listen for gunfire, which had been heard plainly yesterday by the crowds in the Park and gravel-pits. Today being Whitsunday and a holiday, half of London might be there, and all Westminster. It was not Tom alone who was a-tiptoe with anxiety for the fleet, which was certainly engaged with the Dutch fleet somewhere between England and Holland, with nobody yet knew what success.

Snatching up the broadsides, Michael buckled on his beloved swordbelt as they hurried down the lane. In a few moments he was standing beside Tom at Trig Stairs, scanning the bobbing jumble of craft for Sam'l's yellow sculler, and shortly afterwards tumbled into the little boat after Tom, who was already asking Sam'l what new rumors were circulating and if he had heard guns this afternoon.

"This afternoon, no, Master Godfrey. This mornin', aye. Yisterday, aye. There do be those as say they heard 'em Friday," Sam'l added with obvious disbelief.

"And a goodly crowd of us who fancy we heard 'em this hour," Tom observed with a glance around at the river, whose broad, breeze-ruffled surface, dancing with sunlight, did seem more thickly dotted than usual with light craft heading toward Westminster.

Once well away from the wharfside, with the noise of wheels and hoofs and strident voices all fading, Michael listened again. But there was only the lap of water, the dip of oars, churchbells from somewhere, and occasionally a snatch of talk drifting from other boats as the river slipped swiftly beneath them. The familiar shore glided by in the middle distance as if it, not they, were moving. There went the great, gloomy pile of Baynard's Castle, with the square tower of St. Andrew-by-the-Wardrobe thrusting up behind it. There went Puddle Dock and Blackfriars Stairs, and Fleet Ditch pouring its foul-smelling flood into the already ill-smelling Thames. There went the mean jumble of houses elbowing one another in Whitefriars' tangle of dirty alleys. Then, at Temple Wall Michael's favorite stretch of riverbank began, as the shaded Temple gardens gave way to the lawns and lordly mansions of Arundel, Savoy, and the rest, and these to the long, low wall of Scotland Yard.

Midway along the imposing half-mile of brick and stone that was Whitehall Palace, Sam'l put in to Whitehall Stairs. Tom and Michael jumped ashore and set off through the narrow passage past the Chapel and the Great Hall, leaving Sam'l jousting bitterly for his bit of wharf. "They love their brabbles, do watermen!" Tom remarked. "Horn-mad, most of them, that's my opinion . . . Straight on across the court, Michael."

"If we *don't* hear the guns, then will we know the battle's over?" Michael asked, skipping to keep up with Tom's long-legged stride.

"We'll know nothing for certain till one of the ships comes home, that's the hard fact of it," Tom told him.

But the crowd of Londoners, surging restless as the sea up and down the long, grassy reaches of St. James's Park, was alive with rumors. The battle was won; the battle was just begun; His Majesty's hard-pressed Navy had been saved in the nick by the arrival of Prince Rupert's fleet from France; Prince Rupert's fleet was calmly victualing in Dover and knew nothing whatever of any battle.

"God-a-mercy! A new tale every minute and not one of 'em worth a trillibub!" Tom said in disgust. He swung his lute from his back to his front and began to tune it. "Let's give them something else to think of." And so they strolled and sold ballads awhile, but with indifferent success, and finally Tom shook his head, slinging the lute across his back again. "Today they're in no humor to hear anything but news of a victory. I'm just another fly to flap at. Come, we'll cease our buzzing and go try our luck at the New Exchange."

With a last glance around, Michael turned to follow, then suddenly seized Tom's sleeve. "Look! Yonder by the water—it's Susanna!" Joyfully he pointed across a sweep of lawns and trees to the unmistakable figure in sky-blue standing at the pond's edge, idly tossing something to a cluster of ducks. Her hair shone like metal in the sunlight. At last she would meet Tom—and find she liked him ever so much and maybe stroll along with them to the New Exchange or . . . "Don't you see her yonder?" he said impatiently. "Come on! I want you two to say good-morrow face to face!"

"For shame, Michael." Tom was looking toward Susanna with interest, but his tone was firm. "Oblige that finical, pretty lass to curtsey to a worthless rogue like me? No indeed!"

"Oh, Tom!" exclaimed Michael, exasperated. "She wouldn't refuse—she couldn't!"

"Precisely. And I'll not be party to such a scurvy trick. But you run along, if you like," Tom added, with one of his best cuff-flourishing gestures. "You're at liberty! Chuck those ballads into the nearest gutter, and give Mistress Susanna my greetings."

To Michael's dismay he started briskly across the grass in the direction of Westminster town. Michael threw a frustrated glance back at Susanna, only to see her hurrying in the other direction, waving —not to him, but to an elaborately dressed young woman who was hurrying just as fast toward her. As Michael watched, they met, with every evidence of enthusiasm, and began to talk so animatedly one would think they hadn't set eyes on each other for a year. As maybe they hadn't, thought Michael, remembering the plague. He watched them, feeling more and more disgruntled as Tom continued to stride off one way and they began to stroll the other. The strange young woman—or girl or whatever she was—wore a fur capelet despite the warmth of the day and a crimson dress all lace and ribbons and more ribbons in her ringletty dark hair, which was wired to stand out wide at each side of her face and then fall in bobbing, dancing, silly-looking curls. Her dress was silly-looking, too—tucked up to show *two* different petticoats. *She* was silly-looking, thought Michael crossly. And why Susanna was too interested in her silly chatter even to look around, he was sure he didn't know. Or care!

With a face like a thundercloud, Michael turned his back on them and stalked rapidly after Tom.

It was the first of three events that week to have unexpected importance in Michael's life.

Much later, heading back to London after a fruitless hour among the crowds and rumors in the New Exchange, they finally did hear guns—or what might be guns, unless it was the rumblings of a very distant storm. Sam'l rested his oars, and they listened hard, but it was all disappointingly uncertain.

Dolittle Lane, on the other hand, turned out to be a scene of lively drama. They arrived to find that Harry Hobson had been hauled off that hour to debtors' prison, and Mistress Hobson, her five children, and half the neighbors were lamenting in the street. "Ech! Wot'll we do without 'im, wot'll we do!" Mistress Hobson kept chanting, alternately flinging her apron over her face and embracing the nearest child.

"What *will* they do?" Michael echoed in consternation.

"Live well off the rest of us, same as last time," Tom said dryly. He glanced around the little knot of neighbors and gawkers, heaved a sigh, and swung his lute into position. "Here, Michael, start passing my hat—to Mother Floss first. Heaven's a witness, Harry's her best client when he's in funds."

He struck a chord to capture attention, then smiled at the tearful Mistress Hobson, who came from the North Country as everybody knew, and eased into the lightsome chords of "The Countrey Lasse":

> *Although I am a Countrey Lasse*
> *a loftie minde I beare a,*
> *I thinke myselfe as good as those,*
> *that gay apparrell weare a:*
> *My Coate is made of comely Gray,*
> *yet is my skin as soft a,*
> *As those that with the chiefest Wines*
> *do bathe their bodies oft a.*
> *Downe, downe dery, dery downe . . .*

A verse or two of that and half the bystanders were bawling the dery-derys along with him, the forsaken Hobsons were producing watery smiles, and the hat was jingling.

"But we'll have to eat light tomorrow and spare them a groat or two," Tom muttered, as he led the way up the crooked stairs a little later. "Tomorrow and tomorrow and tomorrow—"

"I'll give them my thruppence," Michael offered.

"I'll give Harry my boot in his backside! But I'll buy him out of compter this time. It'll be cheaper in the end."

In this opinion Michael concurred, without quite knowing what he was talking about. He assumed Tom knew—and so did Tom.

And that was the week's second event of consequence to Michael.

Harry owed the butcher, the baker, the chandler, the landlord, but chiefly Mother Floss and half a dozen other tavern-keepers. The total was over sixteen pounds, a figure that struck Michael dumb, but merely caused Tom to push his hat back on his head and whistle thoughtfully, then remark that he hadn't clapped eyes on Jack Stubbs for a month of May Days and had a mind to do so. He departed, returning triumphant an hour later with nine pounds six. "And nary a penny of it to be repaid, since he owed it me already, in a manner of speaking," he told Michael blandly. "Mind you, I doubt your Mistress Susanna would quite understand the transaction."

Michael, himself open-mouthed at the sheer adroitness of contriving that a foist rescue a shifter, wisely decided not to put Susanna to the test.

The remaining six-odd pounds were harder to come by. But by Monday sundown, Tom had scraped it together, extorting a few last grudging shillings from the neighbors, adding the week's rent money, and borrowing the final four pounds from a money-lender in Shoe Lane—to Michael's alarm, for Master Trueblood had never had a good word for money-lenders, saying they charged such interest that you always ended paying double what you borrowed, and often never got out of their clutches at all. "And now we're a week behind with Mother Floss, too," Michael added in some trepidation. Mother Floss could become very unpleasant when the rent was overdue, as he had had ample opportunity to discover. But Tom brushed all that aside, saying he'd dash off some extra ballads to make up the rent, and the other was Harry's debt, not theirs. "And well worth a fit of his sulks, if it keeps him out of mischief and off our minds."

Finding nothing to quarrel with in this, Michael too brushed inconvenient ifs and buts aside.

So, early Tuesday, a reluctant Harry was restored to his family and responsibilities, which now included a sworn promise to hand over ten shillings per week to Tom, who would then hand it to the money-lender. An admirable plan, Tom considered it, fair to one and all. Michael could only agree once more—and devoutly hope that it would work.

"He paid the fellow's debts? From his own purse?" Susanna asked in astonishment when Michael turned up in her kitchen that afternoon talking more about the Hobsons than the Whitsunday battle.

"Well—some from his own purse. The rest he—arranged for," Michael said hastily.

"Did he! I'll not ask how." Susanna reached to untuck Michael's side-locks, then without warning snatched a handful of hair and yanked his head askew to glare at it. "My soul and body! Creeturs!" she said grimly. "Michael Cornhill, you've gone and got lousy and that won't do, not in this house. Old Master's fearful strict about it. Come. Upstairs . . . though how a body's to keep clean of 'em *all* the time is more'n I know," she admitted as she followed him.

"Mistress Trueblood used to comb me for 'em," Michael offered.

"Well, I mean to comb you, too, and comb you clean if I have to scalp you like a red Injun. Sit there."

Michael settled meekly by her garret window with a rag of an old towel about his shoulders, smiling as he reflected that Susanna's ferocious threats seldom had much to do with her subsequent behavior, and idly wondering, as he caught a wavery glimpse of himself in her little mirror, when he was going to grow into his front teeth, and if he would ever acquire an air of elegance like Tom's. When the familiar half-painful, half-comforting tugging and yanking was under way, he remarked, "We saw you Whitsun, Tom and me. Feeding the ducks, you were."

"Well, I never! Too high-and-mighty to say good morrow, were you?"

"Tom said *you'd* be too finical to greet a ballad-man," Michael retorted, adding "Ouch!" as he was instantly paid out for it. "*I* would've come, but for that silly-looking friend of yours," he went on grumpily.

"What silly-looking . . . Ah! That was Moll, that was! That sister of Nancy that lived above Old Joan and me in Cripplegate."

"The actress one?" Michael exclaimed.

"The same. Lawks! Did you mark that crimson dress? I'll warrant it cost ten pounds! Laced all over—real lace, mind you! And that little fur cape . . . Though why she wasn't sweltered I don't know," Susanna added prosaically. "I'd not wear such things this weather, even if I had 'em—not that I'm likely to—no, nor not just to please some fine silken fop of a court-dandy, neither, whether he'd bought 'em for me or no."

"Did a silken court-dandy buy Moll's clothes?"

"He did. He pays her lodging, too, and a good thing, Michael, or she'd be hungry in the street, with both theatres tight-shuttered ever since the plague. Though she did say the King's House opens in a month or so—she had it from Master Thomas Killigrew. All the same . . ." Susanna's tilted nose tipped a bit higher. "She may keep that gallant of hers. I saw him—lawks, he had more ribbon about him than Philip's got in this shop! A stare-about fool! But when he crooks his finger, Moll must come. I'd sooner stay a maid-servant!"

"You mean you'll not be an actress after all?" Michael was disappointed.

Susanna shrugged and attacked a tangled lock as if it had personally offended her. *"I* don't know. But I mean to be boss of Susanna Peach! I'll dance to my own tune or none at all."

"What if you find that husband to look after you? Will Butling, maybe?" Michael said slyly. "Won't he be boss?"

"Eh, that depends!" she retorted. "There, Master Cornhill, you're clean-combed. Come along, we'll put these varmints in the fire."

She led the way down the three narrow flights of stairs, the towel bundled under her arm. Michael followed, stealing his usual glimpses of well-waxed paneling here, a carved lintel there, diamond-paned casements opening on the river at every landing.

"What will you do, if you're not to be an actress?" he whispered. "Could you just stay here? I like this house, I do."

"And so do I. But suppose Old Master died—or Philip took a wife!" Susanna shook her head as she led the way into the kitchen. "No, I must leave it all to the good Lord. No doubt He'll see to me."

She laughed and poked up the fire and thrust in the towel-bundle. But they were both thoughtful as they stood absently watching the flames devour it. Michael was off into a fine day-dream. He would earn—or *find*—a lot of money, maybe even ten pounds, and buy Susanna a crimson dress with real lace, and—no, it would be *twenty* pounds. And he would *buy this shop*. Then Susanna could be shop-mistress, and he would live here and learn map-coloring all by himself just by watching Old Master, and soon become the next-best map-colorer in England and grow rich and famous and take a wife of his own, and the Cornhill family *would* be grand, fine folk after all—the grandest and finest in London.

It was the following day, when he was chattering idly to Tom as they again hung out the window listening for the guns, that Michael chanced to mention Moll's news about the King's House opening and found he had Tom's whole attention.

"Theatre Royal, d'ye mean? Tom Killigrew told her so himself? Well-a-day! Now that's a tidbit to chew over!"

"But what—who is Tom Killigrew?"

"Master of the King's Company of Comedians. My master too, once. I made one of that company when they were still acting in Gibbon's old tennis court off Clare Market, five years back."

"You were an actor?" Caught between interest and doubt, Michael braced himself for yet another version of Tom's personal history.

But Tom merely said, "A reluctant one. It was playwriting I fancied—though little luck it brought me. Still, there was one attempt . . ." He left the window to ferret about in the box of old broadsides he used for scribbling. "—part of one, anyhow . . . Damme, now where could I have put that?"

"The mattress?" ventured Michael, remembering an occasion on which Tom had surprisingly produced three shillings from that unlikely spot.

"The mattress! . . . Ah." With an air of satisfaction Tom extracted from his rumpled bedding a packet of foolscap sheets held together with a bit of twine. "There it is, i'gad! *The Mask of Comedy—a tragedy in five acts* . . . three of them still unwritten," he added wryly.

"Tom! A real play, all your own!"

"Now, don't go building air-castles!" Tom warned him. "No doubt this one's rubbish like all my others. Still, with the theatres reopening, I might contrive to finish it. Mind, you're not to hang over my shoulder, asking if I've done yet!"

"I won't," Michael promised.

Tom plucked the twine off and scanned the first pages, looking as if he might be constructing an air-castle himself. With a sigh, Michael turned back to the window. Outside, another fine, dry afternoon was drawing to a close—another restless afternoon, with St. James's Park again full of Londoners imagining gunfire, and churchbells ringing at unexpected hours because of its being a monthly fast day for the plague with extra services everywhere. Four whole days since Whitsun and still no word of the fleet or how the battle went, no fresh developments at all.

But an hour later, when they took their usual stroll to Paul's in search of news, they found the Churchyard criss-crossed with people coming and going and being restless together. Some voices were uneasy, but most were talking excitedly of a victory, jeering at the Dutch admiral, De Ruyter, and boasting of Sir Christopher Mings.

"They must have heard *something,*" Michael told Tom. "Look, they even have serpents all ready to light!" He was enviously watching a group of boys, who were not the only ones carrying "serpents" and all sorts of other fireworks, obviously only waiting a signal to set them off.

Tom shrugged, and they pushed their way inside the cathedral. Paul's Walk was thronged and Duke Humphrey's seething, but nobody seemed to know anything for certain. Michael, fending off brocaded coattails only to collide painfully with loose-slung swords, was wishing mightily that he were somewhere else, when the first real news began to run through the crowd like fire through a thatch.

And it was victory—clear and certain, with more and more people arriving hatless and shouting to bring the tidings straight from Westminster and the King. They all told the same tale of a decisive battle that had raged the whole day after Whitsunday. Michael, heedless now of shoving and elbows, could fairly hear the guns booming, the crack of masts toppling, the confusion of yells and curses as the high, square-sterned men-o'-war pitched and churned the sea in a reek of smoke and gunpowder. By evening, so ran the story, the Dutch were in full flight—what was left of them. Of a hundred sail, scarce fifty had limped home again to Holland. And the best of it was that English losses were few. General Monk was unharmed, the seamen's beloved Sir Christopher Mings only wounded in the leg. And Captain Bell—little Captain Bell, in one of the fire ships—had set a vessel of seventy guns in flames at the very end of the day.

Oh, it was glorious news, as fine as anybody could wish to hear!

"That's settled, then, eh Michael?" Tom shouted over the jubilant hubbub that had turned Paul's into a gigantic buzzing hive. "There'll be no more heard out o' the Dutchmen now! And no more press gangs, either, to plague a man's dreams and play handy-dandy with his life! Anyway, not till the next war," he added wryly.

"Would the press gangs nab *you,* Tom?" Michael shouted back in consternation. It had never occurred to him to dread this.

"They'd nab a stone image if you warmed it a bit," Tom retorted. "And it might be more useful than I, at that. They could drop a stone image on De Ruyter's head." Tom grinned and added, "Let's begone from here. I'm near deafened."

"I once met a fishmonger's 'prentice who *wanted* the press to take him." Michael puffed as they struggled through the rejoicing crowd toward the portico.

"God-a-mercy! He must've been tired of life."

"He was tired of his," Michael said thoughtfully.

But it was no time for musing, or even for enjoying the half-scary waves of relief that washed over him, hot and cold, when he reflected that if the *previous* press had got Tom, he himself would now be . . . doing what? Sleeping where? Eating how? He shuddered away from such questions. It was a time for rejoicing.

They shoved their way out the great west doors and between the columns of the portico. Beyond, in the open space where sixty years ago the Gunpowder plotters had been hanged, drawn, and quartered to the vengeful cheers of a crowd larger than this one, they hesitated, as the bells of Paul's suddenly began to peal the news of victory.

"A pox on bread and cheese on such a night!" Tom cried.

So they supped in splendor at the Golden Lion, on venison-pasty, ale, and strawberries, and afterwards Michael, too, bought serpents and roamed the dusky alleys helping Harry's boys and some other urchins scavenge bits of wood and trash to add to the pile growing in Knightrider's Street. As the dark came down at last, their bonfire was lighted along with a hundred others all over London, and Tom played his lute and everybody sang and cheered the General and the fleet and Mings, and the serpents flared bright until midnight.

And by noon next day they had learned, with all London, that the glorious news was false. His Majesty's fleet had not won the battle but had been ignominiously beaten. Nine ships were lost or missing, five captains slain; the rest had fled in disorder, pursued for miles by the victorious Dutch. Worse, General Monk was saying he had never had more cowardly officers—that only twenty or so had behaved like men. And Sir Christopher Mings was mortally wounded with a bullet still lodged in him.

It was disaster—perhaps even disgrace. The news was as bad as news could be.

Stunned by the tales they had heard, Tom and Michael walked home past last night's scarcely-cool bonfires in troubled silence. Neither confided his worries to the other; but Michael suspected that Tom, like himself, was thinking about the press.

That was the third event—and the most important of the three.

The Great Press

It was nearly midnight of the twenty-third of June, Midsummer Eve, and still hot and close in the room above the stable. Tom and Michael sat together in the dark, near the open casement—partly to catch whatever breath of air was stirring, partly to watch the lane and Knightrider Street without being seen themselves.

Below, all was quiet, except for the faint cry of the bell-man on Carter Lane, calling,

> *"Twelve o'clock . . .*
> *Look well to your lock,*
> *Your fire and your light . . .*
> *Good-night . . ."*

It was a quavery old voice. Well, he was a very old bell-man. There was a great scarcity of young men these days in London. Few enough middle-aged ones or even tall boys were to be seen in the city's streets. Except, of course, for the despondent little groups standing shackled to a post somewhere, like the three unfortunates slouching at the corner of the lane this minute, waiting for the press wagon to come and collect them for His Majesty's fleet.

It had been a dismal fortnight that followed the shocking news of the defeat. Once the ships had limped home, deserting seamen had flocked into the city by hundreds—never to be got back now, with Sir Christopher Mings, whom they might have heeded, dead of his wounds and buried last Wednesday-week. The Dutch were boasting and revictualing their ships, and now the French were prowling, too, and had actually seized a British island in the Indies. Here at home there was the whole crippled fleet to re-outfit quickly, with the King as usual desperate for gold and seeking to borrow it from London. On top of all, to send the city wild with resentment, the press had begun. Not a legal impressing with money, but out-and-out kidnapping of anything male that moved. Every man who owned a sword wore it everywhere, to prove himself a gentleman and exempt from impressment; if you owned none, you were out of luck. You were run down like a stray dog and asked your birthday later, if at all. Even persons of eleven and a half were for once glad to be rather small for their age. The fury had raged for a week now and showed no signs of abating—rather the opposite. Tom, who had not stirred from the room in the last three days—at dire cost to their larder and ever-shaky financial state—had predicted earlier that evening that the gangs would be coming inside the houses soon, perhaps tomorrow.

"Tomorrow!" Michael had echoed in dismay. "*Then* what will we do?"

"We can't leave it till then, Michael. I must slip out of here tonight. It can't be helped."

"But—where will you go?"

"I know a place. Not a cozy one, but it's safe enough. Sam'l will take me there, and I'll come back when this is over. You must go to the Bridge."

Michael stared at him. "To—the Golden Buckle, you mean?"

"Yes. Will they take you in for a while, d'ye think?"

"Susanna would," Michael said slowly. He found he could not picture Master Haas's reaction—perhaps Susanna could sneak him in with nobody knowing. He could sleep in the coal bin.

"She must." Tom's voice was uncharacteristically urgent. "You can't stay here. You've nothing to give for rent."

That was true enough. They hadn't a groat between them. The loaf they'd finished at midday was one Michael had wheedled from Mother Floss the previous morning, but she would give no more credit and had said so flatly. They already owed her the current week's rent as well as their usual small running bill for cheese and ale—grown to a large one because Tom had not dared venture out. To lodgers in arrears, Mother Floss's heart was stone. Michael had found that out an hour ago when he tried to add just one more supper to their tally.

And then there was Harry's debt—as Michael still called it,

though in hard fact it was not Harry's; the signature on the money-lender's hateful chit was Tom's.

"A pize on Harry!" Michael muttered, not for the first time. "It's all his doing!"

"It isn't. It's all my doing," Tom said calmly. "If I'd kept my nose out of his affairs, Harry'd be taking his ease in Ludgate this minute, and Mother Floss would be in charity with us. So a pize on me."

Michael sighed and fell silent as Tom leaned out the window to listen. The point was academic anyhow. Harry, too, must keep close indoors now, with no more chance than Tom to earn enough for ale and bread, much less anything over for the debt. And tomorrow, when the gangs went inside the houses—?

"There it comes," Tom said at last, drawing back into the black shadows of the room. Michael drew back too, listening as the faint rattle of wheels on cobbles grew louder and nearer, finally filling the night as the press cart rumbled and shrieked and clattered its way into Knightrider's Street and along to the corner where the three shackled men were helplessly waiting. For a short time the air rang with outrage, with yelled curses from the men already prisoners in the cart, with harsh orders and blows and scufflings as the three new ones joined them. Then with a scramble of hoofs and the mingled groan of rusty axles and despairing men, the equipage made off toward Bridewell. Michael thought of Alan Blake and shivered.

"It had better be now," Tom said. He peered once more down into the moonlit lane, then moved to the table where his lute and hat lay beside the small bundle of his books and belongings. "Mind you're up before first light, Michael, and out of here. I won't have Mother Floss seizing you for rent—she'd turn you into a slavey. Con your Latin—ten lines a day till I'm back."

"But how long—?"

"There's no saying. Two weeks, three . . . but I'll be back. Never doubt it."

Michael nodded mutely, forgetting he was all but invisible in the gloom. He sensed, rather than saw, the familiar motions, heard the whispering jangle of strings as Tom slung the lute on his back. He felt for a brief instant a strong arm about his shoulders and the rough, affectionate rumpling of his hair. Then the floor creaked, there was a faint noise on the stair, and all was silent. He rushed to the casement, his throat tight as a fist; the lane was empty of all but moonlight, though there were inky shadows under the houses' overhang. Presently something caught his eye crossing Knightrider Street—a flitting shape already merging with the shadows on the other side. In the instant before it vanished, he glimpsed the seven-shaped thrust of a lute.

He turned back into the room. It was desolate; already he hated it. He knew he could not bear to curl up on Tom's abandoned bed and try to sleep the night, much less sleep in his own with Tom's there, empty. Quickly, he felt about the room, snatching his other shirt from the nail, his jackanapes and clean tucker and Lily's Grammar, bundling them all up together and buckling his sword-belt around the whole. His empty scarlet purse was in his pocket. There was nothing left now in the room of his or Tom's. He glanced around it once more, wondering if Mother Floss would save it for them to come back to—in case they could come back. There was nothing to do but chance it. Swiftly, he felt his way down the familiar stable-smelling stairs and out into the lane.

Fifteen minutes afterwards, he was standing on the Bridge in front of the Golden Buckle, wondering in a panic how he was to get in without rousing the whole house and perhaps the neighbors, too. He had picked up a pebble and was hopelessly eyeing Susanna's fourth-story dormer when he glimpsed a flicker of light through the shop window. He ran to it, tapping desperately, pressing his nose to the diamond-shaped panes, and was rewarded by the sight of Susanna herself, in nightrail and ruffled cap, candle in hand, peering across the dark shop from the kitchen doorway.

In another moment she was pulling him into the house, patting and shushing and examining him anxiously, whispering, "Lawks-a-mercy, Master Cornhill! What's happened? It's gone midnight! Coming through those streets alone!"

"No matter. I had them to myself." The streets had been silent, deserted except for an aged bell-man or two; no need to fear foot-pads this night; they too had vanished. London had seldom been safer—or more sullen. Few householders had bothered, this Mid-summer Eve, to set out the little colored glass lamps or string the garlands of birch and fennel and St. John's wort; and there was certainly no merriment or dancing. "Everybody's hiding from the press," Michael said. "Now Tom's gone too."

He told her about the past three uneasy days. It was a whispered and slightly jumbled recital, punctuated by gulps and an occasional sniff because the concerned scowl between Susanna's flaxen eyebrows and the sympathy that puckered her rosy, freckled face were harder to stand up to than anything. In the end she hugged him so warmly that he had to fight free of her and do a ferocious bit of scowling himself.

"Oh, lud, then, I'm sorry, I'll not cosset you! But where can your Tom hide? What'll he do? Anybody must eat!"

"I don't know—he only said he knew a safe place and that Sam'l would take him there. Oh, I hate the press!"

"It's the devil's own tyranny, it is! Decent family men dragged off like criminals—no chance to bid good-by, even—what's to become of all those wives and young ones? Yes, and Master Soaper across the way here, he says regular seamen are bribing their way out altogether! He says their officers—" Susanna broke off. "Here I stand gabbling, and what's to be done with you?"

"Can't I stay, then?"

"You must, I'll not have you sleeping on the cobbles somewhere. I'll—I'll try to smuggle you up to my chamber. But Master's awake still. I came down to make him a posset—it's how I saw you." Susanna glanced toward the stairway, turned back with a distraught gesture. "Philip's gone too, y'see."

"Philip!" Michael had forgotten his existence. "To hide, you mean?"

Susanna nodded; the ruffle of her nightcap nodded too, around her worried face. It was an old-fashioned cap with ties under the chin; it looked very much as if it might once have belonged to Old Joan. "We suppose so. Though we don't know, and Master's sick at heart, afeard for him. We heard rumors, y'see . . . there was a nasty brabble, at the Bull and Chain in Southwark, two nights back—a stabbing and all. Oh, a bad thing, Michael! It's a place Philip goes . . . he's not been home since then. And not a word as to whether he's dead or alive or in prison or fled to Virginny . . ."

"Perhaps he's pressed!" Michael said.

"I hope he is. Master'd rather see him pressed than fallen into disgrace. Oh, the jolthead! Huffing about with those roaring-boys . . ." She gave a sigh and reached for Michael's shoulder to turn him. "Come—into the kitchen, be quiet. I'll mix Master his posset, then later on, somehow—"

The stair creaked, and they stood like guilty statues, he with his bundle, she biting her lip, as Master Jan Haas loomed up in the doorway. His austere face, harsh with worry in the light of the candle he held, relaxed a little as he looked at them.

"So! It is the creepy-mouse. Nay, don't be frightened, *seuntje,* I'll not bite you. Is it more trouble then?"

Susanna explained, diffidently, and not too coherently, since, as she told Michael later, she didn't want to bother the Master with a lot of details. He was quite able to grasp, however, that the press had left Michael homeless. He muttered and rumbled at this, shaking his white head angrily. But the anger was not for his uninvited guest, whom he showed no sign of rejecting. On the contrary, he was inclined to be a trifle stern with Susanna for leaving Michael to someone else's care in the first place.

"Look at his shirt-ruffle, that *jongen!* It is frayed like an old rag. And he has outgrown his breeches. How can a little boy have care for these things? You must watch over him better, *meidje.* He is your brother!"

Susanna opened her mouth to protest, hesitated while Michael held his breath, then closed it resignedly and ended by promising to do better in future.

"*Jawel,* you are a good girl. Now bring me my posset, and we will all try to sleep, eh?" The old man turned away, only rumbling kindly when Michael tried to thank him. But halfway up the steps he paused, glancing back at Susanna. "Put him in Philip's bed, the *jongen.* I do not like it gaping there."

Susanna nodded, watching with troubled eyes as he climbed slowly toward his room. Then with a glance at Michael—who was watching too and remembering Tom's bed—she led the way into the kitchen to make the posset.

PART III

At the Golden Buckle

Life at the Golden Buckle was very different from life in the garret above the stable. Susanna arose with the sparrows at 5 a.m., roused Michael at 5:01, and lectured him on sloth if he was not ready to accompany her downstairs five minutes later, when she reappeared in his doorway fully dressed and aproned, with her flaxen braid pinned firmly in its heavy bun. Still yawning and rubbing the sleep from his eyes, Michael would stumble after her down to the kitchen to begin his round of duties. These Susanna had outlined for him the morning after his arrival, having apparently lain awake far into the night compiling the list—or so Michael accused her, protesting that Master Haas had said she should treat her brother kindly. He then found out that the coveted status of brother was a sword that could cut two ways.

"He said I should watch over you—and so I will! I'll also watch to see you earn your keep. As for your shirt and breeches—there's a grand box of Philip's outgrowns I'll ask him for—finer than we could buy! Meanwhile, take that rag and shine up the doorknocker till I want you to sweep the shop. After that you may fill the coal scuttle and polish the big brass kettle, then grind some peppercorns to dress the beef—a-plenty of them, it's going bad already in this weather. Step, now! *My* brother'll be no sluggard—and no ingrate to his benefactor, either!"

Susanna had strong views on a person's duties to his benefactor; they seemed to be based on the notion that any recipient of largesse should make himself twice as useful as if he were employed for pay. Still, what the days lacked in the old easy idleness they made up in the stimulous of Susanna's company, the chances to dust the Master's table, and the never-ending charm of living on the Bridge.

The greatest novelty for Michael was having so many windows and being able to see so much from them. In Dolittle Lane, the one window stared straight at Harry; even at the Truebloods', the view had been limited to a tiny back garden or the housefronts across the way. Here, you could pause on any stair-landing and look out over the river, and at London climbing Ludgate Hill toward the crowning hulk of Paul's. At the top of the house, Susanna's little garret had dormers east and west—it was like being in a bird's nest, you could see so much.

But the best windows of all were in Philip's bedchamber, which, as Michael discovered to his delight on waking in it that first morning, formed the *hautpas* of the tall old house—the outstretched arm of the third story, that spanned the street. Its east wall, against which stood Philip's scarlet-curtained bed, was common to Master Soaper's house across the way; Michael often heard the apothecary's pleasant voice murmuring on the other side of the partition, or his wife's shrill one scolding her maids.

The room was narrow and white-painted, with a dark, polished floor and a row of casements at either side. In all the house, Michael's favorite spot was the window-seat under the north casements. Kneeling there, with his elbows on the wide sill, he could look far along the Bridge, past the burnt-out stretch and St. Magnus, and right up Fish Street Hill or, better, straight down onto the horses' broad backs and the tops of drays and coaches and people's heads and the top edges of the dusty iron curlicues framing the shop-signs, which swayed at all levels beneath his eyrie. Everything looked different from this angle—hats big and flat, boots dwindling to tiny feet, ladies shaped like pincushions, and horses like long brown pears. He once saw a kitten clinging high in a hay-cart, that nobody knew was there; another time he spied a silvery glint between the cobbles and ran down to it, and it was the taverner's lost key that the boy from the Three Neats' Tongues had been asking for everywhere. If he leaned out and craned a bit, he could even see part of the Golden Buckle's front, with Master Haas's stern profile visible in the bow-window, half concealed by the angling sign, and below, Susanna's bright head and vigorously swinging skirts as she swept the doorstep. Wherever he looked, he saw enough of interest to have kept him there watching all day, if Susanna had permitted it.

Of course, she did nothing of the kind. If she caught him at gaze there in the window, she called him back instantly to his Latin book, reminding him he was there to improve himself, not to gawk and daydream. Susanna was scrupulous to preserve his hour for Latin out of the press of other tasks; usually it was after they broke their fast at mid-morning. Most of the household chores were finished by then, and Michael would be sent with the pewter pitcher along to the Bear to fetch the breakfast ale, while Susanna heated Master Haas's gill of "burnt wine" and carried it up to the sitting-room. When Michael came back, he and Susanna settled at the kitchen table for their first rest of the day—a rest broken for Susanna every time the shopbell tinkled.

"Lawks, I miss Philip, that I do!" she said one morning as she returned for the third time to her half-finished ale. "Why folk can't wait another quarter-hour for their shoe-clasp or needle I don't know! I'm thinking I'll give up breakfast till Master Haas finds a shopkeeper."

"I don't think he's hunting one," Michael told her. He had often wondered if Master Haas thought the fairies were minding the shop these days, while he brooded above-stairs. "Maybe he'd help out— just for the quarter-hour—if you ask him."

"Ask the *Master?*" Susanna found that notion too shocking to discuss. Doubtfully, she did agree to let Michael take his turn at responding to the bell. "Providing you call me *at once* if it's anything but pins or a corkscrew or some trifle. And remember to write it in the ledger—anything, no matter how small—and—"

"I know how!" Michael told her indignantly, causing her to grin at him and untuck his hair and agree that indeed he should know, since she'd taught him herself.

"Though what Master'd say to it, I can't think," she added with a glance toward the stairway. "A little 'scapegrace like you playing the journeyman in Philip's fine shop. Lud, he'd likely ring me a peal if he knew."

Michael reminded her that *she* was no journeyman either, and thereafter attended his share of the breakfast-time shoppers. With Philip gone, and Master Haas too worried to know or care if the shop were open or closed, there was really nothing else to do. The shop's patrons—all women these days—seemed not even to notice who served them, having their own worries with men in hiding or impressed and the gangs still a-prowl and searching.

Then one morning the search invaded the Golden Buckle, while Michael was minding shop alone. Three rough-visaged bravos walked straight in, brushed past him as if he were not there, and flung open the hall door. The customer fled, and Michael yelled for Susanna, who flew out of the kitchen in time to intercept them at the stair, where she held them momentarily by sheer vivid fury and the power of a lashing tongue. In the few seconds before they brushed her aside too, Master Haas had appeared on the landing above. His looming, black-clad presence and formidable stare changed their headlong rush through the house into a sullen but civil progress. Naturally they found no hidden men. When they had clumped back down the shining stairs and across the shop, followed by Susanna ostentatiously plying a broom, Master Haas closed the door behind them and turned to Michael with a frown.

"They hurt you, *seuntje?* I heard you cry out for your sister—"

"Oh, no, Master, they only pushed me. But Susanna was in the kitchen and you abovestairs, and I had a customer and the money-box out—"

"You? *You* had a customer?" rumbled the old man.

"Yes, Master, it was Mistress Grover from the Sceptre and Heart—" Belatedly, Michael faltered and fell silent, as Master Haas turned to Susanna.

"You have been tending the shop, *meidje?* You and the *jongen?* . . . *Ja, ja,* of course you have, there is nobody else." The old man slowly rubbed a hand over his face, like a man waking, still muddled from a distressful dream. "I am sorry. I should not put such burden on you."

"But indeed it is no burden, Master!"

Master Haas seemed not to hear Susanna. "I have been . . . I will close the shop now. Perhaps sell the house. Why not, it must happen soon or late. It is the only answer." As Michael and Susanna, staring at him, burst into a chorus of protest, he shook his head and waved them to silence. "Nay, nay, I care nothing for it now. What does it matter?"

"But when Philip comes back—" Susanna began.

"I think Philip will not come back. I think Philip maybe stabbed that man, that ruffian at the Bull and Chain, the one we heard about, and is prisoned or fled or . . ."

"But he might only be hiding!" Susanna insisted.

"Or pressed," Michael added. "The press could have nabbed him, easy! Or he could be hiding from *it,* like . . . like a-many others."

"*Ja, ja.* It is possible. So I tell myself. But I do not believe."

"You must believe until it is proved not so, Master," Susanna told him firmly. "S'posing it's true! S'posing Philip's on a man-o'-war this minute, ready to sail and helpless to get word to us—and you were to sell the Golden Buckle! Why, he'd have nary home nor work to come back to." As Master Haas nodded acknowledgement of the truth of this, she went on, "When the fleet comes home again—then you would know—for certain."

Master Haas nodded again. Finally he said, "Very well. Unless—other word comes, I will keep all as it is until the fleet returns."

"And we can mind the shop for you, Michael and me! It's no burden," Susanna assured him.

"We like to do it!" Michael put in earnestly.

A small gleam of humor flickered in the somber depths of Master Haas's dark eyes. "*Ja?* You like to play apprentice?"

"Susanna *was* apprenticed, for four years and a sixmonth! She knows all about shopkeeping, Old Joan taught her. She—"

"Buz, Michael! That'll do!"

"Nay, let him tell me, *meidje.*"

So while Susanna turned rose-red and shifted from one foot to the other and looked as guilty as if she had been thieving the Master's gold, Michael boasted of her competence, and in doing so, let slip the fact that Philip had been depending on it all summer, which changed the old man's half-smile into a fierce scowl.

"*Bloedt!* He left you alone here, that boy? Left the shop, left the good name of his dead father in the hands of a little servant, to go off to his gaming and his bad friends . . . *Flauw!* That is not behavior for a man!"

"Oh, Master, I shouldn't have let him do it—'twas like lying to you!" Susanna was half in tears at his chagrin.

"Nay, peace, the fault was not yours, *meidje*. I hold you blameless," Master Haas said more quietly. "His father—my son—was a good boy, a good man. But this one—" he shook his head. "Perhaps it is only youth. And perhaps it is not. You minded his shop and his name with more care than he, I think. Now, you may continue. Each afternoon, with the young brother to help. For this work you will receive two extra shillings every Friday. And the *jongen* shall have ninepence. In the mornings, I myself will sell the pins and needles!"

But Susanna had her accustomed firm notions of what activities were proper for her venerated master, and pin-selling was not one of them. Having already learned to fit most of her household duties into mere chinks of the day, she soon reduced his shopkeeping to the minimum and by mid-morning was heading for the shop as usual with her mending basket, while Michael, carrying the burnt wine, escorted the old man back upstairs to his freshly-aired chamber and the ever-fascinating table in the window.

Sometimes the Master sent him along the Bridge then with a finished map for Master Danforth or across to Master Soaper the apothecary for a chunk of cinnabar or yellow ochre—but more frequently straight back downstairs to fetch an egg from the kitchen. A plain raw egg. What he wanted with it Michael could not fathom, for he never ate it, or broke it into his wine, never cooked it, either, though there was a copper basin on the big table with a fire-blackened bottom. No, he merely set it aside on a bit of rag so it wouldn't roll and never looked at it again while Michael was there, however long he contrived to linger. It was a mystery, that egg—one of the many mysteries of the Master's chamber—and it finally goaded Michael's curiosity beyond bearing.

"Please, Master Haas!" he burst out one morning. *"Please* would you tell me what you do with the egg?"

After a glance of mild astonishment the Master said, *"Ja,* certainly I will tell you, *seuntje.* I paint with it."

"Paint with it? Truly? Paint with *egg?"* Michael's voice had softened with wonder.

"With glair—so it is called. Glair, the white of the egg prepared just so, in a certain way. I mix with the paint, *ja?* Then it makes the color fast to the paper. Or, I spread the glair after the color is laid on already—for a glaze, you understand. I keep some always for that purpose here." Master Haas stretched a long arm over the table and plucked a small, stoppered flagon from a row of pots and jars. Holding it up before Michael, he shook it gently, so that the colorless liquid inside formed a few delicate bubbles.

"But doesn't it go bad, Master?"

"Nay, nay." The Master's deep laughter rumbled. "I put an equal part of white vinegar with it." He pointed to another bottle, a larger one. "The best white vinegar—after I have strained the egg-white through a clean white linen kerchief. Then there is no spoiling for a long time."

"Vinegar! I've smelled vinegar in this room. And often-times garlic . . . d'you never use the egg's yolk, then?"

"Sometimes, for a special purpose." Master Haas was chuckling at him. "You have smelled my secrets? You have the keen nose, eh? And many questions."

"I have a-many more than those," ventured Michael, greatly daring.

"So? You wish to know the special purpose for the egg-yolk, I suppose. Come, I will show you."

Setting aside his wine, Master Haas turned to the table, broke the egg skillfully, and let the white slip out into a small bowl while the yolk remained in one half of its own jagged brown shell. The shell-half he set into an old candlestick, which held it steady while he stirred its golden contents, adding a splash of water from a cruet. Then, dipping a tiny brush, he painted his own name, "J. Haas," on a scrap of paper, embellishing the capitals with delicate curls and flourishes with what seemed to Michael wasted artistry, since the thin line of yolk could scarcely be seen on the paper. While it dried, he took up the smoke-blackened copper basin, and to Michael's intense gratification resolved another mystery by scraping some of the powdery soot into a tiny pot and mixing in glair to make a smooth black ink. Then, astonishingly, he painted the black all over the entire scrap of paper, egg-yolk lettering and all.

"But why—what happens to the—" Michael began in bewilderment.

"Wait, patience, you will see." The old man waved the paper

back and forth to dry it, then presently took a soft white cloth and rubbed the blackened surface, which began to flake away from the egg-yolk lines. A moment later he held up the result: his name, "J. Haas," inscribed in beautiful white letters on a pure black ground.

"Ohhhh!" Michael breathed, staring spellbound at this sudden magic. "Ohhh—I'd never've believed . . . Oh, *how* d'you ever learn to write those letters so? And please, Master, what's the garlic smell? And what d'you do with that little soft rabbit's foot there, and—"

"Michael!" ejaculated Susanna in scandalized tones from the hall outside the room. "What can you be thinking of! Chitter-chattering to the Master half the morning! Come away, now!"

"Gently, *meidje*. He is only curious, like any lad. He may ask his questions. But not all in one day, eh, *seuntje*? Perhaps another one tomorrow, with the *brantwijn*." He waved away Michael's stammered apology but studied him, still smiling. "You have much interest in my craft, *ja?* I remember the 'likely boy' who wished to become my apprentice. But you must understand, my craft is not like others. To be ironmonger or baker requires only a willing boy and a skillful master. But to be artist of whatever sort—that requires something more, something already in the boy. No master can supply it."

"I understand," Michael said humbly. "One must have a gift."

The old man considered this, sipping his wine. *"Ja,* a gift, certainly," he agreed. "A cleverness in the fingers. But there must be more also—a kind of courage." His dark gaze rested a moment on Michael's puzzled face, but he made no effort to clarify his meaning, merely nodded and repeated, *"Ja, ja.* It is a kind of courage." Then he turned back to the window and his glass, leaving Michael to descend the stairs absorbed with plans, unmindful of the shocked lecture Susanna was hissing into his ear all the way down.

"Yes, I promise—no, I won't . . . but did you hear, Susanna? He said I might ask another question tomorrow. And likely another the next day . . . Tomorrow I'll ask about the garlic. Or maybe—maybe first about why he always draws a boy for East Wind, and an old grouch for North Wind . . . or, no—ods bobs! How can I decide!"

"Well, mind you do decide, for he said one question and one

only! Let me ever again catch you hanging about teasing him, and I'll ring you a peal you won't forget!"

"The garlic," Michael decided happily, at which Susanna, turning pink with amusement, threw up her hands and vowed she might as well spare her breath.

A Night Caller

So on the following morning, Michael learned more magic. One dipped a fine brush into garlic juice and drew a design—then sprinkled gold leaf lavishly with the little soft rabbit's foot. When it was dry, one carefully removed the excess with a soft cloth, and there was the miracle: a shining tracery of gold following just the garlic-juice lines.

On succeeding mornings, little by little, he came to know that camels' hair made the best brushes; that another sort of black, like velvet, came from burnt stag horn; that red-lead pigment faded in strong light; that Master portrayed East Wind as a boy (and West Wind as a merry youth and North Wind a grouch with an icicle beard, and South Wind a dreary fellow with wet wings and dripping hair and frogs pouring from his water-pot) simply because all mapmakers from time immemorial had done so. And one entrancing morning he learned that cinnebar was hard to pulverize and yellow ochre easy—learned it firsthand, when Master Haas set him to work with slab and stone, grinding fresh color for the little pots.

But most mornings there was no danger of his lingering above-stairs, "teasing the Master" for more than a quarter hour, even if Susanna had permitted it. He was too much in awe of the old man, too anxious not to disgrace himself by behaving like an ill-mannered nuisance. Besides, he was well aware that in spite of the kindness, Master Haas's thoughts were chiefly elsewhere, on Philip, Michael was sure, for his dark eyes were sad and troubled as he brooded in his chair and sipped his wine.

He was not the only one lonely for a missing face. Busy as Michael was, doing Susanna's bidding and pursuing his own quest in the Master's chamber, he never failed, at some moment each day, to stand a while at one of the stairlanding windows and scan the river as it swept westward in its curve toward Westminster, searching for a glimpse of Sam'l's yellow sculler and wondering how it was with Tom, wherever he was. Once he thought he glimpsed a flash of yellow near Queenhithe, another time far along the Southwark shore. But Sam'l was as little in evidence as any other waterman, despite his one eye and a twisted hand.

He was wary with good reason. Michael never forgot what he had seen one Sunday evening at the end of his first week at the Golden Buckle. Walking back from St. Magnus after evening service, he and Susanna had noticed that the east side of the long burnt-out stretch was lined with people, all peering through cracks in the wooden palisades or clustered about the gaps where palings were missing. Joining the nearest cluster, they stared downstream at the long wharf flanking the ancient, crenelated walls of the Tower of London. It seethed with activity. A warship was moored alongside; its decks swarmed too. The whole area was a confused mass of people in angry motion; some men were running, some struggling together in little knots, others shuffling toward the ship in sullen double lines. Women were everywhere, pushing through the mob, breaking in waves against the double lines and falling back in disarray. It was several moments before Michael could make sense of what he was seeing.

Then he knew. It was pressed men, scores of them, being herded out of their Tower prison like criminals, hustled across the wharf and into the waiting ship. And the women who rushed among them were searching frantically for sons or husbands snatched away during the past two weeks. Michael, watching appalled, saw the guards roughly fending women off, saw the desperate reaching out of hands, male and female, and was glad the roar of the waterwheels and the river kept him from hearing the wailing, crying, and cursing that must be echoing in the nearby streets. The women were forced to fall back at last and stare hopelessly after the ship as it slipped away with swelling sails toward Deptford. At once another tacked in from the Pool to take its place, more men were hustled toward it, and the whole dreadful scene began to play again.

"Michael, I must go there," Susanna gasped, pulling him back from the palings.

"Go there! Why?"

"To search for Philip. You go straight along home to the Buckle. Master's supped already, he'll not need me. If he does, tell him . . . lud, tell him something, I don't know what! Do as I say, now."

She gave him a push toward the shop, whirled, and ran the other way. Michael obeyed, though reluctantly. He entered the shop quietly, went directly upstairs past the second-floor room where Master Haas sat reading, and on past his own third-floor landing to Susanna's garret at the top. From her east dormer window he could see the Tower wharf plainly in the fading light. Even the distant voices, faint and discordant like far-off bird cries, floated up to him in snatches. The Master did not call for him. Evening darkened into night, the moon rose, torches bloomed along the wharf like agitated orange flowers, and still the bird cries sounded and the dark figures moved in the torch-glare. It was midnight before the last ship moved off downstream in the moonlight, and Susanna dragged home, weary and half in tears, still without sight or news of Philip.

It was only the first of such shippings, such tyrannical scenes. The very next day after the Tower was emptied, Master Haas reported Bridewell prison full to bursting with press captives, growing unruly from outrage and short rations; he had heard their stamping and cursing and threats as far away as Fleet Street, as he walked along. In the week since, Michael had seen scarcely one man in the streets of whatever age; for lack of a porter, he and Susanna had lugged a great box of merchandise from the Custom House to the shop themselves; for lack of a waterman, they had lugged it on foot. And gangs still roamed, invading houses, though it was now a fortnight since Michael had moved to the Bridge.

Then came the hottest night Michael could remember—it was July seventh. He lay wakeful and tossing, while the old bell-man cried ten o'clock, then eleven, and the mutterings of thunder and flickerings of lightning that had played about the sky all evening drew ominously closer. He first thought the quiet rapping on the shop door was another rumbling of the storm. Then he knew it was not. He was out of bed in an instant and pushing open his casement. In the street below, a darker shape in the darkness turned a pale face upward and whispered, "Michael! Come down!"

In a frenzy of hope and bewilderment—the shape looked like a woman—Michael scampered barefoot down the two flights, knocked over the candlestick twice before managing to light a stub, and very cautiously opened the top half of the door just enough to see out of it. A strange-looking, very tall woman muffled in a voluminous hooded cloak instantly thrust a large hand through the space, lifted the latch on the inside, and pushed into the shop, closing both halves of the door behind her. With an urgent "Shshshhh!" the woman glanced toward the windows, then seized the candle in one hand and Michael's arm in the other, found the way to the kitchen, and threw off the cloak—and it was Tom.

Michael hurled himself bodily upon him. As he was caught in a strong pair of arms and whirled around exuberantly, he kept insisting in a piercing whisper that he knew it, he knew it all the time, but all the same—

"But all the same, I made a fair shakes of a woman?" supplied Tom, setting him on his feet again.

"No, you made a regular antic of a woman!" Michael was suddenly weak with giggles and with excitement and hilarity and the simple, profound relief of seeing Tom well and safe. "The funniest woman I ever saw! How d'you ever get by in daylight?"

"No fear! I don't risk it in daylight! But I had to see for certain that you were here and in good heart and looking quite yourself, y'know—" Tom held him off and eyed him critically as he spoke.

"And do I look myself?"

"To the nail—saving that fine new nightshirt, which is a stranger to me."

"It's Philip's hand-down. Tom, are we going home now?"

"No, no, how can you imagine it? The streets are nothing but great traps . . . ah! Listen! That'll help me to get back through 'em safe—I was hoping for that."

The rain had started—torrents of it, accompanied by crashes of thunder and glares of lightning that paled the candle.

"When *will* we go?" Michael was feeling suddenly that he could not bear to part from Tom again.

"When the fleet's sailed and well-away—not before." Tom frowned down at him. "You're not unhappy here? Not mistreated? Get a-plenty to eat, do you?"

"Oh, plenty," Michael was starting to assure him, when an outraged voice from the doorway cut in.

"Mistreated, is it? Lawks, does he look mistreated to you? I suppose you think I wallop him every morning—and Master every night! I starve 'im too, I do—the crusts and rinds is all *he* gets, oh, yes, fuddle-duddle, I can't bother to feed a little worthless Jack-o-Lent like him! Why, 'twould be pure waste, same as clothing him decent would be. A rag or two, a tot of ditchwater now and again . . ."

Susanna might have gone on in this vein quite a while if Michael hadn't tugged at her arm, so tipsy with giggles that she checked her indignation to bite her lip on a grin of her own. Tom, after his first startled glance, listened meekly, eyes glinting with amusement and —Michael thought—with admiration too. This did not surprise Michael in the least. Susanna, poised there in the doorway with her dark cloak over her nightdress, blue fire in her eyes, and the candlelight silvering the two thick plaits on her shoulders, was in his opinion as fine as any duchess.

Tom waited until she wound up with a toss of her head and the remark that he must be Michael's famous Tom. He then humbly admitted to being Tom Godfrey—Michael's famous Tom. "And you are Michael's gold-and-silver Susanna. Your servant, m'lady," he finished, with a graceful bow and his most elegant flourish of cuff-tatters.

"Lawks, what lady?" muttered Susanna. "I'm the serving-maid here—and don't try to cozen me. You've never come to take Michael with you?" she added in alarm. "You dassn't, the press is worse'n ever, you'd never—"

"I've no thought of it. I merely wanted to assure myself that—well—"

"That I was feeding him a-plenty," Susanna finished tartly.

Tom grinned and shrugged an apology.

"You don't look overfed yourself, if I may say so," she added.

"Oh, you may say so, never was truer word spoken," Tom said cheerfully. "But it can't last forever, and I intend to overeat—and overdrink too—to the best of my capacity when I'm able. Are you conning your Latin, Michael?"

"Yes. Truly! Ten lines a day, Susanna won't give me dinner till I finish. Though I scour and polish and fetch coal for her all the morning!"

"Proper shrew, I am," muttered Susanna, who was busy at the cupboard.

"And I help in the shop, too," Michael went on, deciding not to cross swords with Susanna just at this moment.

"The master knows you do?" Tom asked warily. "Where's the grandson?"

Michael explained the altered shop arrangements, boasted a little of his wages, and after a hesitant glance at Susanna told what little they knew of Philip. Then, while the rain drummed down on the kitchen roof loudly enough to drown out the river below, he told everything else he could think of about his life on the Bridge, repeating each smallest detail he had learned about maps and color and describing the ever-changing view from Philip's window, even including the kitten on the hay-cart, which made Susanna go pink with amusement under her freckles and vow he had never told *her* that. Tom listened as he always did, half-smiling, with speckled eyes moving over Michael's face and not much indication of what he was thinking of it all. But when the tale was finished at last, he drew a deep breath, ran one long-fingered hand through his tumbled chestnut hair, and sighed, "Yes, well-a-day. 'Tis a thousand pities the press can't go on forever, Michael, for I can see that you and the Bridge just suit."

"Not as well as you and I!" Michael told him loyally, and at once felt that he could never bear it until he and Tom were together again, back in Dolittle Lane. "Oh, I'm wishing the fleet would sail!"

"Now that's the first I've heard of it," put in Susanna, setting a bowl and spoon on the table with unnecessary clatter. Michael, noting her expression out of the corner of his eye, decided she had taken his remark personally, but before he could make amends she was slicing the loaf and scolding Tom for calling when her larder was near empty. "But we've bread and bonny-clabber, and they're good if plain, and I'll thank you to sit down and eat them," she ordered in the tone Michael always obeyed promptly. Tom obeyed it promptly too, perching his long frame on the kitchen stool and docilely beginning to spoon up the sour-buttermilk, which he ordinarily disdained.

"You *are* hungry!" Michael exclaimed with concern, if not much tact. "Tom . . . where is it, this place you're hiding? Couldn't I—"

"No, God-a-mercy! You could not." Tom reached for a chunk of bread, his speckled gaze traveling around the tidy, dark-beamed kitchen. "It's just—a hideyhole. Not far from here in miles, a mighty long way in comfort. Still," he added, "it's better lodging than a man-o'-war's fo'c'sle. And I have Sam'l—and my friend Montaigne to read."

"But no way to earn a penny," Michael said uneasily. "What of that money-lender? And Harry's debt?"

Tom hoisted shoulders and eyebrows. "Nothing of them. They'll have to wait . . . The press might have nabbed Harry by now, unless he's vanished pretty smartly."

"Maybe they've nabbed the money-lender too!" Michael exclaimed.

Tom laughed but shook his head. "He's far too sharp. But if the press can't find me, he can't either. Provided I vanish pretty smartly myself and get me back where I came from." He drained his bowl, popped the last crust into his mouth, and got up, still chewing, to reach for his cloak.

"You mean to go now?" Susanna demanded. "Are you horn-mad? Listen to that rain!"

"All the better. The gangs'll never stir out in that—not for a useless old crone like me, eh, Michael?"

"Lawks, just look at you!" Susanna gaped at Tom's transformation into the strange-looking woman and clapped both hands over her mouth to smother a gale of laughter. Then she snatched up the rest of the loaf and made Tom stow it about him somewhere and went ahead into the dark shop to peer out into the darker tumult of the rain, turning back to remark that if any gangs were abroad this night, they'd do well to see the Bridge, let alone an old woman crossing it.

"But when will you come back?" Michael said in panic, clinging hard to Tom at the last minute.

"When the fleet's sailed. Don't fret, I'll know when that is; Sam'l can find out. And it's a fine, idle time to be working on my play, y'know. No—I've not finished yet. My thanks to you, Mistress, and God keep all in this house. *Au 'voir,* Michael!"

Then he was gone—swallowed by the dark and the rain so

quickly that Michael never knew whether he turned toward Southwark or toward London.

After that, it was not quite so much fun to live on the Bridge. Michael worried about Tom, about whether he had enough to eat, about whether the hidey-hole was still safe, about where it was. "Not far in miles," Tom had said, but such nearby places as Greenwich and Deptford were reported raging with plague now. He began to understand very well Master Haas's anxiety for Philip, his brooding and unspoken fears, and to feel for him, and to bring him a bedtime posset or clean his boots without Susanna's prodding. One evening, coming into the sitting-room and seeing the old man so still and melancholy in the bow-window, he could not help saying, "He'll come back, Master! See if he doesn't!"

Master Haas turned slowly, as if it took a moment for any voice from the outside to penetrate his thoughts. Then, just as slowly, like ice breaking up on a thawing river, his stern features relaxed into a faint smile. "So? *Ja, ja,* perhaps. And perhaps no."

"He will!" Michael insisted. "He'll come when the fleet sails. That's when Tom will come back—he dassn't until the fleet sails."

"Tom? Who is Tom, then?"

Michael hesitated, because it was hard to explain just who Tom was and delicate to mention that he was a ballad-man and decidedly awkward to confess that he had recently paid an uninvited call at the Golden Buckle. But soon, encouraged by a kindly nod or two, Michael was telling the Master all about his meeting with Tom, and with Elizabeth Botts before that, and Susanna before *that,* and then about the Schoonmakers and the plague and the Truebloods and Alan Blake, who was probably pressed by now, and—far back in the dimmest mists of time—his own appearance from nowhere on the steps of St. Michael Archangel church in Cornhill. That this also involved clearing up the matter of his kinship with Susanna—or lack of it—he only realized when the old man sat back at last, his dark eyes amused but interested, and commented, *"Jawel,* that is quite a tale for one still so young. So—the *meidje* is not sister to you after all."

Michael admitted reluctantly that she was not. "I only pretend it sometimes—though she won't. But we might be kin!"

"*Ja, ja,* you might—the same flax-heads, the same blue eyes and way of laughing—I have seen it."

"And the same freckles," Michael added, warming to his favorite subject. "And—did you notice?—the little brown moles on our necks just here, at *nearly* the same—"

"Michael, hssssst!" came Susanna's voice from the doorway. "Now come away! I beg pardon for him, Master, he was only to hand the book to you—"

"Nay, nay, let him be, *meidje,* he's a good lad. What is this book, then?"

"The one you ordered from Mistress Tyns, at the Three Bibles," Michael mumbled, feeling his ears go fiery as he handed over the parcel. He had run all the way to the shop beside St. Magnus in the new block and all the way back. Then to forget to give it to him—!

"I don't believe he cared, though," he told Susanna when they were back in the kitchen. "It took his mind off—things. Mine, too," he added sadly after a moment.

Unexpectedly, Susanna turned from her dinner preparation and hugged him hard. "Your Tom'll be all right, Master Cornhill, don't fret over *him.* That's one as knows how to look after himself, or I'm a dotterel! Indeed, he's an odd sort, an't he?" She blinked in a puzzled way into the space over Michael's head. "As odd a ballad-man as ever I saw. He must *be* somebody. Or anyway, used to be . . . All the worse that he should turn out so!" she added sternly.

Michael only shrugged and told her he no longer worried his head about Tom's past. "When I fretted about who *I* used to be, you told me not to be a goose and said it didn't matter."

"Well, and so it doesn't. Leastways, not to *me,* I'm sure!" retorted Susanna, and set him to basting the joint for dinner.

There was one thing, Michael reflected as he sat turning the spit and shielding his face from the heat of the flames. He no longer had to wish that somebody needed him. The Master needed him and so did Susanna, so much that he sometimes worried about how they would do without him, when he went home to Dolittle Lane with Tom. Susanna had said she'd ask Master if the half-grown daughter of the Tabard's ostler—Kate, her name was—might come in daily to scour and bake. But who would sort shoe-buckles and hand out bills and make Master's posset and . . . ?

Back in April, in the turnip cart, that was what he had wanted above all else—just to be needed by somebody. It was what he wanted still, if only Tom were back. But he missed Tom more and more, as the days passed, and it seemed each one must bring an end to the waiting, and yet the waiting went on.

Doldrums

July was well into its second half before the last warship vanished from the Pool in the direction of Deptford. Then, at last, the press gangs disappeared from the streets. After a cautious interval, ordinary men began to reappear, one by one. And on July 22nd, a bright and breezy Sunday, Tom came striding along the Bridge, with his hat at its jauntiest and his lute slanting across his back. Michael, leaning on the half-door staring out idly at the morning, spotted him and gave a shout that brought Susanna from the kitchen and caused Master Haas to pause on the third stair and come back down.

"So that is your Tom," the Master rumbled, peering toward the approaching figure as Michael wrested the lower half of the door open and shot out of the house. "Nay, *meidje,*" he added with his low chuckle as Susanna, ever mindful of his consequence, would have hustled him on upstairs. "I will wait a moment for my *brantwijn*. I must meet this ballad-man who teaches that *jongen* Latin and French."

So the conventions—and Susanna's sense of propriety—were disregarded for a few moments, while the foremost map-colorer in England made himself acquainted with Tom Godfrey. Michael, hovering eagerly on the sidelines, proud of the set of Tom's head and the grace of his cuff-tatters, prouder of the old man's simple warmth, did not know which one he admired most.

A quarter-hour later he was standing, bundle in hand, in the bow-windowed chamber, thanking his benefactor for a full month's hospitality, while Susanna hovered in the doorway to see that he did it properly. "And thank you for letting me ask all those questions, and grind the colors. And I'll come back to help in the shop, three half-days a week, Susanna says . . . I mean—if you want me to," Michael faltered, and was relieved to see the old man nod. "It's only till Philip comes home," he added quickly.

Master Haas's smile thanked him for the sympathy behind the awkward phrase. *"Ja, ja.* Till Philip comes home," he repeated.

Sighing, he turned away toward the window, and Susanna beckoned Michael out. They faced each other on the stair-landing, wordless with the wrench of parting, with the realization that everything was changing again. Michael had little faith in Philip's return; nor had Susanna to judge from her expression as she led the way silently down the stairs. Nor had the Master, Michael suspected. He would wait until the fleet came home, but if Philip did not come too, he would sell the Golden Buckle and return forever to Piebald Farm. And how would it be then, for Susanna—and himself too—when the shop passed into a stranger's hands and Master out of their lives?

"Oh, I wish it wouldn't happen!" Michael burst out as he and Tom started for home. "If Master never found out about Philip, then he'd just stay here and—"

"You don't want that fine, sad old gentleman ever to know whether his grandson is disgraced?"

Michael heaved a sigh. "I just don't want everything to change."

But some things had changed already, as he discovered the moment they reached Dolittle Lane. For one, the garret seemed only half the size he remembered and twice as ramshackle. It looked more natural after Tom's six precious books were back on the shelf and their clothes on the nails, but at first it seemed in some distant dream he had lived here.

For another, their lighthearted financial habits had been changed for them. Mother Floss had saved their room, but her price was a fortnight's extra rent, plus the week's arrears they had owed when they left. Nothing Tom could say, neither logic nor blandishments, would move her. She agreed to let them pay the additional sum little by little, instead of in a lump—that was her sole concession.

"And that only from necessity," Tom growled as he flung his lute on the bed. "If I had the whole, she'd have it out of me and our shirts as interest."

"We can go live someplace else!" Michael said defiantly.

"Not now that she's got her claws into us. Unless you'd care to join Harry in the compter."

"Is *that* where Harry is?"

Tom shrugged wearily. "Only God knows where Harry is. I doubt if we ever see him again."

For the Hobson family had departed, leaving a fresh scattering of tavern bills but no address. Somebody else now lived in the rooms across the way. And Harry's debt now belonged exclusively to Tom.

"And to me!" Michael said firmly. "I can pay part of it." He dug out the scarlet purse and showed Tom the two shillings he had saved from his work at the shop. "And I'll still have sixpence or so each week—and sometimes a penny for fetching parcels for Master Soaper. Why, that's a fair bit, that's—"

"That's yours," Tom said with equal firmness. "Think I'd go thieving from children, like Jack Horner?"

"Thieving?" Michael raised shocked eyes to Tom's face. "We're —together, aren't we? I live here too! Anyhow, once your play is finished . . ." Michael hesitated, remembering he was not to nag. "I suppose you can't tell when . . ."

"No. There's no saying."

"I didn't think so," Michael said hastily. "But till it is—"

"Till it is, we'll sell ballads as usual. You'll keep your money, and that's an end to it," Tom said.

Of course, it was not the end of it, for ballad-selling could not support their sudden array of debts. Before the week was up, Tom was forced to accept sixpence to replace a broken lute-string, and by early August the shillings from the scarlet purse had gone to the money-lender, and Michael's shop-wage was buying the breakfast ale. But as Tom bitterly remarked, it was like trying to fill up an alderman's pocket; the more they paid, the faster the money-lender's interest seemed to grow. It was exactly as Master True-blood had warned Michael long ago, and he could not help feeling a touch of panic. Then one Friday—the rent day—he came in to find Montaigne gone from the bookshelf, and Tom plucking mournful strands of melody in the dusky room. For a moment he stared up in flat dismay at the gap in the row of books. Then he flung his jackanapes on the floor in a clatter of buttons. "That settles it, that does! I'm going. Tomorrow. You could manage if 'tweren't for me. Find somebody who could go fair shares on the rent—"

"God-a-mercy, what is the boy blathering about?" Tom demanded, turning to stare at him.

"About taking myself off. And don't be trying to talk me out of it, because—"

"Talk you out of it! I'll not discuss it at all." Tom stroked a thunderous chord out of the lute and set it aside as he rose to light a candle. "Can't a man indulge in a fit o' the megrims without Persons of eleven and three quarters ordering him about and telling him what he can talk of?"

"But you've sold Montaigne! Oh, if I hadn't needed those shoes patched—if you'd never even seen me . . ."

A large, firm hand reached out to grasp his chin, and swivel his head around. "Now, we'll just put a cork in *that* flagon o' woe. I won't say I like parting with my volume, but one day I'll buy another, so spare me your vapors about it." The hand rumpled Michael's hair and withdrew. "Never fret about shillings and pence, boy. Now take those ballads and come along."

Silenced though doubtful, Michael came along, wishing he dared ask about the play. Perhaps Tom worked secretly on it at every opportunity, intending to turn up some fine evening with a handful of gold nobles. But there was no sign he ever worked on it at all.

On the surface, the old rhythm of their life resumed. They sold ballads and searched for news, and kept their loaf—when they had one—in the window-box, and three afternoons a week Michael went to the Bridge. But those afternoons had changed too, for the pattern of life at the Golden Buckle was different. The Tabard ostler's daughter, Kate, now inhabited the black-beamed kitchen and scampered up and down stairs on errands, humming irritatingly through her nose. Susanna kept to the shop—and Michael, perforce, stayed with her. Only occasionally was he sent up to the Master's chamber with a parcel or the letter-post. Once he tiptoed up another flight and peeped into the *hautpas* with its shining floor and scarlet-curtained bed, but it no longer seemed real that he had slept there—the room was Philip's. The Master himself was unchanged, rumbling kindly whenever he saw Michael and inquiring how he did and if the ballad-man still taught him Latin. But there was no chance to watch him work, and Michael no longer felt at liberty to ask him even one question. All that was over—like so much else.

As the August days passed, he became aware of a hollow, empty sensation inside, as if more were over than he knew. He no longer lived on the Bridge, but he no longer quite lived in Dolittle Lane; his life was neither one sort of thing nor the other now. And I'm not, either, he thought restlessly. It was not that he was tired of balladeering, not really—but it had begun to seem oddly futile, to accomplish nothing, to be heading nowhere. He could not put his heart in it. Even when he was standing right beside Tom, clutching the fluttering broadsides and listening to the familiar humorous baritone embroidered with lute-notes—even then his mind kept drifting back to the four bright, busy weeks—ever more distant— that he had spent on the Bridge. He missed it all sorely—not just the bed in the *hautpas,* not just Susanna's prodding him into usefulness, but *feeling* useful and hard-worked. And that was mightily queer, he told himself glumly. He'd never have believed it.

It was no use brooding about it. The old life was not to be recaptured—neither one of the old lives. He tried hard to be his old self, and so did Tom, as if everything were the same. But nothing was the same as before he had lived on the Bridge.

"Lud, where's your mind a-wandering, Master Cornhill?" Susanna demanded one mid-August afternoon. "I've asked you three times for that box yonder. Thinking of the fire you'll light tonight, were you?"

It was a special day, August 14th, designated as Thanksgiving Day for the recent successes of the fleet in Dutch waters, and when evening came there would be fireworks and bonfires and merriment all over London. But Michael could summon little interest in it. He had not one spare groat to buy a serpent or rocket for himself, and he did not feel merry.

"No—just . . . thinking," he said heavily, handing her the box of shoe buckles he had been sorting. "Susanna, d'you ever get to wondering where you'll be and how you'll be earning your bread this time next year?"

"No, and I advise you not to either," she retorted, then changed the subject briskly, making Michael belatedly remember that she was not even sure how she'd be earning her bread this time next month, unless the fleet returned bringing Philip, safe and sound.

It seemed certain, now, that the fleet must come home in September with final victory secure. The very next morning after the August 14th Thanksgiving Day, word came that English fireboats had crept in to the Dutch isle of Schelling and burned a whole town— a thousand houses—along with a hundred and sixty Dutch ships lying in the straits nearby. The Tower guns went off in jubilation; that night fireworks blazed and rocketed again, and fresh bonfires were lighted on last night's embers. The day after that, fresh news arrived: Amsterdammers, in fury at the fiery disaster at Schelling, had besieged the house of John DeWitt, the Grand Pensionary.

"What's a Grand Pensionary?" cried Michael, excited in spite of himself, as he and Tom turned away from the crowd in Cheapside where they had heard the new tidings. No use trying to sell more ballads today, and they both knew it. People were too elated to give ear.

Tom shrugged and hitched his lute around to slant across his back. "A chief minister, I think, in Holland. Like our Duke of Clarendon. You could ask Master Haas if you liked."

"Master Haas?"

"He's a Dutchman, isn't he? Or was born one."

For an instant Michael was too startled to reply. Master Haas was—yes, a Dutchman, of course. But not an enemy! Not "the Dutch"! "That's different!" he exclaimed. "Why, he's lived here ever and ever so long—I don't know how long!"

"My faith, boy, I'm not saying he's DeWitt himself, only that he could tell you about Grand Pensionaries."

But for Michael the thousand burned houses had suddenly become the ruined homes of real people—people like Master Haas— who were now left weeping in their charred and ash-strewn streets, perhaps clutching some random possession—a hearth-broom or a kettle—as he had seen burnt-out people do in London. And the victory had become a sinking dismay inside him.

At the Bridge that afternoon, being sent upstairs to Master Haas with the Thursday foot-post, he seized the opportunity to stammer out his sense that it must be painful indeed to have the country you lived in make war on the one you were born in. But the Master's reaction was unexpected.

"Painful? *Jawel!* It is painful to see men act as fools."

"Fools?" Michael echoed.

"Ja, ja, ja, ja!" The summer-thunder voice reverberated impatiently. "Fools! Both sides! This is not a war, *seuntje,* it is a squabble, a jealousy, as two children tugging at the same toy and kicking at each other. Fifty years now we behave so, this day bickering over a mess of herrings, that day over nutmegs and peppercorns—and next week, kiss and make up and wed an English Mary to a Prince of Orange! We should be standing together against France." He glanced down at Michael and smiled ironically. "I shock you, eh? You have still the soft heart and the wide eyes. *Jawel,* I, too, I felt so when I first fled from my Holland." The old man's voice and expression alike grew distant. "I felt torn apart."

"You *fled* from Holland?" Michael probed softly.

"Ja—it was a quarreling there, too, in those days, a sad and bitter one, but not for herrings. For ways of worship. Men disowned their sons and struck down their brothers because they could not agree on the nature of God. My village split like a melon and destroyed itself in flames, and I was left, a *jongen* of thirteen years, and all my family dead or savage enemies. So I fled and came here on a fishing vesel and found kindness and a roof. Oh, *ja,* I returned to Amsterdam later and learned my craft. But I could not forget this land that had stretched out the hand to me. When I was a man I came back and made a family of my own," he finished, with another smile at Michael. It was supposed to be a cheerful one, but Michael could see it dimmed, half through, no doubt by the same thought that had flashed through his own mind: where was that new family now? One childless daughter at Piebald Farm—and Philip.

"You never told me—all that," he said, chiefly to be saying something.

"Nay, it is not good to speak of what is past—or think of it," Master Haas said firmly. "It is finished, done. Always there is change."

"Yes," sighed Michael.

"Always there are beginnings, also," added the Master with a shrewd glance at him from his dark eyes. "Never look back, *seuntje. Ja?* You understand me? Look only ahead."

"Yes, Master," Michael murmured, and as the old man took up his letters, he went slowly back downstairs. He understood that the Master was again talking about courage—and counseling both Michael and himself.

An End and a Beginning

It was a different matter for Tom, whose need was less for courage than for the patience to stomach debt. Michael could see his temper thinning, his gloom mounting at the drudge's life he'd been chivvied into exchanging for his lighthearted grasshopper's ways. Lately even his hat seemed to have lost its dash and his ballads their wit. A day or two after that mid-August Thursday, Michael came home to find him singing lugubriously of "Nothing."

> *"He that hath nothing can nothing possess,*
> *And he that hath little may look to have less,*
> *But much want and sorrow doth daily oppress*
> *The man that hath nothing.*
>
> *"He that hath nothing, with troubles beset,*
> *Will steal or do something a living to get,*
> *But if he be caught in the hangman's net,*
> *His life is worth nothing . . ."*

"Oh, *Tom!*" Michael cried in protest at these doleful verses. They made him feel like howling. "Ods bobs, give over! Why d'you want to write such stuff?" He hesitated, then burst out with what he could no longer hold back. "Finish your play instead—*that'd* be some good to us! Or don't you mean to finish it?"

Tom was silent; only the lute spoke under his drifting fingers. Then he put it aside and stood up. "I threw the scurvy thing in Fleet Ditch, Michael—with the rest of the dead dogs. It wasn't worth finishing. 'Twould've been laughed off the boards—and it a tragedy!" He hoisted his eyebrows, or tried to—it was a ghost of the old gesture—and walked over restlessly to stare out the window. "Don't fret. We'll come about somehow."

Michael was miserably wishing he had never spoken. Now he knew for sure what he had only suspected. As for just how Tom meant to come about, those dismal verses were hardly reassuring. "But I don't want you to—to steal or do something a living to get and then get caught in the hangman's net!" he blurted.

"So that's what's biting you!" Tom's laugh was short but genuine. "Well, you may put it from your mind, because I'd be clumsier at birding than Jack Stubbs is at lute-playing. A pox on Jack anyhow —I can't find him lately. And a pox on Mother Floss and on Harry too, while I'm at it, and on that money-lending devil—and the worst plague on myself!" Tom's tone was only half-humorous, and his smile was chagrined as he wandered back to tuck his lute into bed. "The matter puts me out of the countenance, I admit it. You'd think with all my scribbling I might scribble a passable play, now wouldn't you?"

"I'll wager it *was* passable. Wager it was *good,*" Michael said in bitter disappointment.

"It was a witless hodge-podge, all gabbling pretension and no pith," Tom informed him. "Never cling to a dead dream, Michael. Truth to tell, I'm not your man for tragedy—on the boards or in real life either! Low comedy's more my forte—or downright farce!"

It was true—Tom scarcely seemed the same man when he was gloomy and everything going wrong. The old blithe grasshopper— that was Tom. Why, thought Michael crossly, did he ever try to write a tragedy anyhow? Aloud, he said, "Then write a farce!"

There was a silence. Then slowly, they turned to stare at each other.

"A farce," Tom echoed.

"Why not?" Michael was stunned by the simple brilliance of his idea. "A funny farce!"

"Why not indeed? God-a-mercy, what a fool I am sometimes. A funny farce . . . But what about? Where in the world o' marvels can I find something to be funny about these days? If it's not war, or plague, it's debt and press . . . and precious little to laugh at in the lot of them."

"I laughed at *you* in the middle of the press—sneaking back to see me in that old woman's cloak," Michael reminded him.

"So you did." Tom stared past Michael. "Well-a-day . . . Then we might start with a man in a woman's cloak . . . and if one disguise is funny, two's funnier, so we'll just add a woman in a man's breeches and jackanapes . . ."

"And a periwig!"

"And a sword. A very large periwig, a very long sword—a very small woman." Tom was beginning to enjoy himself; his speckled eyes were glinting. "But why the devil are they dressed so? And who the devil are the two of them?"

"I don't know . . . rogues, maybe?"

"Lovers?" Tom mused. "No—not before the third act. Wait, patience, I'll have it in a moment."

It was more than a moment, but very soon he did have a sketchy but very Tom-like tale—the mere synopsis sent Michael into giggles—with a wildly variegated cast, which ranged from a villainous money-lender in league with his landlady to a court fop in love with a fishwife.

"Lord, what a mess of catchpenny riddle-me-ree," Tom commented, eyeing his notes. "Could anybody make a play of it, d'ye suppose?"

"*You* could! It's a good Tomfoolery," Michael added brilliantly, and Tom's laugh held its old ring as he vowed he'd try.

After that the problem was that Tom would do nothing *but* write his play. He had no time for ballad-making and would have earned no pay for ballad-selling if Michael had not dragged him out now and then in the long summer twilight to sing other men's verses for an hour.

"Ods bobs, you should see him—he scribbles day and night!" Michael told Susanna one evening in late August as he gratefully accepted a bit of leftover mutton-pie to take home for supper. For two weeks now, he'd seen little more of Tom than his back bent over the foolscap sheets. "Hardly knows I'm there, I'll warrant."

"Bit lonesome, are you?" Susanna asked with a shrewd glance at him.

"Oh . . . I don't mind. If we can just manage till the play's finished, then Mr. Killigrew's bound to buy it and put it on the boards, and we can pay Harry's debt, and then maybe Tom'll write another and another and be a proper playwright!"

"Proper weathervane," remarked Susanna, untucking Michael's hair from behind his ears in an unimpressed manner. "Swinging this way and that . . . And what about you, Master Cornhill, if your Tom gets into this new line of work and stays in it? Scribbling day and night leaves precious little time for teaching you anything."

"Oh, who cares for that?" Michael scoffed. "I can worry about me later," he finished rather lamely.

"Yes. Later and later until it's too late." Susanna hesitated, then added, "You should leave him, Michael. Find something—real."

"Leave Tom? Now?" Michael stared at her indignantly. "Proper cullion you must think me!"

"I don't! 'Twas *you* saying, not a fortnight back, that if Tom hadn't you to feed—"

"That was a fortnight back. Everything's different now." Michael glanced down at the napkin-wrapped packet in his hands, thinking how few nights lately they would have had supper, had he not supplied it. "Tom stuck by me, and I'll stick by him. He needs me." *Temporarily,* added something in his mind. This week, but maybe not next. *Never mind,* he told it crossly as he started home. I might be dead or something next week. Or find a whole bag of gold angels and be rich.

It was another warm, clear evening after a hot, clear day—another in a summer full of them. All along Thames Street, the black pitch that coated the wooden buildings was peeling off in chips from the long, uncommon heat. Since mid-July there had been no drop of rain, and here it was the twenty-third of August. St. Bartholomew's Day tomorrow, Michael thought with a little spurt of interest, which immediately died. There would be no Bartholomew Fair again this year for the same reason as last—fear of plague. Sam'l reported Deptford almost depopulated, and Michael himself had seen the dreaded cross and "God Have Mercy On Us" chalked on a door in Fenchurch Street several days ago. He would be glad to see this summer done; he said so to Sam'l as he stepped into the yellow sculler, which often awaited him at Old Swan Stairs.

Sam'l only growled something, which Michael took to mean agreement and the conversation's end. But once out into midstream, the waterman suddenly asked gruffly where Master Godfrey was keeping hisself a'late, anyways.

"He's writing his play," Michael said. "He keeps to his lodgings mostly."

"Never take oars to Bankside now-days, the two o' ye. Never see no greyhound racink. Never do nothink."

"Well, we're light in the pocket, so we can't."

"Pox on it. You tell 'im I said give't the packing penny. *I'll* look arter him."

Michael promised to pass the message, though he did not think Tom wanted Sam'l looking after him. *I've* got to, though, till the play's done, he thought as he walked up Paul's Hill with his packet of mutton-pie. He'd likely forget to eat.

But starting up the familiar stairs a moment later, he met Tom starting down, looking alert indeed. "Damme! I meant to intercept you. No matter, come along in. Was there anyone in the lane?"

"Anyone in the lane?" Michael repeated blankly as he followed Tom into the room. There was always someone in the lane—more often, a score of someones.

"I mean hanging about—say in a doorway. Leaning against a shop-stall."

Michael squinted and tried to recall the lane as he had just left it: a fish-girl calling fresh sprats, a porter, two urchins playing balloo, Mistress Slade coming out of the cobbler's shop, a man-drake-hawker, an old man peddling spectacles and ivory teeth. "Oh, and another fellow—over against Harry's house yonder, in the shadow—but he dodged off somewhere."

"What sort of fellow?"

Michael shrugged. "The kind that can slide through a hole in the cobbles. Like Jack Stubbs."

"Ah, that sort." Tom relaxed. "I thought it might be that money-lender's bully-boy—I've played mouse to his cat all afternoon. But he's a big Captain Puff of a fellow with a scowl and a swagger and a jolthead's vast opinion of himself. Wears a long iron sword and a ring in his ear—you can't mistake him. And should you ever see *him* hanging about down yonder, walk straight by as if you'd never heard of me, d'ye understand that, Michael? He's not to get his claws on *you.*"

"But what if he gets them on you?" Michael asked in alarm.

"Not a chance of it—I could bubble him forever, he's solid oak betwixt the ears."

"But what does he want of you? Tom! You've not fallen behind on the payment?"

"No, my bluebottle, I've not fallen behind. I've quit." Tom smiled into Michael's dismayed face and waved aside his protests. "Now, come, cease your buzzing at me! The play'll be done soon, then all will be clear and fine as a spring morning. Don't fret about that devil of a usurer, God-a-mercy! He's already had more money of me than ever I borrowed, and I don't mean to give him another groat."

"Then—d'you mean to go on forever dodging the bully-boy?"

"No, I mean to settle my debt to Mother Floss as soon as may be, then change lodgings. After that, the cat may watch this mousehole till doomsday—I won't mind."

He turned back to his scribbled sheets, and Michael knew the matter was settled. But he could not help wondering what was to prevent the cat from sniffing its way to the new mousehole and again taking up its watch.

And he could not help the hollow feeling growing inside him as he looked around the familiar splintery walls and blackened rafters and little leaded casement, and realized that this too was soon to change. Indeed, if what he had told Susanna that afternoon should really come true, everything would change. If Tom's play succeeded and he wrote others and became a proper playwright, there would be no more ballad-selling. And for play-writing, Tom clearly needed no assistant.

Thanks to the bully-boy, Tom consented to go out early into the street next morning and to stay out until they had earned their pittance for the day. But by mid-morning he was striding back to Dolittle Lane and his foolscap sheets. Tired of the company of his Latin book and the scratching of Tom's pen, Michael turned away down Watling Street—though what he was to do with himself the rest of the long, idle hours until nightfall, he did not know. Yesterday and tomorrow were his days at the shop; today stretched before him as empty as his pockets, as endless as eternity.

He wandered up Friday Street and into Cheap, as restless as the fitful breeze that had sprung up from the east, the wrong direction for a London breeze, wrong like everything else this glaring, dusty morning. He felt cut off, adrift from both his makeshift lives, and as near a panic of loneliness as he had been since leaving the Botts's derelict shop that April evening five months before. From everybody needing him, it had somehow got to where nobody did—or wouldn't, soon. Susanna made a great show of it, for his sake; but she had Kate now. Tom asked for only foolscap and a pen. It was not Tom's life that was futile and aimless, it was Michael's own.

It's because I don't truly have one of my own, he thought. Nor haven't since ever so long—since the plague ruined everything . . .

He tried to think back, to wipe out this whole past year and the terrible summer before it, and remember how it felt, the April he was ten and a half, to have a solid, ordinary life of his own, with a father and a mother and a draper's shop and a school and a proper house. And for a moment he yearned for the warm, careless comfort of having somebody else right there to do the worrying and arranging. But he could not make it seem real now. That was some other boy, the ten-year-old who had lived that life. This Michael was nearly twelve, and if he wanted a life of his own, *he* had to arrange it.

I could, if I knew who I was, he thought. Where I came from—what I'm fit for.

Automatically his eyes sought the tall, four-spired tower of St. Michael Archangel. He had always believed the answer must lie there somewhere. Yet he had never tried to find it . . . Well, I did once, he thought, and remembered Alan Blake, the stunned disappointment, the bleak shriveling of hopes better left unborn. But that had been the old almswoman's fault. If he'd gone again into the church itself, persisted, found somebody who would show him the records . . .

And what would he have learned from the records? Nothing.

Exasperated with himself, he turned his back on the four spires and started walking the other way. Likely he'd never learn anything about his family—he was a coney to keep tinkering with the notion. That day on the turnip-cart with Susanna, that had been the end of his fine old Cornhills. He was the last of them. Or, seeing there never had been any anyway, you could call him the first of them.

Better to be the beginning of something than the end of it, wasn't it?

He stopped, with the strange breeze jerking at his hair, feeling some of the heaviness lift from the day. It *was* better—more cheerful anyhow—to think of it so. Not that it changed anything. But you really could call him the first of the Cornhills—the first of *his* Cornhills. His were only beginning. In fact, they couldn't begin, right and proper, till he grew up and found his work and got a wife, and the wife had children, and the children grew up and had other children . . . and here he stood in Cheapside like a bobchin jolthead, not twelve years old and already thinking of his grandchildren. What a ninny! He started walking again with a sheepish grin tugging at the corners of his mouth. All the same, he knew what he meant, and it did make things better. More—hopeful somehow. To feel himself the first of something, instead of a tag end—to think it might be up to *him* who the Cornhills turned out to be.

Barring things nobody could help, that was, like plagues and wars and pickpockets and all the other events that altered cases . . . And that thought made him restless again, or else it was the east breeze, plucking and jerking at him—or simple boredom and idleness. It was witless, it was, to slouch about here idle; he could sort those needle-cases as well today as tomorrow. He'd go along to the Bridge, Susanna wouldn't care.

Half an hour later, like a reward for something he hadn't even done, there came a parcel for Master Haas and Michael was allowed to take it up to him. And when the Master, surprised at seeing him, asked in jest if he could find nothing better to do with his leisure than come to work again, Michael said simply, "No, nothing. If I were let, I'd come here every morning, and bring your burnt-wine and carry your maps to Master Danforth and fetch your egg and dust your chamber and—watch you work, and—grind your colors sometimes and maybe, just once in a while—ask just one question . . . I beg pardon, I understand of course, I only meant—"

The old man cut across his embarrassment. "But you are in earnest? You would do these things, your Tom could spare you?"

"Oh, yes! D'you mean—you'd let me?"

"Your offer is welcome," Master Haas said emphatically. Leaning forward, he lowered his voice. "This Kate—she has a kind heart but a clumsy hand, *ja?* I do not like her about my table; she knocks things, she spills the glair. You may come, yes! Every morning at ten. And ask your questions." He leaned back, adding with a slow smile, "I have missed you."

So abruptly, could life again be filled with interest. Mindful of the bully-boy (whom he had never yet seen) Michael left the garret early next morning—and the next and the next—sometimes with Tom, to sell ballads for an hour, sometimes alone, to dawdle impatiently about Paul's, watching the men build scaffolding to mend the vast roof, until the bells told him half-past nine had come. Then he was off to the Bridge to spend the hours till noon observing what he could of the Master's magic and savoring his company. He refused to think of Philip and the fleet's return or to question how long this chance would last or what good it would do him in the end. He merely seized each day, hungrily, while he could.

A Stroke of Blue

On the sixth of these precious days, the last Thursday in August, Michael arrived at the Bridge as usual in time to share Susanna's ale. Shortly afterwards he was bounding upstairs to scratch on the Master's door and offer to make himself useful.

He found the old man bending over his big table in a flood of morning light, spreading a large new map out and weighting its edges with various objects against the stiff breeze that swept in through the open casement and ruffled the paper. It was that same alien breeze from the east, still blowing—the "Belgian wind," Master Haas called it, grumbling to Michael—which, though it blew seldom, was mischievously troublesome. It was warm air, parching and gusty; it dried up the Master's glair and rumpled his maps, whereas the ordinary southwest breeze merely filled the stair-well, gently ventilating the house from top to bottom. Worse, an east wind could sweep up a handful of grit or chaff from the cobbled street and fling it straight onto his work or into his paint pots, even into his eyes. Yet in the late August heat, one could not endure to have the casements shut against the *plaagziek* thing.

Michael, helping him rig a small screen to protect the fine new map, tactfully did not mention that these inconveniences were nothing to what the rest of London, lying northwest of the Bridge and the waterfront alleys, suffered from the east wind. All the air-borne filth of Thames Street's thousand chimneys—clouds of smoke and soot from breweries, chandleries, bakeries, plus the stench of every gutter from Billingsgate on—instead of blowing away downriver as usual now swirled westward in a fog of choking foulness to envelop the whole city, even the rich houses along the

Strand, and the King's palace itself. People living in Dolittle Lane
were being half-suffocated.

"Likely it'll shift back southwest soon, Master," Michael said
as he wedged a book firmly against the screen. But as he picked up
the empty *brantwijn* glass to take it to the kitchen, his gaze strayed
hopefully to the fascinating map. "Might you want me to fetch an
egg now? Or just the duster?"

The old man chuckled and bade him forget the dusting and
watch him paint if he liked. "But fetch the slab and the muller.
You may grind vermilion as you watch."

The chamber was soon quiet except for the nagging voice of the
wind and the steady rasping of Michael's flat-bottomed stone
against the slab. As the strange black crumbs reddened as if by
sorcery under his rhythmically circling hand, he watched the Master's familiar ritual—the unhurried selection of a fat camel's-hair
brush, the dissolving of gum arabic in honeyed water and the subsequent filling of a tiny cup, the careful mixing of pulverized indigo
into the liquid, the testing of the mixture on a scrap of paper until
it showed the precise delicate blue he wished. Then—as Michael's
muller slowed and his breathing grew shallow—the Master turned
his attention to the map. It was a map of a great sea, studded with
islands and edged by saw-toothed coasts. Master Haas dipped his
brush, rolling it in the paint pot until it was full and glistening.
Then, with a firm, sure sweep he laid a stroke of blue along a
curve of the coastline, feathering it out alongside a promontory before he lifted his brush. It was a perfect stroke—the color smooth
and even, shading from dark near the shore to light farther out.
Michael let out his breath in a sigh of admiration as he resumed
his grinding, his eyes and thoughts alike absorbed in that fat
brush spreading color on the sea.

"So—tell me what you are thinking, *seuntje*," rumbled the old
man presently, without stopping his work.

Startled by the unexpected question, Michael nearly answered,
"Nothing," but instead ventured, "Of what you said once, Master—
about a kind of courage. I keep wondering what kind you meant
and how a person ever finds out if he has it, or has a gift, or . . . I
beg pardon, I shouldn't plague you."

Master Haas made no reply, and his stern old face showed no

change of expression. He merely swept on another smooth and perfect wash of blue, then paused, regarded Michael a moment, and suddenly held out the brush to him, saying, "Try it!"

Michael stared at him, then at the brush, then unbelievingly back at him. "D'you mean—me? Try it on the *map?*"

"*Ja, ja,* so I mean. Why not? There is always a first time."

"But—but, Master! What if I don't do it right?"

"Then the map will be ruined," said the old man calmly. But he still held out the brush to Michael.

Michael's eyes clung to it, then moved to the map itself—and suddenly he, too, was calm. Of course he could do it right. He *would* do it—right or wrong—somehow or other. All he needed was that brush. He took the brush, dipped it boldly in the pot of indigo, rolled it exactly as the Master had done until it was full and glistening, then laid his own broad stroke of blue along the coast line. It was a fine, even stroke, shading smoothly from dark to light.

And once it was done, he was so weak with fright at his own temerity that all his bones felt turned to water. As Master Haas took the brush quickly from his shaking hand, he raised shocked eyes and saw that the old man was nodding with satisfaction even while he rumbled with laughter and saying, "*Goede!* Very good!"

"It wasn't," Michael gasped. "It was the dear Lord's own luck. I couldn't do it again, Master. I couldn't, not if you gave me a million gold nobles, not in a year o' Sundays!"

"*Ja,* I know, I understand. But one day you will, perhaps. You have the courage. We have found it out."

Michael looked at him wonderingly. "Have we? Because I—took the brush from you? Or—?"

"Because you did not hesitate to mark the paper. A beautiful, fresh, white paper—it frightens, *ja?* 'I am pure and virgin, I am perfect already,' it says. 'Who dares to mar this so-perfect white?' Only the artist says, 'I dare. You exist only to receive my thought, my image, my stroke of blue!' That is the kind of courage I meant. Now. We will discover if you have also the gift, the—possibility in the fingers themselves, *ja?* And in the eye."

Breathless, Michael whispered, "We can do that, too? This very morning?"

"Nay, nay, it will require more time. I must first instruct you in this and that, then I will set you little tasks and watch how you perform them. Perhaps you will stay now on the Bridge, a day or two, three—I cannot say—or must you go to sell the ballads?"

"No. No, I'll stay, Tom won't mind," Michael said quickly. They'd sell few enough ballads anyway until this east wind shifted; it made loiterers move on, blew away Tom's voice, and ruined everybody's disposition. "I'll go to Dolittle Lane and tell him this evening soon as Susanna closes shop—then I'll come back."

But at sundown when he climbed to the room above the stable, breathless with haste and his news and the choking swirls of soot, he found Tom gone. The lute was at home, occupying the bed as usual, the scribbled sheets littered the table. But no Tom. Vaguely troubled, Michael went back down and stood a moment in the lane, squinting against the blowing grit. A dirty paper plastered itself against his leg; he peeled it off irritably, telling himself there were a hundred places Tom might be but hoping each second to see the familiar, easy-moving figure appear from one end or other of the lane. Instead, another figure hunched around the corner from Knightrider's Street—a hulking, high-shouldered figure with a conceited swagger and a long iron sword clanging against his fleshy thigh. Michael, hurrying on instantly as if he had never heard of Tom Godfrey and were only passing through Dolittle Lane by the barest chance, shot a glance out of the corner of his eye as he passed the newcomer, and spotted a single gold earring. It was the bully-boy, right enough, come to hang about, wind or not. Now Tom wouldn't and couldn't come home till he'd gone, and that might be hours.

Sharply disappointed, Michael made his uncomfortable way through the stench and gusts of coal-smoke to Paul's Wharf, where Sam'l had promised to keep a watch for him. He felt cheated not to be telling Tom this minute about the stroke of blue, and he was disturbed about the bully-boy, who had seemed so easy to dodge that Michael had all but dismissed him from his mind. He could only hope Tom had not—otherwise he might walk straight home into a trap.

Sam'l, as he rowed Michael back to the Bridge, scoffed at these fears but seemed more blackly uncommunicative than usual, and ended by saying he'd try to find Tom.

"Oh, will you? And tell him I can't come home for a while," Michael shouted against the wind. "Several days, maybe longer."

"I'll do all I can," Sam'l promised.

Michael parted from him, hoping rather uneasily that he, too, had done all he could. But when he reached the Golden Buckle, Susanna was firm in her recommendations to leave Tom's problems up to Tom. "Lawks, how d'you think he got on before he knew you? Just you think of yourself, now, and work your best!"

So Michael worked. For the next three days, while the east breeze steadied and freshened and kept the Bridge lively with blowing trash and shortened tempers, his world narrowed to the bow-windowed chamber and the ever-enchanting table. Master Haas set him strange and precise little tasks—such as to color one square of paper indigo, using gum-and-water with the largest brush, then wash sap green on another square, using a smaller brush and glair then repeating it all with ochre and vermilion. Each color, each brush, handled differently, and Michael was able to see with mortifying clarity just how much about handling them he had to learn. But the Master made no comment, merely examined his blotched and painstaking efforts, put them aside without change of expression, and set him another task.

He spent half a morning tracing the word "Oceanus" off an old map, lettered and decorated in the Master's most lavish and fanciful style, then the other half doing his best to reproduce it freehand with the original in a drawer. One day he colored a whole alphabet of decorative initials, drawn by the Master with skillful speed, painted by his own clumsy, anxious hand at a tortoise's pace. But that morning—it was Saturday—the Master's stern mouth relaxed into an almost-smile as he studied the stiffly careful work, and he nodded a little, and rumbled something under his breath before he put the sheet aside. Encouraged by this out of all reason, Michael swept through his afternoon's tasks with some of the dear-Lord's-own-luck that had guided his hand in the stroke of blue, and afterwards even attempted—quite on his own and privately—to draw one of the puffing wind-figures, the gentle boy-figure of the east wind, giving him an expression of gamin malice to fit the real thing banging against the casements. Master Haas saw this, too, when he came into the kitchen that evening and surprised Michael showing his effort to Susanna. And it was then, lifting his dark gaze from the paper to the boy's face, that he told Michael he had the gift.

"Master!" Michael breathed, feeling his cheeks go hot and his fingers icy. "D'you just *know,* all of a sudden? Because of that— that nowt-head drawing?"

"Nay, because of what I have seen in the work, in the tasks. The drawing—it is not much yet, it is a nowt-head, *ja?*" The old man gave his deep chuckle and tossed the paper aside. "But it will improve. *Jawel,* I will show you how, *seuntje.* You have the gift in the fingers, the will, the courage also. Now we begin. But you must give me all yourself now—all your days, and leave the pin-selling to Susanna. And the ballads to your Tom. Come at eight each morning, eh? Can you arrange this? And I will teach you, as I was taught, by Mijnheer Blaeu."

"Oh, *Michael!*" cried Susanna. Like some jubilant silver-headed bluebird, she swooped down upon Michael and spun him round and round, while he wondered how he could be dancing absurdly about the kitchen and yet feel himself floating high above the Bridge's rooftops, all at the same time. Can I arrange it? he kept thinking wildly. What of my shop-wage and the suppers and the bully-boy and . . . Oh, I must arrange it! I will arrange it!

"I'll go tell Tom," he panted, as Susanna released him at last. "I'll go right now."

"Lawks, it's ten at night, Master Cornhill, wait till tomorrow, after church. It's too dark now."

"I don't care . . ." A swift glance out the kitchen window showed the west still light—still windy, too; straws tumbled in midair and a torn broadside flapped across Michael's line of vision like some erratic bird. But the streets were deep in dusk, full of shadows that could conceal a lurking figure. To go now might mean leading the bully-boy straight to Tom. "Tomorrow, then," Michael agreed reluctantly. *"Before* church, early! As soon as ever I can go."

He ate his bread and radishes without tasting them and went straight to bed, eager for the night to be over—though sorry to see this day done. It had been a wonderful, a miraculous day—a day of untold consequence for him.

Saturday, September the first, 1666. He would never forget it.

The Belgian Wind

Michael was never sure what woke him. Not a noise—there was only the deep night-song of the river and the never-ceasing chatter of the water-wheels. Not the "Belgian wind" either, though it was still rising. Over a spiteful gust that spattered debris against the *hautpas* wall just behind his head, he could faintly hear the wavering brazen chime of the clock on St. Magnus. Three o'clock. He turned over, restless, wishing the wind would stop, wishing it were full morning and he on his way to Tom.

Tom would be overjoyed to hear of his good fortune. Master had said so; Susanna had said so. Michael knew so himself. It would not matter about the shop wage and the suppers—or the ballads either—how did he suppose Tom had got on before they met? Besides, the play would soon be finished. And the bully-boy *wouldn't* catch Tom and haul him away to compter—*hadn't* already done so, three days back . . .

Oh, why didn't I slip away somehow to make sure! Michael thought. So busy with my own affairs—he'll think I don't even care!

That was probably what had waked him.

Michael flounced over again in bed, punched at his pillow, and ended by sitting up and staring moodily through the gap in the bed-curtains. There was a faint, rosy light somewhere outside the north windows. He slid down from his high mattress and padded across the cool bare floor to peer through the uneven panes of the casement. A fire, it was. A house burning, maybe two or three of them, somewhere just eastwards of New Fish Street—Buttolph Lane, it might be—or Pudding Lane, where he had stopped at the baker's to buy raisin-buns that day after he had found Alan Blake . . . Michael frowned, stared more intently, moving his head to find a clearer pane; the glass distorted the distant flickering, made the flames look much higher than they probably were. They even looked as if they were in New Fish Street. He unlatched the casement and pushed it wide, heedless of the dangers of night air and the gritty malice of the wind. The fire *was* in New Fish Street. That was the Star Inn catching now; he could see the shape of its roof and chimneys stark against the light of the flames. Figures were running into the street—people and horses. By this time, no doubt the Watch and the parish constables would be there too with their leather buckets and hand-squirts. Maybe they could save the Star, or part of it anyway. It was a nice old inn, with a good trade.

Well . . . reluctantly, Michael shut the casement. Susanna would ring him a peal if she found he'd been standing in an open window at three o'clock in the morning. In daytime, he could have run down to the end of the Bridge and watched the excitement. But by daytime he'd be on his way to Tom. He climbed back into the tall bed and closed its hangings against the flickering glow from the fire. They'd get it out before long—they always did.

The next thing he knew, Susanna was shaking him, exclaiming, "Michael! *Michael!* There's a fire, a bad one, get up, folk are coming here for shelter—"

"I know there's a fire," Michael mumbled rather crossly. "Haven't they got it out yet?"

"Lawks no! With this wind? It's burning all down Fish Street Hill—St. Margaret's is like a great torch, and no saying how many houses . . . I'm afeard for Thames Street."

"Thames Street!" Wide-awake by now, Michael tumbled out of bed and over to the window to stare in dismay at what the fire had done in the past two hours. The Star Inn was gone forever, and so were the Sun, and Master Brandon's Swan and Bridge, and all the others on New Fish Street, along with shops and homes and goods, both there and in Pudding Lane behind it—all he could see was smoke, in billowing yellowish clouds edged with black and shot with flames. And he could smell it, here in this room, though the window was closed still. On the Bridge the early London-bound stream of produce carts and hay wagons was already clogged as it met an unexpected flow from the other direction—people pushing barrows loaded with odd lots of belongings, carrying children and birdcages and bundles, leading horses or a cow.

"Yonder come Master and Mistress Padnoll from the Sun!"
Susanna exclaimed. "The little girls too—I'd best run down and
fetch them in. Master's sure to say so—old friends like that . . .
Dress yourself fast, Michael, this day'll be a busy one, I fancy . . ."

Busy, yes. Frantic, more likely, Michael thought as he hurried
into his clothes. And likely he'd have to wait till afternoon now,
to go see Tom.

Still wriggling one foot into its shoe and simultaneously fasten-
ing his shirt buckles, he took a last anxious look out the window.
This fire was a bit *too* exciting. It was uncomfortably near and
seemed to have got nearer in the last five minutes. St. Margaret's
Church did indeed look like a great torch—and it had never looked
closer to Thames Street and to St. Magnus right at the end of the
Bridge. Thames Street—with its sail-lofts and pitch-smeared warehouses, dry as tinder, stuffed with tallow and hay and coal and
spirits and oil and tar and tow. Abruptly, appallingly, Michael
remembered the fancy he had once had of Thames Street as a row
of giant candles with the hand of God reaching down to light them,
one by one. As he ran from the room, he heard the wild peal of
St. Magnus' bells, being rung backwards in the universally recognized fire alarm.

A scant hour later the pealing had ceased because the bells
themselves had come crashing down from their blazing tower. St.
Magnus, where Michael had expected to go calmly to church as
usual this very morning was, unbelievably, an inferno. Worse,
flaming bits of its timber roof were blowing every which way, even
across the river, and alighting in flocks like malignant birds on
wharfs and stairs and on the Bridge itself.

"Master, we must leave, we'll be roasted to ashes right here in
our own house!" Susanna wailed as a streamer of flame shot out
suddenly from the garret of the Three Neats' Tongues Inn, in the
"new block" at the end of the Bridge. The three of them—Susanna,
Michael and Master Haas—leaving the ground floor crowded with
refugees from the lanes around Fish Street, had climbed the stairs
to take a look out the *hautpas* window. It afforded a terrifyingly
clear view of the fire's progress and of the chaos in the street below,
where Fish Street fugitives, joined now by some alarmed Bridge
residents, were milling in a frenzy around the wheeled traffic,
which was trying to turn back southward, only to find the narrow

way choked with curiosity-seekers coming northward to see the fire.

"No," Master Haas said firmly. "We stay here. Better perhaps to be burned—or leap from the kitchen window into the Thames, *ja?* —than to be crushed like beetles down there. And they make a firebreak yonder." He pointed down the long, palisaded open stretch, burnt bare thirty years before, which lay between their window and the "new block." Several figures moved frantically just south of the new buildings—a space efficiently emptied of crowds by the heat of the vast bonfire that was St. Magnus. Michael suddenly realized the few scampering figures were tearing down the wooden palings and flinging them over the edge regardless of the swarm of boats darting about below like agitated water-bugs.

"Oh, bless those good men, whoever they are!" Susanna gasped. "That'll save the rest of the Bridge—God willing."

God was willing, and the fire spread no further southward, chiefly because the mischief-making wind steadied as it grew stronger, sending the flakes of burning debris directly west and northwest. But it fanned the blaze already started; with hideous speed the new block on both sides of the Bridge became a nest of flames. Smoke rolled in the air-currents, stained the blue morning sky, obscured the waterfront buildings, began pouring from what seemed the river itself, as the clattering waterwheels under the first two arches perished, leaving an eerie silence. Through it the backwards-ringing peal sounded from St. Lawrence Poultney and a dozen other parish churches in the neighborhood.

By midmorning, St. Lawrence Poultney was itself afire, Old Swan Tavern and the Stairs were mere cinders, and the fine two-hundred-year-old Hall of the Fishmongers was blazing with a horrid gaiety.

Then the hand of God reached down and began to light the giant candles of Thames Street.

For Michael the day had taken on the unreal quality of a dream, in which he recognized nothing, believed nothing that was happening. It was a day totally isolated from both yesterday and tomorrow. Yearning only to wake from the nightmare, he hurried from one to the other of the unfamiliar and extraordinary tasks that kept coming up to be done because the house was full of fire-refugees—for Master Haas had flung open his door to all comers and kept pulling them in, helping with their charred bundles, rumbling comfort, passing them on to Michael and Susanna. Michael bounced howling babies, fed toddlers their gruel, carried possets to their stunned elders, who sat staring at the little heaps of possessions they had salvaged, apparently unable to comprehend that they were now destitute and homeless. Between times he pushed and squirmed and struggled his way through the tangled traffic of the Bridge to the grocer's in Pepper Alley or the baker's or the Tabard on Southwark Bridge Foot to fetch the food and ale Susanna was constantly serving to their unexpected guests. And occasionally he stole a minute to run upstairs to the *hautpas* or up another flight still for the broader view from Susanna's garret to watch the sinuous line of flame wriggle its monstrous way westward like some side-winding serpent, its mouth at the water's edge devouring the Waterman's Hall, Coldharbour, the Steelyard, snapping after the laden boats that fled from it, and its tail whipping northward toward Eastcheap. Ahead of it rolled the smoke in sulphur-yellow billows; behind it the shape of everything familiar vanished.

Then Susanna's urgent voice would summon him back downstairs and out for a basket of eggs, or across to Master Soaper's for soothing syrup for a wailing child.

It was at the apothecary's shop that he heard the first low rumblings of panic. *"It's the Dutch have done it—mean to burn us all in our beds, they do!"* . . . *"Dutch? I heard it was French Papist spies. . . ."* *"No, it's the sneaking Dutch at the bottom of it—paying us out for burning that town of theirs last Wednesday fortnight. . . ."* *"It's Eyetalians, they're throwing fireballs—my brother saw one hisself. . . ."* *"Well, Eyetalians are papists too. . . ."* *"It's a plot, such a fire's not nat'ral. It's a Papist Plot. . . ."* *"Or Dutch . . ."*

Terrified, Michael hurried home and after some difficulty got Master Haas away from his guests to stammer out what he had heard. "And they were saying they'd—they'd catch all the foreigners and kill them and—"

"Peace, *seuntje*. It is lies," the old man told him. "Lies and fear and rumors, spread by rattle-tongues. Do not listen to them. There is no plot."

"But they said—they said St. Lawrence Poultney took fire on the *steeple*—that 'twas a fireball—"

"No. A burning brand, carried and dropped there by the wind."

"But—but Master, do you remember the Rathbone plot? Last April?" Michael's voice sank to a frightened whisper. "They meant to *burn London*—on September third! That's tomorrow! And there've been ever so many prophecies. . . ."

"*Ja, ja,* scores of prophecies, for scores of years. It is a fire like others, *seuntje*—begun by carelessness, blown very fast by this accursed Belgian wind. It is a bad, a very bad fire. But London will not burn."

Susanna was similarly reassuring. "From here it looks a sight bigger than it really is, Michael. Don't fret, they'll get it out. Lawks, London'll never burn!"

They were both wrong. London was burning.

The nightmarish day wore on. Scores of parish churches were ringing the backwards peals now, a jangling, nerve-racking sound that yet failed to shut out the vicious roar and crackling of the flames as they ate steadily west and north. The river swarmed with boats and lighters filled with weeping fugitives, with gawking sightseers, with household goods—bolsters, chairs, often a pair of virginals or a lute, kitchen kettles, feather beds. Michael saw many such things simply floating on the water. Fire-flakes showered over the whole unlikely scene. By noon, Thames Street was alight for nearly half its length—Michael could see that plainly from the kitchen window. What was happening in the smoke-obscured lanes just northward was all too easy to imagine. Suffolk Lane, for instance. The Merchant-Taylors' School might be ablaze this minute, the familiar door beneath the sculptured rose a mass of flames.

About mid-afternoon the royal barge came down the river from Westminster, threading its way through the turmoil of other craft to land at Queenhithe a scant two hundred yards ahead of the fire. Michael, again hanging out the kitchen window, saw it and yelled for Susanna. "It's the King his own self, look!" he said, pointing to the little group of men stepping onto the wharf. The figure in the lead was unmistakable even at this distance because of its height and the very long black periwig.

"It is! And t'other tall one's the Duke of York." Susanna nibbled at her lower lip, frowning as she watched them, looking as uneasy as Michael felt. Obviously things were serious to bring the two royal brothers to the scene themselves.

"If only the wind would stop!" Michael burst out. "It just blows harder and harder. Susanna, can you spare me for half an hour? I've a mind to find Sam'l or somebody who'll take me across to Dolittle Lane—"

"My stars! Are you horn-mad? You'll do no running about the streets on such a day! Tom'll likely come here—I've looked for him to turn up these two hours." Susanna untucked Michael's hair, turned her worried gaze back to the horrid spectacle on the river-bank.

"But what if he can't come?" Michael whispered. "What if the bully-boy caught him—and he's locked up tight in Ludgate or the Fleet, and the fire—"

"Now that's enough such tarradiddle, Master Cornhill!" cried Susanna, so sharply that he knew the same thought had crossed her mind. "We've trouble enough right in this house without you borrowing it in a bucket! Go make yourself useful and quit fretting. And *stay on this Bridge!"*

Michael stayed, but he could not quit fretting or prevent himself from scanning the Bridge at every opportunity for a glimpse of a broken plume.

Meanwhile he was useful enough, for most of the refugees who had filled the house all day were gathering their courage and their children and departing to seek other shelter, leaving bundles and pictures and cooking pots to be collected later. Michael was kept busy stowing these pathetic, awkward heaps in the unused second-floor bedchamber or crowding them into the *hautpas*. A few even overflowed into the Master's own bow-windowed sitting room, so impregnable a haven only yesterday. As it will be again, Michael told himself fiercely. Someday—when the fire is stopped. The difficulty was in imagining it stopped. Fire now seemed a condition of life, something that had been going on always and would continue forever. Yesterday seemed the dream now, and this windy, crackling, blazing destruction the only reality.

As evening approached, the hectic light of the fire grew brighter; with darkness, the individual flames became horridly visible—licking over steeple roofs, creeping between houses, streaming from upstairs windows, spurting up in places no one had yet suspected them to be. The moon, which last night had bathed the city in its cool glow, went unnoticed unless one happened to glance up and see it there, a white stone in the wine-red smoky sky. Some time near midnight, Michael, the Master, and Susanna left the Padnoll family to bed down in the shop and climbed wearily upstairs, pausing by common consent at the window of the second-floor bed-chamber. Silent, they stood amid the forlorn clutter of their neighbors' goods, staring with sinking hearts at a single blood-red arch of fire that stained the night along half a mile of riverfront and leaped in a great bow up the hill of the City as far as they could see.

"May the good God have mercy." Master Haas sighed, and Susanna echoed the prayer as they left the window to grope their separate ways to bed. Michael, too, closing his bed-curtains as tightly as possible against the ruddy glow, whispered, "God have mercy on London," and meant it with all his heart. But the phrase was unhappily familiar. In spite of himself, the image on his mind was of the fluttering plague-notices tacked on door after door after door last summer—and God had shown no mercy to London then.

No one slept much that night. The fire slept not at all. Michael pulled back his curtains at daybreak to see a strange red sun rising into a smoke-darkened sky, the fiery arch broader, the flames whipping like evil banners in a wind that was still gaining strength. It was much harder today to see from the Bridge what was happening; the rolling clouds of smoke and the fire itself were in the way. At nine o'clock an old friend of the Master's from Gracechurch Street, an engraver, came with his smoke-reeking bundles and his granddaughter and the news that there was no water whatever in the city's heart. The Bridge waterwheels had perished early; as the fire spread the wooden pipes in the streets had been broken open in panic, and all their contents had run to waste in the night.

At ten o'clock the wind rose perceptibly.

At half-past ten, hurrying back from the Bear with a pitcher of ale, Michael stopped on the drawbridge to search the swarming boats once more for a glimpse of Tom, who surely should be here by now—*would* be here if he were able. . . . He did not see Tom.

But he did see a well-known yellow sculler just putting in to Pepper Alley Wharf with a load of people and goods.

A wild glance around showed him the draper's young apprentice gawking from the doorway of the Sugar Loaf nearby. In an instant Michael was beside him, thrusting the ale-pitcher into his startled hands and shouting instructions to carry it quickly to the Buckle, give it to Susanna, tell her not to worry, not to worry about him at all . . . He was already running toward Pepper Alley as fast as he could go.

Monday

It was hard to breathe, but still possible to land at Paul's Wharf, when Michael scrambled out of the sculler there about eleven o'clock, exchanged final shouts with Sam'l, and started up the smoke-fogged hill toward Dolittle Lane—normally a five minutes' stroll away. Today he had a quarter-hour of furious struggle even to reach Knightrider Street, then could not force his way eastward to the lane. The whole area was a tangle of traffic, confusion, and fear. Frantic Londoners were fleeing with their belongings toward the city wall, only to find the exits choked with another crowd pushing in—mostly men from the countryside, crying their carts and horses for hire at prices that made Michael gasp. To avoid the chaos, he dodged along tiny foot-passages between buildings, once straight through a cookshop's rear door and out its front, hard put to keep his bearings because steeples and other landmarks had vanished in a pall of smoke and his eyes kept watering. But at last he was pounding up the rickety stairs, coughing and breathless, already despairingly sure he would find Tom gone.

The lute was gone too, and so were Tom's five remaining books from the shelf and his own Lily's Grammar. But Tom was *not* locked up somewhere, Sam'l had seen him only last night, when Tom had come to Trig Stairs especially to ask Sam'l if the Bridge was saved. Then he had hurried away—where? So Michael asked himself as he stood panting and gulping in the empty garret. And where might he be this morning? Master Bennet the stationer might know . . .

Down the stairs again, out into the reeking smoke, up the lane, and through more twisting alleys to Paul's Churchyard.

The whole broad open space surrounding the vast hulk of Paul's was like an anthill overturned; people ran every which way, arms burdened, heads down against the swirling wind and smoke. At first Michael could make nothing of it; then, as he hurried around the roof-menders' scaffolding toward the Lamb and Inkbottle, he realized all the burdens were papers and books, and all the apparently aimless scurrying was really between the various doors of the cathedral and the dozens of stationers' and booksellers' shops in the Churchyard and Paternoster Row. Of course! They were carrying their stocks into the stone safety of Paul's in case the fire came this far. . . . And there was Tom, heading for the north door with a double armload of ballad-paper flapping in his face and his broken plume snapped clean off. Michael flew to him and was greeted with a shout of consternation.

"God-a-mercy, and I thought you safe on the Bridge! Sam'l *was* right? The Bridge is whole?"

"South of the Square, 'tis."

"I hoped you'd stay there."

"Oh, Tom, I couldn't! I—I thought—"

"No matter," Tom broke in swiftly. "You can help, now you're here—run to Master Bennet's and fetch a load. I'll wait for you just inside." A few minutes later, when Michael shouldered his way through the north transept door with a stack of new books, Tom motioned him away from the ant-lines hurrying to and from the nave and led him down a staircase into the parish church of the Stationer's company, St. Faith Under Paul's, which occupied the vaulted crypt below the choir. "If the nave's safe, St. Faith's is safer, so some of us are reckoning," Tom puffed as he struggled free of his load of paper. "I'll wager the others'll be shifting their stocks down too, before the day's up. . . . Just stack those books along the wall there, Michael, then come away, there's a-many more to bring."

Stooping to obey, Michael noticed a shabbily familiar Lily's Grammar tucked behind a couple of type-cases, and beside it Tom's five tattered volumes and his lute. With an odd, helpless little lump in his throat, he turned away and hurried back up the stairs.

For what might have been an hour or two or three for all Michael knew, they hurried up and down the stairs, through the jostling crowds and out into the wind—heads ducked, eyes stinging from the smoke. Into the shop for a new load, back into the wind, and the whole buffeting, difficult round-trip over again. There was no chance to talk—and nothing to talk about, Michael thought confusedly. Better not to think, either. Just load up with books and follow the half-plume through the chaos, back and forth . . . Then all at once it was done, the last load was transferred. Tom pulled Michael into the partial shelter of a buttress and sagged beside him, mopping his face with his sleeve. Both of them were sweaty, sooty, and dazed with exertion, and Michael suddenly near tears, he could not have told why.

"Tom—why didn't you *come?* I thought—the bully-boy had got you! And then—oh, the fire—" To his total dismay, his voice twisted away into nothing, and he was sobbing. He felt Tom's arm come around him, hard.

"There. It's bad. But we must bear it, we've no choice. Come, we're thirsty, that's half what's wrong with us. The Golden Lion might have ale—no chance of getting near the water conduits . . ."

Still talking, Tom was propelling him rapidly across the Church-yard and up Ivy lane, as he had done that very first morning. The Golden Lion was a turmoil, but somehow Michael was soon holding a mug of ale and eating a chunk of bread and feeling a great deal less hollow and unreal. As soon as possible they pushed their way out again, and after a glance at the billowing ceiling of smoke that was turning daylight into a dirty ochre gloom, started hastily for Ave Mary Lane, for Tom's only plan now, he said, was to work back down to the river and across and to the Bridge and let the fire burn on without them, for he'd had his fill of it.

But they could not cross Bowyer Lane; the mob around Ludgate was impassable. The crowd was pushing all one way now—out of London—but here at the narrow archway between the prison's tall towers, it was jammed like a cork in a bottle and had lost all power of movement. People, horses, carts wedged together, everyone shouting something over the noise of the wind and the backward-pealing bells, everybody carrying something—bundles, babies, the sick on stretchers, and always those strange things, useful or use-less, that they clung to through everything—a painting, a chamber-pot, a feathered hat. A whole city full of people, Michael thought dazedly, trying to rescue chamber-pots and feathered hats.

"Come! We must get out of this!" Tom was pulling him free

of the crush and back through a slit of an alley into Paternoster Row. But it was hard to head eastward against the tide fleeing west—and against the wind, which had risen almost to gale force now and shrieked like a chorus of devils as it shot through the narrow defiles between buildings, carrying soot and great curling flakes of ash and occasionally a handful of glowing debris. They had only managed to squirm their way back to the Golden Lion when they saw that a tangle ahead of them—a coach and a cart jammed sideways across the street, the horses rearing, people yelling—blocked their way completely. Back down Ivy Lane they went to Paul's again.

"This way—around the choir," Tom was shouting into his ear. "Clean around to the south, we'll try for Carter Lane . . . God-a-mercy, what's that poor lady up to?"

At the same moment, Michael glimpsed a familiar lanky figure and exclaimed, "There's Master Niggles!"

It was indeed Niggles the cunning-man, standing with a bundle on his shoulder and another under his arm, passively watching the young woman Tom had noticed. She was sobbing angrily, holding a tiny blanket-wrapped baby and struggling to wrest the handle of a handcart from a gaunt-faced gypsy parson Michael remembered seeing around the Boar's Head. Tom was already striding forward, crying, "Well-a-day, if it isn't the Patrico! And glad I am to find you—Black Jack was just inquiring for you! Ah. I thought that might remind him of business elsewhere. Your servant, Mistress!" Tom managed a sketchy bow before he reached to catch Niggles, who had hastily turned to follow the fleeing gypsy. "Not so fast, my bravo. Are those your bundles?"

"Pox on yer, we was only a-meaning to haul 'em for her out of Christian charity!" Niggles flung the bundles at the woman's feet, shouted, "He'll make off with 'em hisself, he will!" and pelted away through the smoke.

"We won't! We'll help you, Mistress! Won't we, Tom?" Michael cried. "Where were you going?"

"My b-brother's house." The woman was clutching her baby, half-weeping, looking wildly from one to the other of them. "Leadenhall Street, near Aldgate—but you can't . . . there's my husband, too—"

Only now did they see the pallet on the ground behind her and the pale young man with the bandaged head lying on it as if asleep or dead. Tom muttered an exclamation, exchanged a glance with Michael, then began swiftly to rearrange the piles of household goods and clothing on the cart. In a few moments they were all hurrying toward Cheapside, the woman carrying her baby and a small valise, Michael lugging several inconveniently shaped objects tied in bolster-cases, and Tom pulling the cart with the sick young husband lying atop its remaining load.

By this time Michael could well understand why Tom had not managed to get to the Bridge yesterday; he wondered if either of them would get there today—or ever. It was mid-afternoon now, maybe later; impossible to judge in the strange, sulphur-colored light. Refugees were still hurrying in every direction, though the going was a bit quicker in Cheapside, which was wider than any of the streets near Paul's. *And once we reach Poultry,* Michael told himself, *a-many of the people will fork off toward Bishopsgate or the Posterns.* But the closer they got to Poultry, the closer they came to the fire. They could hear it plainly—a horrid *rattle-rattle,* like cruel iron wheels clanging over the cobbles, and underneath a hissing, terrifying roar. Once Michael looked down a lane they were passing and saw straight into the fire's bloody eye, with the top-heavy houses leaning black against it. As he watched two fierce clouds of flame and smoke puffed out at once from windows on either side, folded together with a great *whooosh,* and the whole end of the lane was in flames, roofs and walls collapsing into glowing rubble.

Twice they saw men—churchwardens, likely—running by with ledger-books and armloads of ecclesiastical silver and pewter. Another time they glimpsed a mob in the next street chasing a tall man in black, waving bread-staves and yelling about Papist plots—and Michael's heart turned over, until he reminded himself fiercely that Master was still on the Bridge, would stay on the Bridge, and would surely, surely be safe there. And somewhere just short of Poultry they suddenly, unbelievably, met the King himself, spurring along Cheap on a tall bay horse.

Poultry was nearly impassable—the roadway dug up hours ago when the broken pipes still had water, then left so, all rubble and scattered cobbles. Michael shifted his grasp yet again on the ill-shaped bundles. By now he knew every jutting, hateful knob and handle of them through the soot-grimed bolster-cases. One was a chamber-pot, he was bitterly sure of it; another an iron hearth-skillet that grew heavier by the minute, and its legs more like talons clutching his shoulder. He had sorely bruised his left heel somehow; he was sticky with sweat. Beside him, Tom was bent double, both hands behind him tugging the cart, his face glistening; beyond tottered the young woman. They seemed to have been struggling along so in this shrieking, dismal half-light forever, choked with blown smoke, wincing away from the skin-shriveling heat of the fire. It rattled and roared ever closer.

In Cornhill, fire-fighters with brass hand-squirts swarmed about one of the fire-engines—a big dripping barrel on wheels—and other men with tall, hooked poles were pulling down the handsome old houses to make a firebreak. Sections of plaster, roof-leads, venerable timbers black and crusted with age, all tumbled helter-skelter into the street to lie blocking the way and making passage all but impossible as well as dangerous. One timber glanced off the end of the cart, barely missing the sick young man's head and dislodging a box, which hit the street and burst open, spilling beef-prongs, pepper-mills and spoons in every direction. Half-crying with discouragement, Michael bent to scoop up what he could, dropped one of his own bundles, grabbed it up again, left the rest lying and followed Tom's shout to the far side of the pavement, where they stumbled past the debris somehow, frantic with haste, for the fire was suddenly in Bearbinder Lane. Michael saw it through his tears, then glimpsed the Gresham Grasshopper high in the swirls of smoke and knew they were passing the Royal Exchange, then presently heard on his right hand the sweet bells of St. Michael Archangel ringing wildly. He did not even look up, only wondered fleetingly if the reason he could no longer hear St. Mildred's and St. Stephen's and Grace Church and all the others that had dinned all morning was that they were no longer there to ring.

A few straining, stumbling moments afterwards, Tom hauled the cart across Gracechurch Street. Abruptly, they were in a different world—day before yesterday's world of late afternoon and gritty wind only intermittently befouled with smoke as it swirled and backed on itself before howling westward. They had got behind the fire. Ahead stretched the long row of Leadenhall's market stalls, and beyond near Bricklayers' Hall, the house of the young woman's brother—and then they were there, and it was done.

In a quarter hour they set off again, Michael limping a bit because of his sore heel, but feeling feather-light to be rid of the clawing skillet. The distracted brother, himself ready to move his household should the wind change, had pressed upon them chunks of bread and a double handful of shillings—which they had gratefully accepted, for as Tom said, there was no saying when they'd get more.

"Now for the Bridge again, Michael. We'd best stay this side of the fire. . . . Maybe through the wall by Aldgate, then down to East Smithfield—or by Mark Lane down to the Tower. Then—if we can find a boat . . ."

But they could not even get close to Aldgate, which was clogged with carts and weeping refugees and the little fire-engines filling their barrels at the conduits outside the gate. Mark Lane was as bad. They were forced back west, down Leadenhall again.

But we'll get back through Cornhill all right, Michael told himself. It's scarce half an hour since we came along there. He listened for St. Michael Archangel's bells and thought he heard them still pealing but could not be sure. "D'you think . . . St. Michael's couldn't burn, could it?" he asked anxiously. "All that stone—"

Tom only said, "God knows," and grimly hurried him on.

It *couldn't,* Michael thought. Anyway the men were making that firebreak; it couldn't spread north of that.

They arrived at the head of Cornhill just in time to see the fire burst through. The desperately pulled-down houses did not even delay it; in fact the debris of old timbers, left lying where they fell, conducted the blaze from the south side of the street to the north as swiftly as if a powder-train had been laid. As they watched, flames licked voraciously the whole length of Cornhill from St. Michael Archangel to the Stocks Market, roared with terrifying speed from bottom to top of the houses, shot glowing tongues ten feet out of garret windows, rolled sulphur-edged black smoke from the cellars.

"Run, Michael!" yelled Tom, stumbling backwards.

"But it can't, it can't burn! I was—going back—someday—"

Michael found himself sobbing uncontrollably, thinking, now I'll never know, I'll never know who I am, and it's too late, too late, too late, too late.

Tom yanked him away, and they fled along with the fire-fighters, the householders, the wildly fluttering pigeons, every living thing, up Gracechurch Street toward the north. Behind them, Gresham's jaunty grasshopper was suddenly enveloped in a sheet of flame and within a few moments the six sweet bells of St. Michael Archangel broke one by one from their burning ropes and tumbled in a final deafening jangle to the stones and silence.

In the end, they abandoned all hope of reaching the Bridge that night. Michael could not stop his desolate, hopeless sobbing—for St. Michael Archangel, for himself, for the pigeons, for London— and even Tom was almost too tired to move. They took refuge in St. Ethelburga's churchyard near Bishopsgate and slept the night on the ground. But night never came, for the great garish arch of flames lighted up the sky as bright as noonday and crackled on with ferocious jollity. While they slept, crumpled like dropped dolls against one of the tilted tombstones, the fire cracked St. Michael Archangel's five-hundred-year-old stones and gutted the church from top to bottom, consuming the bones of long-dead parishioners in the cloister and expunging forever the devil's claw-mark in the belfry window. Then it swept north again to devour the Truebloods' house and all of Bartholomew Lane and Throgmorton Street and Draper's Hall and the Botts's house and all the places of Michael's memories and origins. Before he woke to the windy murk of Tuesday, half the city lay in ashes.

But worse, much worse, was still to come.

Tuesday

It was mid-afternoon on Tuesday when they saw the Portugee. By then they were west of the fire again, just emerging from St. Martin le Grand into Blowbladder Street, and heading for Newgate.

How they had reached there Michael never clearly remembered, except that they had gradually made a wide circle northward in the ever-rising wind, keeping just inside the city wall. Single details stood out clearly: his painful heel, the sourish ale they had found after long, parched yearning, the strange sight of the Guildhall burning—not with flames but glowing all over like polished brass, like one enormous golden coal. For a long period—or anyway it seemed long—Michael was burdened with somebody's baby-cradle; for another long time he lugged one handle of a trunk and Tom the other. Twice they went in and out through Moorgate hauling at demented cows. Somewhere there was a mob of terrifying women, screaming like banshees, and to avoid them, he and Tom scrambled over a stone wall and plowed through an herb bed, and the fresh scent of thyme rose briefly through the stench of the fire.

All through those hours, the fire had been blazing along Cheapside. (The Mermaid Tavern was gone, and Mary-le-Bow and the fair houses of Goldsmiths' Row.) By midafternoon, as they hurried south down St. Martin le Grand, it was devouring its way north up Foster Lane, only a few hundred yards to their left.

"Fairly singeing our heels, it is," Tom panted, keeping a firm hold on Michael's hand as they pushed into Blowbladder Street and headed through the familiar obstacle course—now a nightmare—of the Shambles butcher-stalls. "God grant we can make it through Newgate . . . Hoy! Another mob! What poor devil have they got this time?"

It was a small, bewildered man without hat or cloak, being

pulled and pushed and belabored by a disorderly knot of citizens all yelling, "Papist!" and "Dirty foreigner!" and "Kill the Frenchy!" in a way that made Michael's heart leap into his throat. As he and Tom were swirled roughly into a doorway like flotsam flung by a whirlpool, a couple of militiamen managed to reach the victim and hauled him to a nearby fire-fighters' station, one of a dozen hastily set up since Monday noon.

"Praise God for that!" Tom puffed, as he dragged his sleeve over his sweaty face. The fire was close and hot.

"But what's he done?" cried Michael. Pinned in the doorway, he was craning to see over intervening heads and bundles and fire-fighters' ladders to where the fire-post officers—both lordships of some kind—were questioning the crowd. Then he heard the mob's leader, a stout, respectable-looking man, hoarsely shouting his oath that the dirty Frenchman had thrown a fireball into that cookshop yonder, as he'd seen with his own eyes—and Michael's pity changed to horror. "A fireball! Tom, did you hear? He threw a—"

"Rubbish! Don't believe every dotterel who screeches slander. Look at the poor wretch for yourself!" Roughly Tom turned Michael's head back toward the foreigner—who immediately, to Michael's remorse, seemed again only a bewildered little man babbling some outlander's language. "My faith, he can't speak English—likely his only crime. But he's no Frenchman," Tom added as the lordship's questions shifted to French, and the answers to a French so broken that Michael could understand nothing but the repeated word for "bread."

"It's the Portuguese ambassador's servant," Tom translated. "He threw no fireball—'twas bread he saw lying in the street, which, being a pious man, he picked up and set on a shelf inside the nearest doorway—an old custom of the Portuguese. He says the King of Portugal himself would do the same, that it's godless not to . . . so there's your dirty Papist French firethrower."

Shaken and confused, Michael watched the crowd, including lordships and accused, surge back along Blowbladder Street toward the cookshop at which everybody had been pointing. A piece of bread! To be nearly killed for it . . . Yet that other man swore it was a fireball. . . . Everybody believed him . . . *I* believed him, thought Michael, until Tom . . .

His thoughts flashed in terror back to the agitated, rumor-spreading voices he'd heard in Master Soaper's shop, and the mobs he'd seen—the one chasing that tall old man in Cheap yesterday and the screaming women this morning. And not an hour ago, he'd watched men force their way into a house and drag out the house-holder, yelling, "Jesuit" and beating him only because he wore a black silk coat. Master Haas always wore black . . .

"Michael! *Come,* Michael. Don't hang back, I see a way through."

Peering over his shoulder as he stumbled after Tom, Michael saw the knot of people milling outside the cookshop—for all the talk of fireballs, still not burning. But it would be soon. The whole street would be soon; the fire was only a few houses behind. As he looked, a burst of flame from a nearer roof made the crowd scatter, the little Portugee closely flanked by the two militiamen. "They're arresting him!" Michael cried, feeling his stomach knot like a fist. "They still believe it! Tom—will they lock him in prison, will he—"

"God-a-mercy, how should I know?" Tom demanded, grabbing Michael's hand and yanking him toward Newgate. "He might be safer there than elsewhere, on such a day . . ."

But the Bridge is safe, thought Michael, desperately hoping it was true. Mobs were everywhere, they believed anything, and panic was like another evil wind today, sweeping rumors about the chaotic streets. In the hours since dawn he and Tom had heard every sort of wild tale, told as gospel—that Papists had seized the Tower, that armies marched in the next lane, that fifty thousand French and Dutch were landing to sack London. Tom said one had best believe nothing or say good-by to reason and swallow it all.

"God knows we've no need of French or Dutch to sack London while we have Londoners!" he added grimly as they reached New-gate at last. "It's a thieves' gala and the carters' paradise! Five pounds yesterday to hire some broken down two-wheeler—today it's forty! Hoy, Michael! See that big barrow? Lend a hand push-ing; maybe we can follow it through the gate."

Five minutes later they had squeezed through the city wall in the wake of the barrow, among a tangle of shoving, hysterical people so frantic to escape that Michael was in danger of being knocked down and trampled underfoot. But Tom wrapped a hard arm around him and somehow got them both around the corner into Old Bailey Street, and under an archway.

"What is it? Did they hurt you?" he gasped, frowning anxiously into Michael's face.

"No—not me—the poor Portugee . . ." Tears stung Michael's eyes, spilled hot across his cheekbones. "It's Old Master!" he burst out. "What if they get Old Master? They might, they might! He's Dutch, and what if they fetch him and say those lies—why, he could be prisoned, or *hanged*—"

"Now, peace!" Tom seized him sternly by the shoulders and gave him a little shake. "That'll be enough talk of hanging. He'll come to no harm, your Master Haas. . . . Wait, hark to what I say! D'ye think that tigress of a Susanna would ever let such riff-raff in his door? I'll warrant she'd murder first. Isn't it so?"

"I—yes, it's so, but—" Michael swallowed what felt like a rock, leaned his sweaty and tear-scalded cheek against the archway only to find the stones hot and gritty with soot. With a convulsive effort, he fixed his thoughts on Susanna's blazing eyes, which could stop even press gangs momentarily. Momentarily. "Oh, pray God you're right!"

"Amen," Tom said. "Stay close to me now, we'll try once more for the river. Come."

They half-ran, half-stumbled, down St. George's Lane but had scarcely started around the hulk of Fleet Prison when its doors burst open and a tatterdemalion horde poured out, accompanied by guards who at once abandoned their charges and scattered into the smoky alleys. The reason was soon apparent—a burst of yellow light beyond the prison southward. Ludgate was ablaze. As they stood paralyzed, a crimson shower of sparks and burning debris flew toward them over the city wall and descended like evil birds among the wooden shanties close-packed around the prison. Behind Ludgate, they could see Paul's tower, itself dark and whole, but circled all about with fire.

Dolittle Lane is gone, Michael thought with a wrench of disbelief as they turned to flee. *Carter Lane is gone—and the Boar's Head and the cobbler's shop and Harry's house and the stable and the garret and my truckle bed . . . I'll never see any of them again, not ever.* He tried to feel something, but he had reached the end of what he could feel. His middle hurt, and his throat, and that was all.

Tom gave up the struggle toward the river. They fled straight north outside the city wall—swerving wide around Newgate, now blazing too, past Pie Corner to West Smithfield, and thus by Long Lane back to Moorfields where they had carried goods for people earlier in the day. By this time the fields were covered with homeless Londoners and their salvaged chairs and mattresses and lumpy bundles, and queer and forlorn they looked, here on the trampled grass. Beyond surprise, Michael saw a fine oaken clothes-chest with polished brass handles and a cow tied to one leg of it; a big beef-cauldron full of books; a child bedded in a wheelbarrow; a gilt-framed portrait hanging crooked on a tree. Everywhere were children and women trying to dress or feed them in the relentless, shrieking wind. And over all lay the eerie, brassy half-light and the stench of the wind-driven smoke.

It was wretched enough, but it was safe, and Tom found a space close behind the wall where they could drop wearily on the sooty grass and rest. After a bit he roused himself, counted over the shillings left from the handful the young woman's brother had given them yesterday, then went in search of a baker's shop in the un-burnt streets outside the wall, for neither of them could remember when they had eaten last. Michael dozed fitfully, jerking awake in terror each time the thump of an explosion cut through the howl of the wind and fire—for they had begun blowing up houses with gunpowder over near Cripplegate. Finally he simply sat, helpless to think of anything but the near-murdered Portugee and the menacing talk at Master Soaper's and the roving, malevolent, mindless mobs for which even Susanna could be no match.

As the sun sank down into its reeking crimson pall, Tom came back with a stale penny loaf for which he had paid twopence, and they gave one of their shillings for a little pail of milk from the cow tied to the clothes-chest. But Michael's stomach was a knot of lead inside him, and he could not eat. By full sunset, the fire had leaped Fleet Ditch and was half a mile beyond the walls, de-vouring Whitefriars and everything north to Holborn Bridge. Of the ancient city within the walls, only the eastern rim was still unburnt, and only one huge building—Paul's.

Somewhere around eight o'clock a shout from some boys, who had climbed onto the top of Moorgate, brought news of the ultimate disaster. In a few moments the wall alongside Moorfields was lined with watchers—among them, Michael and Tom—and more were scrambling up by makeshift ladders and crevices. There was little talk, only an awed catching of their breath as each reached the top.

Nearly six hundred feet long and a hundred feet high and set atop Ludgate Hill, Paul's was always clearly visible. It was terribly so now. The evil birds of flame had lighted on the roof-menders' scaffolding, which had fallen onto the lead roof. Now, before Michael's unbelieving eyes, the whole vast expanse of lead was reddening, glowing, achieving a terrifying, impossible brilliance before it collapsed in a molten mass. It took with it the great supporting timbers. The roar of their going reverberated over the wind's noise, thundered on and on as the timbers crashed through the vaulted stone ceilings of nave and choir, sending huge chunks of ancient masonry rumbling ninety feet down to shatter the pavements of Paul's Walk and Duke Humphrey's Walk and North Alley, and finally to burst through the choir floor into St. Faith's below. Michael, his eyes stinging and raw but still staring, felt as if he were standing there himself by the Si Quis door—or in the bake-oven reaches of St. Faith's, where half the books in London, including a Lily's Grammar, Tom's five volumes, and a lute, awaited doom.

It came, in a *swoooosh* that was near explosion. Within moments the windows were golden slits as the stationers' riches turned the whole interior of the cathedral into one huge furnace. Thick oaken doors flew open, stained glass burst from the tall windows pursued by dragon-tongues of flame; scarlet molten lead from the two acres of roof cascaded over the walls and snaked down every alley on Ludgate Hill like rivers of liquid fire. Then the stones themselves—Paul's massive, invulnerable stones—began to burst with terrible reports, hurling chunks like grenades in every direction, and peeling off strangely in great, flying flakes. It was all clearly, horribly visible, and it went on and on.

St. Botolph's Bishopgate rang nine o'clock, and the silent watchers on the wall still stood, their grimy clothes flapping about them, their eyes slitted against the heat and blowing grit. Somewhere to

Michael's right, one man had produced a prayer book and in a hurried, gasping voice was reading by the bright strong light from the burning cathedral as it ended its six hundred years. ". . . Thou makest his beauty to consume away, like as it were a moth fretting a garment . . . For a thousand years in Thy sight are but as yesterday . . . as a watch in the night . . . We consume away in Thy displeasure . . . afraid at Thy wrathful indignation . . . For when Thou art angry all our days are done; we bring our years to an end, as it were a tale that is told . . ."

Michael found himself clinging so tightly to Tom's hand that he could scarcely unclench his fingers. A woman next to him was crying, and he thought maybe he was too, but he wasn't sure. He wasn't sure of anything in the whole world, not anything. Beside him, Tom stirred and gave a strange, hoarse sigh, half moan.

"Ah, God-a-mercy. *Paul's*. Poor London. Poor darling old London. Come, let's not watch it any longer."

Stiffly, wearily, they clambered down and stumbled to their patch of cindery grass and sat down close together. Tom put an arm around Michael, and so they slept eventually, leaning against London Wall. It was a sleep broken by nightmares for them both. Time and again, through the long hours, Michael woke with a start or a cry, the last time not because of a fiery, mob-ridden dream, but because of a queer stillness, a change in the whole world. He jerked his head up from Tom's shoulder, tense and frightened, and felt himself drawn back, with Tom's soothing mutter in his ear. "It's all right, easy—"

"But what is it? What's different?" he whispered.

"The wind's different."

It was so—he realized it at once. The malicious Belgian gale had shifted from east to south, at last and was dropping rapidly. While they lay with every sense alert, afraid to hope, but with hope growing like a green sprig anyhow, it dropped still more, turned into a fitful breeze, and began to die away.

The Shore Ahead

Sometime around mid-morning on Wednesday, Michael and Tom clambered wearily through the tumbled stones of St. Magnus the Martyr and stood at last where Michael had scarcely hoped to stand again—on London Bridge. Pausing among the ruins of the "new block" they stared ahead to the Square and beyond it down the Bridge with something like disbelief. There it was—the familiar housefronts and jutting signs, whole and uncharred. They seemed unreal—or rather, so blessedly real and normal that for an instant the three days and nights since Sunday seemed only one more nightmare. So strong was the illusion that Michael half turned to look over his shoulder.

It was no nightmare. It was terrible truth, what lay back there—a desolate wasteland with the bones of chimneys and towers sticking up, and ugly little flames still playing in spots. The ash swirled over it like dirty snow. No problem about getting to the Bridge this morning; one could walk straight across the city, one could *see* across from Moorfields—though once down the slope and in among the ruins, it was all but impossible to tell where you were, even where the streets were, in the bewildering absence of landmarks. He and Tom had spent near an hour wandering with burning feet through the black labyrinth of rubble that only Saturday had been London's heart, wading ankle-deep in smoking ash and threatened on every side by perilously balanced husks that had been walls and belfries and people's homes. It had been like slogging through the debris in some vast hearth, in which the fire was not quite out.

The fire was *not* quite out. Far along westward, at Temple Stairs, the river flamed red with the reflection of the battle line. Northward, several new fires had broken out near Cripplegate in spite of the houses cleared away with gunpowder there yesterday. And in Mincheon Lane, just eastward from the Bridge, the Clothworkers' Hall roared like a blast furnace from the oil stored in its cellar. But the wind was quiet. Except for the fluttering, tearing sound of the great torch in Mincheon Lane everything was too quiet, with no traffic grating over the Bridge, no waterwheels clattering under it, no churchbells except the faint ones on the far perimeter of the city.

All the days *before* Sunday were the dream, Michael thought, staring at London. And now I've waked up. To this.

"Don't stand there looking, Michael, it'll do no good," said Tom, who had been standing at his elbow, looking too. "Come. What you need's a sight of Master Haas. That'll make things right again."

But nothing could make London right again—not even finding the Master safe at home. "And if we don't find him?" Michael said.

"We'll find him, safe and sound! Remember what the King said."

Michael would never forget that, ever. "Oh, he's a good king, isn't he, Tom?"

"My faith he is! Whatever they may say."

Good and approachable and a comfort to his Londoners, King Charles had been that morning as he rode slowly among the homeless throngs in Moorfields, unattended except by a few of his gentlemen. Yesterday, King and gentlemen alike had been on the firelines, passing buckets and helping to blow up houses. Today, standing almost close enough for Michael to touch, His Majesty had assured the refugees that there was no plot—that he himself had questioned some suspected plotters and found none to accuse, no sign of malice—that he would defend them all from any enemy and by the Grace of God live and die with them. And for a start he was sending bread tomorrow to the value of £500 and more the next day.

"I'm hungry," Michael said, feeling suddenly as empty a shell as one of those crumbling towers. Empty, tired, numbed by too much emotion. He hoped the Portugee was one the King had questioned and exonerated—hoped beyond hope the Master had never been accused. But he dreaded like doom the moment, fast approaching, when he would have to find out.

Tom began picking his way through the jumble of fused glass and burnt timbers left from the vanished "new block," and reluctantly Michael stumbled after him, dragging his gaze away from the awful ash-white ruin that was Paul's. He was remembering the terrifying *whooosh* as the flames found St. Faith's and all the books and ballad-paper and Tom's lute—and no doubt his play, too, Michael thought with a sudden lurch of his heart.

"Oh, *Tom*—" he began, then bit it back. No use to wail and weep over one more loss. His middle was hurting again; he clasped his arms about it as he followed Tom on aching legs. There could be too many changes—in a city, in a person's life. There had been too many in his, this terrible twelvemonth past.

If I find Master safe, he told himself—then, maybe . . . He did not know how to finish the thought, but if the Master were there in the bow-windowed chamber, maybe the world would begin to turn right side up.

A moment later Tom was saying, in a resolutely cheerful voice, "Well? Shall I knock?"

Wordless, Michael stared up at the familiar front of the Golden Buckle—at the sign hanging by one hook, at the broken pane in the bow window. The blue door stood wide open. Inside, the shop was still topsy-turvy with the goods of burnt-out neighbors, but the neighbors were no longer there. Nobody was there. For one terrible moment Michael was certain nobody was in the house at all. It looked desolate, deserted. Then Susanna passed the hall doorway, glancing toward the street—whirled back to stare, wide-eyed—and started for them with an incredulous cry.

"My soul and body! Oh, God be praised!"

Michael stumbled to meet her on legs gone wobbly, and for a few blissful seconds was enveloped in her special smell of ale and beeswax, hugging and being hugged ferociously, being clung to and obscurely solaced, while Susanna, half-crying, half-scolding, reached an eager hand beyond him. "And Tom, too, big as life— oh, Lawks, I can't believe you're here and safe, the both of you! *Whyever* did you run off like that, Master Cornhill?" Pushing him to arm's length, she gave him a frantic little shake. "I vow, I've a mind to throw you into the Thames! The worry you've caused—I near had a fit o' the mother, I did, and Master—I was feared he might set off after you, straight into the fire—"

"Oh, I'm sorry, I'm sorry! But he *didn't* follow, did he? He's here and safe too?"

"Safe and sound."

"There!" Tom said. "And didn't I tell you so?"

Michael drew a long, tremulous, cautious breath—his first in hours, it seemed. "And—nobody bothered him? No mobs came, or fetched constables, or—"

"Oh, they came." Susanna eyed Michael sharply. "How did you know? Saw the broken pane, I suppose."

"We saw—mobs and such—in the City. A-many of them." Michael swallowed a fresh lump of dread. "What did they *do,* Susanna, did they hurt him?"

"No, no, I bolted the door, and shoved the bench against it, and the churn atop that—they never got in. Master Soaper was here, he helped me. But they came screeching and yelling under the window, calling Master a dirty Dutchman—his own neighbors! That coxcomb of a 'prentice from the Angel and old witch Wickford and that brushmaker across the way—and oh, Michael, *that* hurt him, I could see it did. Twenty years on this Bridge—why wouldn't they know a good old man when they see one! The stupid, lackwit nowt-heads—"

He'll never stay here now, Michael thought. Philip gone, London burnt, even his own neighbors turned against him. He'll go back to Piebald Farm forever.

"*Meidje!* Is he come, is it Michael?" came the well-known deep voice from the stair, trembling a little now with emotion and haste.

Susanna ran to him, begging his pardon for not telling him at once, and Michael and Tom followed, to hold a thankful reunion in the dim, tiny hall at the foot of the stair. Master Haas embraced Michael as if he would never let him go and for a while could not speak at all. Afterwards he led them both in to the kitchen table, commanded Susanna to find food for them, and sank heavily into a chair himself. Then it was Michael who could not find his tongue or any proper words. He sat trying to chew and swallow while Tom described their efforts to reach the Bridge. Finally he put down his spoon and blurted the apology he had longed but dreaded to make.

"Master—forgive me—for running off like that, I never meant to fret you, but I *had* to find Tom, I—"

"Peace, peace, I realize, I have no blame for you, *seuntje*. It is good, even, that this happen. *Ja,* good, I am waked up now. I know many things I knew not before."

"Before—the fire?"

"Before the fire—before I lost you in it—before I find out this so-faithful *meidje* is more loyal than old friends, than my own flesh and blood—before we sit together here last night, she and I, each wondering if ever we will see the flax-hair almost-brother again." Master Haas leaned back in his chair, sighing, but with a look of deep relief. *"Flauw!* Men are fools—*ja,* Tom, it is so, eh? They grieve for what is worthless and cannot see what God puts beneath the nose."

Bewildered, Michael looked a question at Tom—who was intently studying the old man's face and did not notice. *What* was good? To see the London he had once thought kind turn on him so cruelly? "But you'll have to hide like a thief, in your own house! Till—" Till you can go away forever, Michael thought, but could not bear to say it.

"Oh, nay, nay, that was a madness only, it will pass," Master Haas said quickly. "I will keep within doors for some days, and the fear will go, and reason will come back, and no one will think it of me that I would throw fireballs into this poor city—which is my own city, too, *ja?* My own poor city."

Michael gaped at him, unable to believe what he seemed to be saying. "D'you mean—you will stay in London?"

"Ja, of course I will stay." The Master appeared as surprised as he.

"Lud, Michael, what ails you?" Susanna put in. "London's his home, isn't it? Same as it's ours."

"But—" Michael had been sure beyond question that Master Haas would start tomorrow for Piebald Farm. Feeling dazed and stupid, he said, "But—it's nobody's." He walked to the kitchen window, waved at the charred and hideously transformed riverbank. "It's all gone! There's nothing left—just cinders."

"The people are left, *seuntje*. They will rebuild all—their homes and shops and lives. London will rise again from the ashes. Like the bird of fable—you know that bird, eh?"

"The phoenix," said Tom.

"The phoenix, *ja!*" Master Haas smiled at Michael. "You do not believe this?"

Michael could not answer—or smile either, and his eyes returned of themselves to the blackened shore. They can't rebuild that, he thought. Too much is gone, too much has changed. *Everything.* Dolittle Lane and Bartholomew Lane and Cheapside and Cornhill and St. Michael Archangel and even *Paul's.* Nobody can rebuild six hundred years. "Nothing would be the same!" he whispered.

"Nay, not the same, but we cannot look back, *seuntje.* I have said this to you, *ja?* Always look ahead."

"But how can we—now?" Michael burst out.

"How can we not?" answered the old man gently. "There is no place else to look."

In the silence, Michael groped his way out of the fire's chaos to a future that might still exist. Scarcely breathing, he turned from the dismal scene beyond the window to search the Master's dark, insistent eyes. "Do you mean—you'll *teach* me still?"

"Of course, I will teach you. Why would I not teach you? *Seuntje* —you imagine your whole life in ruins, like that London? Only because you must start new? Come, leave the window. Sit here at the table with me—the *meidje* too, and Tom, *ja,* Tom. He guesses already what I have to say, eh?"

Michael was not listening, he was repeating, "You'll teach me," over and over under his breath, trying to get himself to believe it. Once, on Paul's Wharf, he had seen a man brought back to life after drowning, and he had always wondered what it felt like. Now he thought he knew. It was like waking up, like—being born, maybe, strenuous but exciting. He found himself back at the table, his mind struggling with a dozen thoughts at once, groping for the obstacles that must be there—something was always in the way. . . .

"So," Master Haas was saying. "Now we will clear these ruins, *ja?* and make again the foundation stones for all of us. And the first is that we live here, all three now, at the Golden Buckle. And the *meidje* keeps the shop and the *jongen* learns and Kate is maid-servant. Is like a family, like brother and sister truly, eh?" He looked from Susanna's face to Michael's, and gave his deep, rumbling laugh. "It is good, *ja?* Is what you always wanted?"

"Oh, Michael, d'you hear what he's saying?" Susanna breathed.

Michael was listening now, he was hearing, but he could not grasp what it meant. Besides, he had found the obstacle. "But Tom—" he began.

"Tom what?" Tom demanded. "The devil wi' Tom, let him clear his own ruins!" Gently he added, his speckled eyes searching Michael's face, "Our arrangement was only temporary."

"I know, but . . ." Michael swallowed and wet his lips, hating to mention it. "Tom—was your play in St. Faith's, too?"

"It was not. God-a-mercy, were you fretting yourself about that mess of tarradiddle? Why, I finished it off Friday midnight and took it Saturday to Master Killigrew in Drury Lane. And there it is still, unless he's tossed it out a window. The least deserving thing in London, it must be—but it's safe."

"Oh, Tom! I'm glad, I'm glad . . ." Something large and burdensome lifted away from Michael; something small and joyful began to expand inside him, making him fill his lungs with a gasp as he turned back wide-eyed to Master Haas.

"And Tom also will stay here," the Master was assuring him. "Until he wishes to go his way. *Ja*, Tom?"

"*Jawel, Mijnheer*," said Tom gravely.

"But Master—" This time it was Susanna knitting her silver eyebrows. "You've forgotten—Philip."

"Nay, my little one, I have not forgot Philip. I think Philip will never come back here. But no matter if he does. Philip has made his choice." The old man took her hand in both of his and patted it firmly. "Now I make mine. It is all planned, I have thought of everything while we sat waiting here last night."

Carefully and fully now, he explained his plans for Susanna. The shop was to be her own, as it had been Philip's. The earnings from it would support her and Michael, pay a fair shop-rent to Master Haas, and leave a bit to set aside if she liked. Moreover, she must abandon her garret to Kate now, and move down to the second-floor bedchamber—once Philip's parents'—as befitted the mistress of shop and house.

Susanna could only vow in a strangled voice that it all sounded like a fairy-tale.

"And I am fairy godmother, eh?" Master Haas's deep chuckle rumbled briefly. "*Ja*, with whiskers. But it is not only old *grootvader* who grants wishes to the almost-brother and sister while pleasing himself. Also is the good God granting my wish—for one like you, Michael—one with the courage and the gift."

To Michael this seemed the most miraculous thing of all. He said wonderingly, "You *want* to teach me. *Me.*"

"*Ja*, you—a nowt-head *jongen* of no consequence, eh?" Master Haas smiled. "To me you are of great consequence—an heir for my treasure. Not sacks of gold. I have nothing, only this house. It shall be Susanna's. I speak of the treasure in my head, my eye, my fingers." He held up both hands, slowly turned them over. "I cannot give it to the poor, I cannot use it up, I thought I must take it to my grave. You are the gift of God, *seuntje*, an empty cup sent to me to pour my treasure into before I die. You understand me?"

Michael nodded, wishing with all his heart he had a treasure to give the Master—a million gold nobles, sacks of rubies, all the *brantwijn* in the world. But the Master wouldn't want those. He wanted only one thing, and that Michael could give him. "I'll work, Master!" he promised fiercely. "I'll sweat and slave to learn it all!"

"*Ja, jawel,* and I also will sweat a small bit. Together we will make a great work, eh?"

"Michael, it's the luck of the Cornhills!" Susanna whispered.

It was only a se'enight later that Tom arose one morning and announced that his stay at the Golden Buckle was done. "It won't do to have a rogue of a ballad-man hanging about Mistress Susanna's fine shop, now that business is picking up. Lends it the wrong air altogether. And I confess, Michael, I've a hankering to go my own way again and eat when I choose and sleep when I've a mind to and get my shirt into a decently comfortable dirtyness. I'gad, it near blinds me, that it does!" Tom extended an arm and looked irritably at his ragged shirt sleeve, washed by Susanna to a whiteness wholly unnatural to it.

"But you'll come back?" Michael asked anxiously. "You'll come to see me?"

"Oh, often. Always. We'll not lose touch, I promise."

"And you'll—" Michael hesitated, feeling a bit awkward. "You'll let me know, if you—well, need something you don't have? Because I'm certain Master—"

"I'm certain of it too," Tom interrupted. "But if I need something I don't have, I'll do without. I'm no clapperdudgeon—yet!"

"Well, I beg pardon. But ods bobs, Tom! Where will you sleep? And what in this world will you do with no lute, no ballads, no printshops, even! How'll you live?"

"How indeed? It's a question that intrigues me mightily," Tom remarked in a cheerful tone. "But it's no cause for worry, y'know. Why, God-a-mercy, I've more talents than ever I had shillings. I'll find a new trade. Or pick up one of my old ones."

"D'you mean—like tutoring? Or lackeying? Or acting?"

"Or ratcatching," Tom mused. "Or—d'ye know, I was a bellman once, for a six-month. Lived entirely in the dark—woke at Angelus, dined at midnight, went to bed at dawn. Now that'd be a change, that would. Restful."

"But what about your play, Tom?"

"Ah, I'll keep bedeviling Killigrew about that, never fear. The poor man'll buy the hotch-potch for a pound or two just to keep me quiet." Tom plucked his hat from the bedpost, gave a graceful stroke to the brave new scarlet plume Michael had found for it in the shop, and dropped it with a flourish onto his head. "And if he doesn't," he added as he led the way out of the *hautpas* and downstairs, "then I'll do without that, too."

"But . . ." Michael began, then let it go. Tom was leaving, it was no use trying to stop him—and he was right. But . . . but . . . but . . . a thousand buts. When they stood together outside the shop door, Michael could not help voicing one more, as his glance moved to the black ruin to the north. "But how can you do without *London?*"

"I shall try Southwark," Tom answered promptly.

"Southwark!"

Tom smiled into Michael's blank face, then turned him right about, away from the ruin toward the unchanged southern shore. "Maybe fame and fortune lie yonder! Maybe I'm on my way to them this minute—maybe this Bridge is the bridge to my future! Who knows?"

"Who knows?" Michael echoed, beginning to smile too.

"Or maybe it's that whiffling little catchpenny play. More kinds of bridge than one." Tom gave a hoist to his eyebrows and added, "Don't forget all that French and Latin, Michael—you might need it yet." Then he rumpled Michael's hair, gave a farewell pat to his shoulder, and swung away down the Bridge. He did not look quite natural without the lute—but his new scarlet plume showed like a beacon over the heads of the shoppers.

Tom was *my* bridge, Michael reflected, as he watched the bobbing red plume out of sight. He was glad, mightily glad, to know they would not lose touch. Feeling strange and biting his lip rather painfully, he turned back to the doorway, then paused for a final glance toward the London shore. Men were moving purposefully about among the rubbish and skeletal chimneys, as they had been for several days past, carrying papers and surveying instruments. It was true, they were going to rebuild London. Master Haas was right. He was right about most things, and Michael was beginning to understand some of them.

Even change. Always there was change, there was no preventing it and no undoing it, either—and all arrangements were temporary. Everything changed except one's courage. But as long as that remained, a person—or even a city—could look ahead.

Afterword

Many things in this book really happened. The Great Plague, the Great Fire, the wars with the Dutch, the false news of victory followed by the true tidings of defeat, the wholesale impressment that resulted—including that night-time scene at Tower Wharf—all these were actual events of the years 1665 and 1666.

The many prophecies of fiery doom were real, too, and the strange coincidence of the Rathbone plot, which did call for setting London ablaze on September third, just one day after the actual blaze started, by accident, in the ovens of a baker in Pudding Lane.

Since so much of my account of that long-ago summer was already based on fact, it has pleased me to get the weather right, too. Samuel Pepys, sharpest-eyed observer of his times, often mentions the weather in his famous *Diary*. I have his word that it rained the night of July seventh and was fine on June sixth; that on the evening of May tenth, strange lightning without thunder flickered for hours around the sky. The unnatural heat and dryness of the whole summer, and of course that Belgian wind, was recorded by many besides Master Pepys.

The vanished London of 1666 is real, from the smell of the plague-filled churchyards to the Devil's claw-mark in the window-sill of St. Michael Archangel's belfry. I've taken pains to locate buildings accurately, including real shops on the Bridge (though my Golden Buckle is imaginary) and real inns on Fish Street Hill. There are even a few real people in the background—not only De Witt, De Ruyter, Sir Christopher Mings, General Monk, King Charles and the like, but Master Padnoll of the Sun Inn, and Master Soaper the apothecary, whose strong opinions on the Bridge's healthfulness and the merits of cold water were really his, too.

Susanna's Old Joan was based on one Joan Dant, a Quaker peddler of great industry who left a fair-sized fortune to the poor when she died. And there was truly, sadly, a Mistress Phillips (I've called her Mistress Blake) whose misfortunes during the Civil Wars were just as described by my (fictional) old almswoman, and who was truly hanged in 1647, proudly saying the words I've quoted, and leaving behind her ten children, one an infant in arms.

Two ballads I've used—ascribing one to Tom—were actually penned and sung by ballad-men of the day: *A Countrey Lass* and *Nothing. Barbara Allen,* still known and loved, was then a recent Scottish import.

Finally, every detail about the Fire came from eyewitness accounts of people who themselves heard the horrid "rattle-rattle" as of "a thousand iron chariots," and saw "above ten thousand houses all in one flame." All of them mention the strange sight of the Guildhall burning "in a bright shining coal, as if it had been a palace of gold." All tried to describe the indescribable, as Paul's "great beams and massy stones" crashed down and "stones flew like grenades." The poor Portugee and his bread were as real as the mob from which he was rescued. And before the fire was wholly out, Londoners really were wandering through the ruins over ground "so hot as almost to scorch my shoes," gazing desolately at "nothing but stones and rubbish . . . so that you may see from one end of the city almost to the other."

But Michael Cornhill himself is my own creation, as are Tom, Susanna, Master Haas, and the others who live their imaginary lives and play out their story in this book.

E.J. McG.

Eloise Jarvis McGraw

Eloise Jarvis McGraw has been writing stories and verse since childhood, but only for her own satisfaction. When she and her husband, a former newspaper man, had children, she began writing books for young readers. Ten books later, she is still at it and so is her husband. The McGraws have a son and a daughter, five grandchildren, and a wire-haired dachshund who is the sole survivor of a once extensive animal family. Mrs. McGraw's previous books include The Golden Goblet and Greensleeves.